SGP .

This book should be returned to any branch of the

SKELMERSDALE

FICTION RESERVE STOCK

Lancashire County Library
Bowran Street
Preston PR1 2UX

Lancashire
County Council

www.lancashire.gov.uk/libraries

'With stampeding pace, theatrical slanging matches and a murky landscape of docks and backstreets, *Hooky Gear* injects fresh venom into the London crime thriller.'
Big Issue

Praise for *Crumple Zone*

'Fresh, insightful with truly interesting characters and some of the best dialogue this side of Elmore Leonard.'
Maxim

'A great dollop of vicarious tourism to savour without risking anything worse than the odd callus from compulsive page-turning.'
Time Out

'I was hooked – a rare treat: intelligent, funny and written by one of the few guys around who can do everyday dialogue convincingly.'
Sunday Express

HOOKY GEAR

Nick Barlay

SCEPTRE

Copyright © 2001 by Nick Barlay

First published in 2001 by Hodder & Stoughton
A division of Hodder Headline

The right of Nick Barlay to be identified as the Author of
the Work has been asserted by him in accordance with the
Copyright, Designs and Patents Act 1988.

A Sceptre paperback

10 9 8 7 6 5 4 3 2

A CIP catalogue record for this title
is avaiable from the British Library

ISBN 0 340 75005 7

Printed and bound in Great Britain by
Mackays of Chatham plc, Chatham, Kent

Hodder and Stoughton
A division of Hodder Headline
338 Euston Road
London NW1 3BH

for the loose people of a loose trilogy

There was a man in the land of Uz

Me & Duane are leggin it. Like I mean proper fuckin leggin it. Me like the wind. Duanes locks flappin. Over the wall, into the back garden. All shins and knuckles scrapin bruisin an hands cuttin on barbs an broken glass. Then over the next wall an into the next garden.

Its one them dead still summer nights. Like I can hear a 24-hour grocer blowin his nose 500 yard off down Green Lanes. So anyone with basic ears – which is most people an animals especially dogs – can hear the sounds of me & Duane leggin it through the gardens an parallels of the Harringay ladder. Over the walls an fences, me like the wind, cash-box under my arm.

Jack Be Nimble, they told me. An I be the nimblest, well breezy, burglar *lite*. Other hand Duane, him like a slow-motion kangaroo, hangin in the air all flappy while 10 dogs tune their yowls an 10 tucked-up fucks swallow their snores.

Even all this would be knockabout kids stuff it really would. Only for 2 things. Number 1: we aint kids no more an so it aint suppose to be like this. An number 2, number 2 is Duane gettin his dreds caught in the wire holdin up a climbin plant. Which is a wistaria in fact. But this point dont help ease the panic on Duanes face nor make his usually clever hands any cleverer.

—— J, Jesus, fuck man, Duanes hissin, sweat pourin off of him. Fuck, J, help me man. Free up my locks. Come on man *come on* . . .

So me & Duane would be proper leggin it all the way home only now I'm playin surgeon with his fuckin hairdo. Which is snared in the fence splinter an plant wire. More I try more twisty an frazzed up it get like the before bit of a shampoo ad. I dump the naff little cash-box in among the overgrown roots. Then I reach in my pocket. Some decisions are tough but.

—— I'm gonna have to cut you loose, I go, foldin out the scissors feature on my penknife.

—— Wha? goes Duane eyes turnin to slits. Fuck you is. Yaint cuttin nuthin.

—— I have to. No other way.

—— Bollix. Dont touch nuthin.

—— I have to, I go as a womans head lean out the window above us. Fuckin told you to ditch the locks in case of this type of emergency. Now look at us an tell me what you see.

—— Bollix. Dealin with my religion you know it. Just free me up an dont be doin no snippy shit back there . . .

Other times I would take his point but Duanes religion is holdin the partnership way back. So I go ahead an cut the offendin piece anyway. Leave about 7 inches hangin in the wistaria. Which hurt me much as it do Duane I swear cos I'm thinkin about all the DNA they could get if they ever do a 2+2 on us. Theres years of testin could be done on them locks. By now the womans yellin. The high notes cut right through the dark.

—— WhAt do yU think youre doIng in my gArden?

Which as it goes is a question me & Duane have often been asked an to which we got a whole list of prepared statements. This occasion we dont bother mainly on account of the helicopter. Which is to say soon as Duanes free we's fuckin proper leggin it again as her voice get drown out by the slashin air above us. Duanes cussin me off with abusive words. Why I dont know. I put it down to the pressure. *Last time I'm out shoppin with you*, hes gaspin.

3

Yeah like police ambush happen every time. Helicopter aint my fuckin fault, I tell him.

Helicopter aint even unusual for the Harringay ladder. Theres often one hoverin over some testo'd turk tryin to powder his snout off of the dash of his Audi while hes hammerin 60. Thing is now they think they got better than boy wonders. Which is why theys hoverin in a holdin pattern over the alleyways, judderin windows, workin through all the junctions like a grid. Maybe their thermal imagin ran out battery cos they got a mega searchlight blindin up an down, pannin 3 lefts follow by 3 rights.

—— Jesus man. Fuck man. Oh Jesus, Duanes goin for no good reason as the light swing over an we press our faces into the dry brick tuckin in our hands an arms best we can.

Shadows spring across the houses. A whole fuckin black wistaria creep up the road. Fence posts stick through our heads like arrows. For a second my nose start to edge out the alley. I mean if they catch you in that searchlight what can you do? All you can do is look up into it an do your routine. *Laydeez an gentlemen a funny thing happened while I was makin my getaway tonight . . .* Thats all you can do cos youre fucked.

Soon as light passes over we's up again, duckin in an out an over, weavin like a coupla right geezers, no-hopers, washin line sheets wrap round us like phantoms, knockin bin lids an scarin sudden cats. It look daft I know. Feel fuckin daft let me say. But underneath wha look like panic we still got our old instincts. They aint deserted us. They cant.

Understand I got wife an kids an in a way a whole empire an I'm a king an hittin 30 years. But sometime a king must prove all over how he got to be king. Like there is this moment, halfway up one the last fences, when me & Duane catch eyes an we bust out laughin, pretty out of breath an everythin but still. Him with glintin face an showbiz grin like when he was 11 an won young rapper competition at Willesden Sport Centre. They said he had sensational voice an so he did till his balls dropped. Plus his overall sound got all nosey from skunk an kuf. Age 15. Use to laugh at him till mine done exactly the same.

Rememberin a load of stuff make me laugh more. Understand for a moment its old times I'm enjoyin. Old times when we was basically too stoopid to plan. When things was always pear-shaped. When we got away with most things just because. When I had no life management skills wha I have now. When no mission was impossible enough cos we had empires to build an I loved to be the bogeyman. Maybe still do. An so yeah I'm grinnin like a bastard too with the sheer buzz of bein hunted. Me like the wind. No danger too big. No risk too small. They cannot touch us. They just cannot touch us. They cannot touch me.

An I'm still grinnin as we's about to merge out the alley. Then we hear crackle from round the corner. Duane grab my t-shirt. That sound we know too well. Crackle come out of standard-issue radio. Our grins all parch up like they was nothin. Too much to lose the both of us. We switch straight back to desperado mode. Which is a mode you dont get on Sony Playstation. Which is wha we was tryin to steal first place. Like 35 of them an 2 kilim carpets worth £2,000 apiece all out a lockup that we hardly even got to unlock. Only time to grab first thing I spy. Which is to say a naff little cash-box now in someones garden. A drug-free voice talk into the radio. It go: *Uncle Zulu 7 maintaining position sir . . .*

Duane look to me for direction. He always do this in time of crisis. Cos in the end its me & Duane not Duane & me. Me I'm thinkin, listenin for other voices. Bushes hang over from the gardens, the streetlamp is out an the waves of rotor off of the helicopter is coverin our breathin. Me I'm quiet anyway. Only one person ever more quieter an he decease some time back. End of the alley its left to Green Lanes, right to Wightman. An no car. No fuckin car. Monica is gonna go mental when I take hers for the school run in the a.m. Had to leave it though. Probably best. It was just for one nights graft anyway.

Still, old days never have left it. Old days clutchburn through the roadblock grinnin with a finger out to the fucks. Go back for it tomorrow. Have to now. Thats if they aint seize it. Duane still lookin so I turn to him an flick my fingers out like scissors. Which is our sign for splittin up. Only Duane thinks I'm takin the piss.

—— 2 year growth you shucked off, he goes all sour. Jesus man.

—— We'll go back for it tomorrow I swear ok?

—— Fuck man yaint even funny. You got nuff explainin to do to Uncle. You get me? Steada laughin.

—— Least we got somethin, I say knowin I'm just settin myself up for the knockdown.

—— Bollix lickle boxy for your flavoured rubbers innit.

—— Yeah but—

—— Aint even gonna relocate it innit.

—— I know but—

—— We go'a sepray up innit.

—— Thats wha I'm tryin to tell you.

Helicopter above go silent in some slipstream. Whole night silent now with the silent people tryin to will the helicopter into a sweet dream. Stuck in their ABC flats wonderin wha their neighbours above or below could of done on a night like this. Us wonderin whats round the wall. Necks on stalks. Listenin out.

Then come the sound of someone playin jolly riddims with loose change. Over an over. We get down floor level an peep out. There he be. The one an only. A Lone Ranger on full alert, shirtsleeve order, hands in pockets, playin a gallop with his hard earnings, eyes fix on the helicopter. Sad button-up policeboy if ever there was one waitin for the big *go go go*.

Only wha he dont know is there aint gonna be no *go go go*. Not for him. Not on the no-promotion shift miles from the action. Nobody an nothin left nor right. An they must of known when they left him here. Like they must of told him 100% clear: *You must stay right here and guard this dark an godforsaken alley with your life you cunt . . . Yes sir*, he would of replied, *you can depend on me sir . . .* Muggy bonehead should of stayed down Safeway supervisin palettes. But still, fate bein wha it is, here we all are, me & Duane an the Lone Ranger, cunts for a night. An its gonna be him or us wha other way is there?

Duanes ex-ABA an KO'd some hardcore in his time. Me I done ju-jitsu an busted Duanes KO hand one time. Accident but still. Thing is this time none of that is called for. Sensible Duane with his sensible hairdo wait for the windows to start judderin again. Then he creep out the alley. Right up close. An from behind he stick a leg in the soft bit under Lone Rangers botty. You can hear the air travel vertical up from botty to bonehead excruciatin him in no time. Then the sound of his knees hittin the pavement. Loose change conductin a last gallop all of its own. Lone Ranger dont even hear us runnin. Me like the wind. Most of Duanes locks flappin. Sweat pourin off of us. An in my gut buzz an fear turn into the same.

—— Go straight back to yours, I tell Duane like he really need tellin.

Then we separate up, Duane for the Lanes, me up

Wightman. Then we is both of us walkin, not lookin back just walkin, walkin away like both of us know how, wipin our faces in our t-shirts, helicopter fadin off, just walkin our routes to safety. Wherever the fuck that is. Cos basically theres this big pear shape in my mind. An I cant see the automatic way out. The easy way out.

So wha can I do but head home even though I'd rather stick my head in a bush in Finsbury Park till dawn. Which aint wha youd call a recommended activity. But home is where Monica is. Which is to say home is where my alibi is an I have to go an thats all there is to it. But at a normal pace. Breathin normal. Lookin normal. Thinkin normal thoughts. Normal as I can after all this, after a full-on fuckup. Normal as anyone can on one them dead still summer nights up the Harringay ladder.

Take me 20 mins back up Archway. Schlepp right up over the hill over Hornsey Lane to avoid Holloway Road an Archway roundabout just in case. Just my night to run into some uniform throwin a pisshead out the 7/11 or buyin stale doughnut an micro'd coffee an sayin to himself as he spy me: *Lo an behold up, there goes an enemy of the public if ever I saw one.* An then hes gonna have to do somethin about it. It happens.

So I schlepp up the hill over Suicide Bridge. From up there it this city twinkle like a 18-century cheveret. Which is a type of fancy writin table with many little drawers an the one I teefed one time turned out to have a load of tom in it. Which is to say jewels. An they the lights look like jewels in drawers on legs like tall buildings. Thats how I see it.

I stop up to catch my breath an smoke. View calm me. Brung the kids up here one time an explained about suicide. They got it straight away but Jade said it was sad thinkin about suicide when you didnt really feel like it. Thats wha come floodin back. Thats wha come floodin back to me. Remember thinkin as I look down about all the trucks pilin up the A1. Suicide thinks the fall is gonna kill him. But it dont. Its the trucks. The 5-axle 40-tonners on the dawn run north from Tilbury. Or Dover. Or wherever.

Suicide lyin there like a bag of twigs. Still alive if that kind of life is ever worth livin which it aint. Was in the paper. Geezer lyin there all busted. Then come the artics, huntin an gatherin like they done since time. Since the origin of man theres been trucks pilin up the A1. An mashin up suicides. So they aint strictly suicides no more. Cos its the drivers wha kill em. I know cos I was one them drivers. Nothin I could of done. Nothin at all. It wasnt my fault.

An all this is wha I told Kylie that same time. But she was too busy dribblin down off of the bridge to notice the type of traffic or understand the small print of suicide. If she was older I would of told her other things about the trucks. Such as that each an every truck is a wedge a proper wedge. Which is to say a livin an not a suicide. The driver hes makin a livin is all. Him an his vehicle. *My home is my artic*: thats wha that jolly fuckin arsehole was most likely singin with the smell of bacon an brown sauce sarnie on his breath. Tin of Tango keepin his 3 brain cells activated.

Which is to say he would of made his brek stop long before he ever picked up the signs for the A1. After that he aint stoppin for nothin else, specially not for no hopeless case. The Highway Code dont say nothin about stoppin for bodies. The Code dont mention them. An even if. An thats that. 5 bumps as 5 sets of wheels go over, each bump smaller an more smoother than the last. Driver never had no paperwork, no tachograph, no insurance. Disappear into the night.

Thats wha happen. Thats the haulage business for you. An maybe if Kylie had a couple more years on her or 10 I would of told her about the haulage business in more detail. Then maybe one day she would see things the way I see them. She would see how theres a lot of dodgy hauliers out there.

Thinkin like this about death an trucks an children lead me to think again about Uncle. AAAA1A Hauliers is buried in among the scores of AAA111A1A firms mostly locksmiths clutterin the openin entries of the phone book. But I mem up all special numbers for security. Uncle prefer landline call after a nights graftin so I always carry a 10p or 2. Only this time I'm gonna need some serious sheks to explain to the bastard wha went on up Harringay.

I dial from Highgate Hill an imagine him sittin in his grubby office in an industrial depot wedge between Beckton an Creekmouth. Left of him he got his haulage scheds clip up on the wall. Right of him he got the newspaper cuttins wha obsess him, cuttins wha relate to his plots an his runnins, like hes proud of everythin he ever done. Stuff like: *A corrupt police officer who split the proceeds of a drug haul was jailed last night*. Stuff like: *Home Office officials pocketed thousands in a passport scam, a court heard*. Stuff like: *A decomposed body was found on a traffic island near the A13*.

Top all that the gaff reek smoke an drivers balls. Uncle he sit in the middle in his swivel chair, his eye glue to his long-range night-vision telescope, while his number 2, Arno, wheezy old dickhead twice his age, play solitaire on a packin crate. Phone on Uncles desk ring a load of times cos its always Arno wha has to get up an answer it, like he was blonde teenage receptionist.

—— Yeah? go Arno eventually like it was his last breath.

—— J.

Receiver bang down on the desk an after a big drama queen second Uncle come on.

—— So whass happenin? go Uncle impatient like the tower block he got sighted in his scope is more pressin than business.

—— Right old fuckin caper is wha.

—— Yeah?

—— Too fuckin yeah. They was swarmin.

—— Where you callin from?

—— Wha? I go, thinkin whys he askin me that.

After another second silence he go:

—— Touch anyfink?

I'm about to say we got some *bollix lickle boxy* but somethin in Uncles voice stop me. Like hes overbluffin his hand. Any case, fuck it, like Duane said, we'll never find it again so theres fuckall point mentionin it. So I go:

—— Did we fuck.

—— Get in?

—— Yeah but—

—— So you musta—

—— Jokin. No fuckin time. Tellin you they was all over us like crackwhores.

Uncle grunts.

—— See wha I'm sayin? Someone—

—— You din touch nuffink yeah?

—— They was already there innit. Poppin out of lampposts an drains an everythin. Bushed us innit.

—— So you din touch nuffink.

—— Like wha? I go, confuse.

—— Like anyfink you musta touched. Like a small item. Like a well useful small item.

I wanna tell him hes talkin riddles. He never brief us on no useful small item. How could he know so soon wha we got or didn't? I got my story now an all I can do is stick to it.

—— I'm tellin you we never had time.

—— Nuffink yeah?

—— You got bad line your end? I told you—

—— Yeah alrigh.

—— No . . . No it fuckin aint alright. I wanna—

—— Shut up. Go home. I'll bell ya.

Fuckin arsehole hang up. I hate the fuckin arsehole. Leave me & Duane high an dry an dont blink. I done too much explainin in my time to that tosser. But hes my High Road to the Big Coin. Cos of everythin wha his dad hand on to him includin, for a laugh, the pawnbrokers tag of Uncle. I graft for the father. I graft for the son. Thats how it is. Thats how I see it. Cos it this city is all about seekin down the Big Coin an takin hold one way or other for you an yours. An its when you feel things closin in that you start worryin about the future of the Big Coin in your minds eye. An that get me walkin again. That worry always get me walkin again. Only now home faster than ever.

Cut through the walks of the estate an over Dartmouth. All cushty on the front line except a car window bustin in some distance off. Kids doin their quota is all. Hard-workin kids if truth be told, out every night 7/52. Check 10 ways Chester then cross into Croftdown. Other side the street stand in the shadow lookin at my house for least 3 mins. Light on upstairs in the bedroom with blue flashes mergin out the curtains which is Monica watchin adult movie on Sky. No further police. No fat bastards in cars eatin doughnuts. Listen a while more then stick my trainers in the clothes bin back of the library. Wonder if Duane done the same on his way. Trainer prints in the gardens equal surefire evidence. Walk home barefoot like a hunter of olden days. Or like a empty-handed nonce of nowadays. Whichever. Aint funny.

Less funny when the front door turn out to be Chubbed up. I mean all 3 sets of 5-levers plus the Banham double-turned. I mean why? Why she gone an done that on a night in? So I have to fumble at my own fuckin door, no shoes an everythin, lookin like I dont know, which altogether really fuckin pins the ribbon on the nights daftness.

Front door finally open with a lot less silence than is my standard. But inside is a lot more silence than wha I expect. I mean I cant hear nothin. I mean no sound of adults moanin in the adult movie. I mean it aint like Monica to leave out the sound. Thats wha does it for her. Shes a moaner. Truth be told a screamer. Always has been. Cant help it. Ok when the kids were younger. Now theres explainin to do an when we argue Monica make out to Social it was me wha cause her to scream. Which is true. An the kids back her up an say Daddy made Mummy scream. Which is true. But you try explainin all that. Result: injunction number 1. Still, time heal.

However now theres fuckall sound an I'm standin listenin to this fuckall sound in this my home. Squirrel on a fence post I am. That still. Sniffin. Soon come the sleep smell of Jade & Kylie, sweet an a bit pissy but nice pissy, kiddy pissy. Which reassure me no end but. Push the door closed with my finger. No Monica smell. Not fresh anyway, more like hours-old deodorant. Pad over the carpet. Sticky hot all over. Livin room to the right. Curtains drawn. Windows closed. Flower smells from the mix bouquet I got Monica for her birthday. Golden plumosas an parrot tulips from Columbia Road. Ive always liked flowers. One day I might be a florist like the ex-Great Train Robber. The flowers waft at me as I listen.

From the bottom of the stairs, just outside the living room, you can hear the whole house, hear into every room upstairs an down. Every house has a spot like that, like a navel, like a dead centre. So I'm dead still on the spot, smellin the flowers an listenin through all the rooms an scannin the toys left all over the floor. Kylies drawin book open on the 4-seater sofa. A red monkey dog woman, her latest project. Got a big laughin mush still waitin for teeth.

Then a trail of jigsaw pieces from different jigsaws. Fairy castle mix in with pony farm.

My life innit. My history in toys. An books. Before J & K 2 books is all I had. Antique guide an SAS survival manual. Now theres picture encyclopedias on ancient Egypt with foldout pyramids. I was gonna get them a Playstation because all their friends have them though I dont reckon J & K is into 007 an secret agents an shootin each other in the head. Still you never know. They can grow into it or out up to them. After 15 secs I know there aint no danger. But none of this is sayin nothin about where the fuck Monica is.

Up the stairs 2 at a time. See straight through to the empty bedroom. Bed made up. No Monica. Her mobile chargin. TV on. No adult movie. Florida dirt bike finals instead. Then I'm goin left to where J & K is snug an sound asleep. Ease Kylies thumb out her mouth. She look like her mum scaled down. Got her personality too, also scaled down. Remind me of how it was. An Jade still got makeup on her face from the school play which she done tonight only I couldnt be there for obvious reason.

Then I'm stalkin everywhere for Monica like just in case she locked herself in the armoire-cupboard. But its pretty fuckin obvious. Shes left them home alone. Fuckin kill her. Then maybe she been abducted. Could be. She believe in alien abduction. But no way theyd touch her car innit. 4-wheel Vitara in pink. Occur to me to look out in the street for it, not expectin to see it cos Monica dont go for a dump unless she can drive there. Still park same place as yesterday. Unbefuckinlievable. She fuckin know the routine. Inside out. Can you do? Nothin. Except kill her when the time come. Fuckin moron. I am gonna kill her. I'm gonna fuckin kill her I swear.

First I'm takin a shower. Cant kill her till she get back anyway. An when she get back I'll have the upper hand bein hygienic. But this is secondary issue innit. Big issue is it just aint right. None of it. The whole fuckin night. Specially her. No kitchen table note nothin. No lipstick words on the bathroom mirror. Throw my garms in the laundry basket an wha do I notice her new bra is wha. One the new ones she got for her enhanced front. Not the full job, she said. *Enhancement*.

Well whatever cos in the end a lot of successful burglars wives get siliconed up. Its a known fact. Trouble bein you cant steal a tit job. You have to commit the dollars. So her bra lyin there all on its lonesome without her in it is just further provocation. Takin the proverbial P. Whatever the proverb is. Which is to say she must be out wearin one her other new ones. Not even out in her car. More like just out. Walkin. Like takin her enhanced proverbial tits for a walk. Whatever the proverb is.

Instead I go console myself with the grout an tile I done in the shower. It look the business it really do. Beautiful hooky tiles. Genuine licensed William Morris most of which Uncle got it bein his finger wha done the pointin. He flogged his end bargain basement. But @ £5 each they was *luxury* basement. Fetch £8 open market. But its them tiles wha brung on the grout cos I aint exactly DIY.

Not inside my own home. More like Take It Yourself from other peoples.

But the grout really is all my doin. As is the well-selected antique furnishins. Which is to say I come home to my Victorian bathtub with brass fittins. We dine on a Georgian dinin table match up with Venetian 8-back chairs. She got a armoire-cupboard like a 6-level carpark for her an her fittins. An course the longcase clock, aka grandfather clock, that she love, that matter fact they repo'd off of me when they come down with a warrant only 4 month ago. They stuck it in the police catalogue only nobody claim it so they had to return it all wrap up for me like it was Chrimbo twice a year. The muffs was gutted. Me I couldnt believe nobody notice their grandfather clock aka family fuckin heirloom went walkabout. Unclaimed goods it was. Except for the fact of it bein mine.

I'm listin again. Its a way I have of relievin stress. Standin under the water with my eyes close is also good for stress but listin is the best. It calm me. An it bring home wha I done. Its all part of wha I done. Wha I done for my family. Wha I done for her. Wha I done in general. Nights like this you have to go over wha you done.

An classic tiles, tables, 4-seater Alcantara super-suede sofas, armoire-cupboards an speciality clocks is just the beginnin of wha I done, wha I done in general, wha I done for her. Cos truth be told I give her the one thing money cant buy. I give her lifestyle. Thats wha I really done. Thats wha come top the list. Thats wha allow her to spend half the day gettin ready to go out an other half gettin ready to go to bed. An in return wha? Wha she done for me except get sarky with her tits, put sackloads of kuf up her snout an write off 2 previous pink Vitaras? To say nish about tyin me down with kids she neglect.

So I hope Duane is sittin tight round his with Trudy massagin his bare feet an strokin his short lock. Cos round mine its gonna be *Nightmare on Elm Street* when the sly bitch get back.

Dry off quick cos I wanna bell Duane but as I go across the hall Jades there. She come up to me all sleepy-headed, school play makeup all smeary, an sort of go back to sleep standin up, arm round my waist, head buried in my dressing gown. She already got more long black curly hair than her mum.

—— Wha you doin up so late baby? I go, holdin her face.

—— Woke up, she goes.

But theres more to it cos her eyes is all blurry from cryin.

—— Wheres Mum?

—— Dont know.

—— How was the play?

—— Din go.

—— Wha you sayin you didnt go?

—— Din go. She shrugs.

—— Whats with all the makeup?

She dont say nothin. Just shrugs an carries on standin there, half sleepin.

—— Jade honey whats with the makeup? Cos you was suppose to be cuttin off the villains head in scene 6 innit . . .

—— He'll have to cut it off himself, she mumbles.

—— Wha?

—— Thats what Mum said.

—— Wha? Why didnt you go? Why couldnt she take you?

—— Cos Mum she said . . . she said we all had pissy fists.

—— *Pissy fists*?

—— Yes an thats why I wasnt allowed to cut peoples heads off. But I wanted to.

—— I know you did sugar, I go, liftin her up an carryin her back to bed. Dont worry we didnt practise for nothin. Theres plenty other villains out there whose heads is gonna have to come off one these days. An when the time come you'll know how.

—— But Dad theres no play till next year an I'll be too old then.

—— No you wont. You'll never be too old to do the business on someones head trust me. Now go back to bed cos you still got 3 more days' school an I promise there'll be other plays ok? Ok?

It aint really ok an Jade aint really convinced but.

—— Wha time Mum go out? I ask as she get back into bed.

—— Dont know, she say closin her eyes an snugglin down. When the nose man came.

—— Who? Jade, wha man? Jade, I go, tryin to gently roll her shoulder, Jade . . . Jade, baby, wha man? Wha nose man?

—— Dont know, she say as she fall asleep.

An a split second later shes far far far away dreamin already like nothin happen, her face in her green sheep name Duane. For a split second after that we's just normal, just a normal daddy an his little girl at bedtime. Then instinct kick in. It come like a mental wave of fear, like the same mental wave that kick in once already tonight. Uncles questions go through my head like a high-speed dub.

Fast as I fuckin can I'm dressin again in the first fresh

garms I grab. Meantime I'm diallin Duane an its ringin. Meantime I'm chalkin out a massive line off of the top of the polished oak of my occasional table. Then I'm lickin all the rest out the wrap an chuckin it. I'm doin all this not to help my heart which is already bustin out my chest but cos all the bad signs is suddenly rushin to get to my place like they was late for their annual general. An the biggest baddest sign of all, which come as I'm tyin my laces, is the sound at the front door of the police batterin ram.

Which is wha they like to call the knock. Real carin community policin, batterin up my mahogany timber to say nothin about my girls dreams. I hear J & K stirrin as I'm headin to their room. Meantime fuckin Duane still dont answer. Meantime the door rip in, glass explode, an theys well in, shoutin, swarmin in all over an shoutin. *POLICE POLICE POLICE*. Like I needed tellin. Like anyone did. Can hear the girls callin for me. Me I'm like the wind, outside their room tryin to calm my babies down as the first muffs mount the stairs.

Through the banisters I see their faces is all pale an para an Judgment Day mean from breakfastin on nothin but adrenaline an hate. Scrambled with beans. Still, bein the host I manage a friendly smile. Which really fuckin put the brown sauce in their pants.

—— Alright boys? I go.

Then I see they got guns. Why they send arm response I dont know. Unless someone told them I was arm. Someone bein a grass. A grass who know me. Uncle? Monica? Duane? Pointless names race through me. For a second they dont know where to point their guns. Hands up down sideways as 2 then another 2 pile on to the landin. Tell all this to your mates over a pint an it would all be a bit of a giggle. But inside me is the same big Q wha I cant stop askin myself over an over: Where the fuck is she? Where the fuck fuck fuck is she?

Then I get my hands in the air just like they tell me. Kids screamin. Then the next moment my face is down on the floor just like they tell me. Kids still screamin. I mean right down in the £60 a square metre velvet pile Wilton. Spreadeagle an surrounded on all fronts with a gun more less at my head I'm still tryin to order the muffs to shut the fuck up for the sake of the children. Like any of them is gonna pay attention. Like any of them give a toss.

Theys too busy mashin in an out of all the rooms in my home, clearin them one at a time. Each boomin their favourite words at the top their different voices like they was hand-picked for choir.

—— *CLEAR BOSS . . . CLEAR OVER HERE BOSS . . . ALL CLEAR HERE . . .*

No respect for carpets. Or fixtures. No respect for the basics. Or for children. Even from down on the floor I can sense wha theys doin which is eyein up all my prop. An if I'm bein frank, they got their reasons. As my brief once told the court: *My client would be the first to concede that the investigating officers were acting in accordance with their intelligence*. Too fuckin right they was. But intelligence or no theyll always target the *hardcore minority*. Once them words get in a lawmans head life become simple.

After that the investigatin ponce go to his or her source, source bein some *associated nominal* the muffs can turn. Source equal grass. Grass get a little somethin. Everyone play join up the dots. Which is wha lead, intelligence or no an sooner than later, to the comin the hell an the high water at the same time in the same place. Which is to say at this time in my place. Which is to say theys here as much because of me as because of someone else, i.e. their source. Some fuckin grass who know me. Some associated nominal who know me so well that they also know my gear.

Which is to say theys here as much for me as for my gear i.e. my widescreen home cinema system. Which is hooky. My antiques – hooky; carpet – hooky; domestic appliances – hooky; toys an childrenwear – hooky; duvets an general beddin – hooky. Etc. etc. etc. an so forth. Well I got connections an thats how it is wha can I say? You dont need no intelligence to act. But who am I to talk from my worm-eye situation on the floor. Anyway now all thems askin Boss, Boss bein the fat-arse ponce with brown socks an a list, the same thing:

—— *Boss, wha about this? Boss, wha about that?*

Boss is answerin them with nods an shakes but mostly nods. Especially when they find the trousers I been scurryin in all night an realise the tools there be in the back pockets. Pliers, cutters, pick. Bein home equipped is almost as good as *going equipped*. Back up by any forensic they get off of the trousers. An so course the trousers get a kingsize nod from Boss. An all the items get bagged like they was jewels out a cheveret. Just to wind Boss up I tell the cunt they aint my trousers. He just look down at me like hes gonna take everything I say into account, no matter how stupid.

Then he read me my rights an tell me wha I been arrested for. Which as per usual is on suspicion of bla bla an fuckin bla on the fuckin bla bla night of fuckin bla. So they fill in the blanks an score lockup number 1. Big deal. Other hand proof is another lockup altogether. Background I see Jade seriously upset. Kylie holdin on behind her with one hand, other thumb in her mouth as shes sobbin an snifflin.

—— The policeman is stealin my toys Daddy, Jades goin as one the cunts go by with all her videos.

Nothin I can do sweetheart, I tell her. Nothin I can do now. Its traumatic for J & K cos they get attach to their gear. Me I got a fluid perspection on things. An in my hand I still got the phone. Hopin its gonna get answered an the sounds is gonna tell Duane all he need to know. None them up-with-the-lark fuckups has noticed. Or heard. Mainly cos theys all too busy shiftin gear they dont appreciate. Theys suppose to be official hauliers an they cant stump up a *mind the picture john* between them. Theres muffs for you. Down the fuckin stairs an out to their van with their para faces turned all beamy like they was judges at a lap-dancin competition.

But whether they notice the phone or not dont make no difference. It cant make no difference either way right now. Cos round Duanes all the phone is fuckin doin is ringin.

So wha happen? Me & Duane is *clock up inna Babylon House*, as Duane put it. Thats wha. Which is to say the police station. First they separate up the partnership. Me in one custody suite. Duane in the other. Then course they pressure us. They reckon they got their 36 hours. Me I know we got as many hours as it take Libby to garm up an steam down. Which is usually about 2.

Meantime they try tactics. Like for instance tellin me Duanes bein cooperative. An same time tellin Duane the opposite. When that dont work they give us needle. Call Duane nigger. Imply to me I suck his cock. Understand they just want us to perform. Thats all theys lookin to do, just provoke us into a massive off. Then they can do us for that. Bang us about *and* do us. Win-win. But once they

31

was turnin to insults we knew they was just frustrated an angry. Cos by that time theyd fucked it. An they knew it. Truth be told we all knew it. The pressure was just them goin through the motions just in case. The pressure was just cops bein muffs. But by then it was all over. Bar Libby of course.

So how they fuck it? Have to say all credit to Duane for it was him wha really done the fuckin. I mean it was all over even before they got us to our cell bein as how Duane went an pulled the oldest one in the book an put right the elementary mistakes of the night. Not that me or Duane ever pulled the oldest one before. Among the ones we pulled that one never came up. But lets just say this time the opportunity did come up an it didnt need no Midas to make it golden. Just Duane.

Wha happen was this. Cops is loadin in all the goods. Which is to say checkin them in at the desk. Whatever handful of selected items they reckon is gonna be the surefire evidence they need. With all the activity at the desk nobody notice Duane sidlin up to the goods. Nobody see his moves. Nobody see the moves of his hands. But they dont have no problem hearin him. *This aint mine*, he cries pickin up exhibit number 1 an greasin his dabs all over it. *This dont belong to me*, he goes, depositin a fine thumbprint on exhibit number 2. *I never seen this before in all my days*, he goes, pressin home a first-rate palm print. His moves is poetic. His hands is athletic. His poise would catch the selectors eyes. Duane he should really burgle for England, let me say. Course by that time I'm joinin him in this loony but as I say not exactly original plan.

Before the dawn patrol are wide enough awake the damage is done. Dont need me to point out this contamination aint never suppose to happen. After that its a matter of clenchin our arses, takin the pressure, an hangin on for Libby.

My brief Libby McDonald. Libby The Lip McDonald. A right assassin. Even jacked up on platforms her eyes is barely above the trench which is her black shapeless garms. An her red lipstick is like a danger warnin under her blonde hair which Monica, bein a hairdresser, says is a *stylish geometric crop*. Whatever. To me shes always been well fuckin sinister which is wha I like about her apart from her outstandin legal abilities. Also shes Scottish. Not that you take it for granted. Only when she tells you shes from Aberdeen do you hear her voice goin back to its roots for sentimental reasons. But then after a couple double vodkas one time she come out an fessed up that she'd never seen the inside of Scotland in her life. Brought up home counties. Finishin school Monte McCarlo. Social life in selected postcodes. She told me she puts on the accent when she thinks its gonna work for her. She said a lot of people think the accent is earthy an totally sincere. *Its the accent that sells engine oil to men*, she told me. So there you go I remember thinkin, deceit is a lawyers thing too.

She leave the fuckin muffs pop-eyed though. Thats for def. When she turn up round 5 a.m. she commit a turkey shoot. Which is to say she hit them with textbooks they never even heard of an turns their big ideas of the law into pork scratchins. Soon their jaws is all achin an sore from droppin to the floor so often. An after that she clean up with engine oil an jargon wha smart Lieutenant Duane began with his hands. By 5.45 a.m. we is on our way . . .

Or we would be. Or more like them they are, Libby an Duane. Yeah right. How come? Cos it fuckin never happen this way. It just never did. Wish it had. Really badly do. But there you go. There you go. I mean yeah they took us down, yeah they pressure us, yeah Libby turn up. But the rest is just rose specs. Me mullin, dreamin. Me wishin. Yeah true to say Libby outlip most people most of the time. But I suppose this is the exception wha prove the rule. Could she do? They had the gear. I had no alibi. They had the circumstantial an the trousers. They reckon fibres from the trousers match the scene. Like you can just hear it:

—— *In your original statement you said the trousers did not belong to you. Is that correct?*

—— *Yes.*

—— *Do you often keep other peoples trousers in your laundry basket?*

Yeah right. They even got the Lone Ranger to put me in the frame for assault even though he never saw nothin. I mean with all that goin for them they never even had to humour Libby. Which is somethin theyd do for free anyway with 99% of briefs.

Then there was the other thing. Which is to say the speciality trick they hold back for extra surprise. I knew thered be one. But of all the tricks they keep up their lumpy sleeves I didnt think Monica was gonna be up there too. My first thought was: no way she grassed me up. Her husband an all that. Father to her children an all that. Mind you some people would say thems both 6-figure reasons for grassin. But not me. Not her. Like I'm tellin myself *no way she be their source*. Then I was lookin at her lurkin. The way she just appear from nowhere. The way her tits come up over the horizon of her new bra like the dawn. The way she never tried to look for me. Or at. An I remember I lost it. Couldnt help shoutin down the corridor so as everyone could hear:

—— WHOS WITH MY BABIES YOU FUCKIN BITCH?

One the police told me to calm down cos they left a woman officer with the children. *A woman officer*. I was like:

—— A FUCKIN WHA? YOU LEFT A WHA WITH MY BABIES?

This is wha come floodin back. But still. I mean the gear, the circumstantial, an Monica, the Undisputed Queen of Injunctions, would altogether of sunk a lot heavier cunts than me. I remember Inspector Brown Socks. He give me this look. Its that muff school look that says: *Theres plenty of ways to skin a cat*. An I have to say I'm round to his way of thinkin. I dont even get to square it with Handbag. She stay behind uniforms. She let it be known that she dont want no violent robber in her life let alone in her home with her children. Yeah in *her* home. *Her* children.

—— Bitch is plottin, said sympathetical Duane. These things happen cosa someone close to you innit.

Too right. Which lead to one them daft conversations you have with everyone you know as your life come to bits. With your mates its who grass who up an who was to blame an who did wha wrong an where everyones dick ended up an all that bollocks. With my brief its:

—— You should have let me know youd moved back in with Monica.

—— Libby it all come down same time wha can I say?

—— When did you get back together?

—— Cant date it Libby. Its love wha done it—

—— My arse.

—— Well one shag or other then. Husband an wife innit. You know how it is.

—— Nope.

—— Thats cos you got a heart like flint.

—— No, thats cos I know how to divorce.

Yeah right. Libby warn me all about them dangers, goin back in with the fuckin bitch. Maybe not in them words but. An it hit home. It hit home how I fucked it big time. How they got me. How she got me. An even so I remember strange things about Monica that night, which is to say little aspects that nobody but me is ever gonna know. Like why I got horny at the police station when I was thinkin about all wha she done to me. I dont know why I did but I did. The way she seem to smile like Mona Lisa when all my previous came up. Shopbreakin an larceny an stealin from unattended vehicles. Then burglary an handlin an more burglary. Young Offenders. Scrubs. You spend a lot of time thinkin how its all gonna go down in court. *Fast* bein the answer. Least there was 7 good years. Fat years, fat with gear an coke an sex an kids an house an pink Vitaras. Mostly in her name as Libby point out.

This is wha come floodin back. In this way the next 2 week or more, 3, disappear in daft conversations. *On remand* conversations. Visits. Daft an dafter conversations wha end it all up, a whole life, wind it all down an write it off like a bad debt.

Uncle never call, the bastard. Probably too busy pastin up his cuttins. *A man who assaulted a police officer was in custody yesterday following a police raid*. So after a few day I try an phone him. Get the breathless Arno instead who cant get a sentence finish without soundin like a deep-sea diver out of oxygen. Go like this:

—— You fucked . . . summin J cos . . . hes steamin at y . . . you.

—— Whassa then?

—— Do I . . . know?

—— Musta got some notion.

—— Only . . . a . . . about his . . . mood . . . which is fuckin dark when . . . ever your . . . name . . . come up. One day its . . . all gonna want explaining.

—— Well wha can I say when I dont know myself?

—— Au . . . r . . . revoir?

—— Prick.

—— . . . Dont . . . be like that.

—— Cheers Arno. Thanks for nothin.

—— Dont m . . . mention . . . it.

Then wha? Then a lot of bye-bye looks. Daft words about how time is, how you do your time, how it flies, stuff like that. An then the even dafter words with the kids. All that thinkin about wha to say an how to say it an then finally sayin it an then course them not gettin it straight off. An then me wonderin about explainin it again clearer. An then bottlin it. Just totally bottlin it. Chickenin out the last an only time I see them properly of tellin them the truth. Hopin like a fool someone else is gonna tell it to them the right way. Like who? I mean the last an only time I seen J & K before the verdict I remember Jade ask about the weather. Like we had nothin else to discuss. She come out with:

—— Does night come when the rain stops?

Could I say? Wha can you say? I give her a full an frank explanation of this phenomenon. Then I just thanked my stars I dont have no son cos of the footsteps I'd have to explain. God almighty. 7 good years. Wife. House. Kids. Gear. Ciffial 4-piece bath mixer in chrome an gold. Matki Colonnade 900 shower surround in Celtic silver. Trips an holidays all over. Sandy beach to ski resort. Everythin. Fat years. Fat fat fat years. I been ridin it. I have. An now they got me again. They skinned a cat. Justice work fast when it want. So this is it. This is wha come floodin back.

He cometh forth
like a flower

£4.99

Des and His Res

I just come out of prison
And all the rents they had risen
So I took the bus round my mate Des
Cos he had this totally fuck-off res.
I mean we shared a cell but he wasnt no don
So I reckoned he would sort me, being just another ex-con,
With a bed, with brekkie,
A bit of en suite and free lekkie.
So I go round Des's res
And Des comes to the door and he says:
I know you are my mate
And you say you are straight

But I'm afraid it has got to be NO.
You see I have moved on and let my past go.
I said: But we was mates in stir.
He said: You are right mate, we were.
Now fuck off.
The cunt.
So well after dark around five,
I crept up his gravelly drive
And I shit on his porch.
Des he come out with a torch.
I said: Have a heart.
He said: Dont fucking start
And twatted my nut on the grate.
So before it is your fate,
If you have a mate what is called Des,
Dont bother going round his fuck-off res.

This is wha I'm readin at the bus stop outside Scrubs. 9 month an all I have to show is one daft pome writ by the dumb bastard mate of Des wha I had to share a cell with last. An I fuckin hate pomes. Especially when you have to listen to or read one a fuckin day for the last 4 weeks we was together. Especially when he always scratch a pome on the back of the paper as well, like a B side. This B side is about the time he ask his *ex-girlfriend Julie for a load of spondooli*. Dont need me to reveal wha she told him to do.

Sittin outside Scrubs an readin about mates an exes press me to think about wha to do. They release people early just to fuck up their surprise party. So I have to think wha to do, where to go, who to go to. How Duane never come to visit. Which I know he couldnt. I told him not to. For both our good. To keep him out the picture. He got off. Never even got charged. Nobody ever asked about his short lock. He had Trudy. Which is to say a good alibi. But still. Day you come out is the day you regret all them para decisions you made way back when. Like about no visitors like Duane. Or any of the people I count as friends. Like Fran an Sensi. Whoever. A whole list of them. They never come for the same reason. We all know the score. Least Duane send parcels.

But family is suppose to be different. All I know is I had a family when I went in. Now I dont. I was robbed. She never brung them. Never even once. I wrote letters an everythin. I asked all the questions. Like why she accuse me. Like why she exaggerate it all up, why she large up the truth like a carnival float. Like where she was on the night of bla bla. An who else was there i.e. *the nose man*. But mainly I ask why she done wha she done. An course about J & K. But she dont answer nothin never. She dont have to, everythin bein in her name to stop anyone takin it off of me, anyone bein anyone exceptin her. But there was the once she wrote. Only it never even come from her the letter but from her solicitor, Spunk, Sadist & Tool. *Our Client is free to sell your property and fuck you up . . . Our Client intends . . . Our Client insists . . . Our Client wishes to make it clear . . . Our Client is in residence at an undisclosed address . . . Our Client is not obliged to disclose la di da . . . If you should attempt in whatsoever manner to see your own flesh and blood without prior agreement from all parties Our Client will press for the harshest penalties . . . You are therefore reminded of your obligation to suck hard and without prejudice upon the cocks of the aforementioned. Otherwise we will have you put back in stir till you rot you pig . . . Up yours.*

Thats the gist anyway. Maybe it would of been hard on J & K an all that. But still. End the day its reality. *Man must take them licks* as Duane would say. We all do. Even J & K know that some days are better than others. They know that because they cry. An if they can cope with cryin they can cope with Daddy bein where hes been all this time. As long as you give them regular information they can work it out. They can cope. Better than their mums an dads even. But it still surprise me how quick a family get fucked up. Because of no information. No letters nothin. Which is to say nothin but a long silent lie. Her lie. The lie of wha she accuse me of. Also, at the end the day I suppose its sad.

An the sad cuntery dont exactly end there. Cos then theres my prop which I aint got no more. Toothbrush, razor, pants, drivin licence an 10 sheks is all. No deluxe items. Suitcase round Duanes. An a secret stash that dont amount to half a dozen rough weekends in Southend.

Then theres the question of my arse which I still got only its wanted. By headbreakers like Uncle. 9 month certain people have been waitin for me to explain one night up the Harringay ladder. Cos its me not Duane wha has to answer for it. An its me not Duane who has to face him one day, maybe take revenge on him one day too. Maybe def.

All this is strife enough but then you have to add to it the boil on the side my nose. Last 3 month its been swoll up.

Ache every time I breathe. Which is often. Monica knew how to keep wha she call the *grease triangle* under control. She always had cleanser for eruptions. An a whole range other lotions to keep my skins PH balance just right. Scrubs youre a nonce if you worry about boils. Never fuckin mind PH balance. An now wha? Fuckin Handbag gone AWOL an nobody exceptin some pugnant slapper from Canning Town is gonna fancy me till the boil clear. If it clear. An even if it clear it could flare up again at any time. It could even get connected to my emotions.

Top all that its only rainin. Drizzle that coat me in muggy exhaust. An shitty Du Cane Road dont exactly give me that breezy freedom feelin. Wouldnt be the first to want to turn round an go back in. Cos nobody even notice another con slinkin out into the real world. The builders carry on dumpin cement bags across the street. The hospital workers carry on slackin off of the night shift. The train carries on clackin across the bridge. An the black crows dont stop flappin round the towers of Scrubs. Which is to say it aint like the earth move. An over the whole dump a sky so grey its blindin. Just as well it aint Monday too. Thats it, thats the whole list. Shit or wha. Even John Lee Hooker would call it a day an trade his guitar for a Kleenex. Which is to say, which is all to say, if it wasnt for my attitude I would be depressed now.

The way I deal with it is to do wha come naturally: I tell myself I'm in danger. Clench unclench my fists. Danger fix my mind. Its the only thing that do. Pomes sure as fuck dont. Anyway the pome is just a little cover to stay still, watch the street, make sure the builders dont equal no guised-up murder posse an the hospital workers aint prepared no cemented-down body-bags. Not that Uncle is gonna organise it that way. Hes got his people. He would of got someone inside, like in the kitchens, to scorch my eyeballs out with fryin oil or trim my ears into points like a rat or give me the ring of glory cut all the way round from up the top my skull to under my chin.

Thats where the danger was innit. Inside. But nothin happen inside. Just crowds of cons shiftin in an out, whole crowds of them always in transit. Drug test 28 days. Suicide every while. Never alone. Never be alone. Only everyones always alone in their flat brown shoes, shufflin about, tradin porn, grabbin snout, stealin puff, passin pills, disputin wha they committed or didnt an thinkin up new ways of committin it better when they get out. Whatever. An then there was Des's mate. The fuckin pote was on barium enemas for slow-transit constipation. Very slow in his case. Least he didnt stink. Least he couldnt fart. Least he didnt shit up the gaff. I guess he was storin it all up for Des's porch.

But wha does all that add up to? Wha can you call all that? 9 month just dull the senses. First you cant think of nothin exceptin your dick. But youre sharin day in an out with geezers who got real enthusiasm when it come to wankin. Some them even keep a diary: *Feb. 8 – wanked like a bastard*. Enough to give anyone the queaze. Put you right off your custard. I mean you start comin over all Cliff Richard. I mean it lead to your dick becomin a grey area.

Actually me I got sick of feelin it. For the first time in my life I got sick of my own dick. Can I say? Most geezers the opposite. Most get para thinkin they must use it or lose it so they keep wankin like it was premium insurance. Every day theys like: *Yep it work at 7 a.m. . . . yep it still work at 3 p.m. . . . an yep the 11 p.m. check is good.*

Thats how the day go by. Thats wha 9 month eat up your brain with. They call it a balance of constraint an rehab. Wha else? I miss takin the kids to school. For 9 month. Wha else? Nothin else. Nothin else happen. Nothin nothin nothin. So unless Uncles got into Satan an witchcraft an the boil on my nose is a hex, then whatevers gonna happen to me in my life is gonna happen here, out here in the almighty here which is outside.

Screw the pome an chuck it in the street. Builders van crush it in no time. At least litterin ease me back into the criminal way. Then I head for the payphone edge of the Scrubs. Almost dial home. Stop myself twice. Then I do it, dial home, let it ring in a house thats empty an most likely for sale. Dial Duane instead. Need a place to chill. To think. After that who know? After that at some point my thinkins gonna come full circle. It just is. It will. An then course I'm gonna have to stalk the bitch. Can I say? I'm just gonna have to. Which is to say I'm gonna have to stalk down my old life. All of it. Wherever it be.

Duanes mobile is off an the rest of wha he know is on his answerphone: *Maybe we be in, maybe not. Eeda way say your piece.* I start sayin it just to delay goin back in the rain when Trudy pick up.

—— J? she blabbers. J . . . No . . . Ma god . . .

Cant help laughin down the receiver. Trudys *ma gods* always kill me an I'm picturin the way her head sort of drop an her springy blonde curls sort of spring forward all at once when she say it. Then she throw her hair back in reverse, trouble bein her *ma god* always come with a plus 1 so the whole thing start again like a superquick replay.

—— Ma god . . . Youre back . . .

—— How you been Trudy?

—— Me? Yeah, fine, fine, great . . . When did you—

—— Bout 5 mins ago.

—— Ma god, J, wow, ma god, you never said, you should—

—— Surprised me too.

—— So, I mean, you . . . alright an everything? I mean—

—— Yeah yeah course. Pissed it . . .

—— God, J, we missed you, everyone did . . .

Trudy sort of swallow them words cos she know the *everyone* aint so obvious. An specially cos she know I know she been seein her best friend, the one the only Who Else. This is as close as I got to speakin with Monica in 9 month. So theres a bit of a silence which aint suppose to happen on the phone. Then I go:

—— Trudy, look, I'm, you know, gonna need—

—— Yeah course J. I know. Dont let whatever, well, you know, whatever *whatever*, if you know what I mean, get in the way an everything. I mean . . . we'll talk an everything yeah?

—— Yeah course.

—— I mean you just caught me. I was halfway out—

—— So how things at Stunners Hair an Beauty?

—— Fine. Lightly tinted with apricot shades for spring, goes Trudy laughin. J . . . Ma god . . . Ma—

—— I'll let you get on.

—— J, wow . . . I'm just blown away. Hearing your voice just like that. Duane—

—— He about?

—— Duane? He, er . . . Take a deep one J . . . Ready?

—— Ready . . .

—— Hes up Mothercare.

—— No.

—— Yeah. Ive still got a week or 2 . . .

—— No.

—— Yeah J, serious . . .

—— Well fuckin hell. Number fuckin 1. Can I say? That make you a family unit.

—— You know . . .

Yeah I do know, I'm about to say, I do know.

—— Congratulations Trudy. Boy or girl?

—— Boy.

—— Duane Junior innit. God help us.

—— Tell me about it, she laugh, an he dont even have a name yet . . . You tried his dad on the mobi?

—— Its off an now I get why: he dont want no giveaway background noise innit.

—— He better get used to the background noise. Thats all hes gonna get next 16 years trust me . . .

Yeah right. I laugh. I try to laugh. Truth be told I almost cry.

—— So . . . I mean, youre coming round yeah?

—— Course I am Trudy but—

—— I'll leave a key. You know?

—— Yeah, usual place.

—— Yeah. An help yourself to anything. An J, the spare rooms yours long as you need you know that.

—— Wicked.

—— An I'll cook a bite when I get back yeah?

—— Wicked. Wha time?

—— Bout 6 half 6.

—— I'll come round then.

—— J, ma god, ma god, telling you, its so good to have you back. Duanes been pining I swear.

—— Yeah? Well, me too Trudy, I been pinin too . . .

—— J, ma god . . .

—— Well, I'll be seein the 3 of yous later . . .

—— Yeah, she laugh, brilliant. Laters J . . .

—— I'll bring a bottle.

I hang up an I'm fuckin kickin myself for sayin that. Dont have enough for a teaspoon of cough mixture an now I'm committed to quality wine. Normally I'm lavish but. Anyway. It add to the list. The list of things pilin up like a life. Which is to say I got about 8 hours to do the followin:

No. 1:   Stalk the bitch an get arrested.
No. 2:   Call Uncle an get murdered.
No. 3:   Go back-gardenin in broad daylight for a useful small item which I cant ignore but which could lead to both the above.

In the light these choices, savin up for quality wine is entertainment. Same breath I cant stop the slush comin up as I think of all the entertainment we had, me & Monica & Duane & Trudy. About all them times. Sun an rain an all that. Sun an rain. Ma god. Ma god. This is wha come floodin back. All the times we had. I spit it out the slush. I have to. Cos truth be told I'm well pissed off. Well pissed off. Well fuckin pissed off. About wha been meted on me.

About wha been done to me. About wha been taken from me. About wha I been accused of. About not bein allowed to see my children. About goin from 9 month in fuckin 10 by 6 to a fuckin spare room. When me I got a house. With en suite bathroom. With a Kyomi Arc bath. An Myson heated towel rails @ £900 each. His an hers. An my own kingsize deluxe bed with my own beddin. With my own lush pillows. An atmospheric lightin an everythin.

An so I make a plan with myself. I say to myself, I go: *J, youre gonna stay well fuckin pissed off for as long as necessary, for as long as it take*. An then I say to myself, I go: *J, youre still in East Acton so its gonna take a long time an youre gonna need all the stamina you can muster up just to reach Duanes in Muswell Hill.*

Thats wha I tell myself. An I keep tellin myself the same thing, over an over as I'm walkin fuck knows where, through a place I never notice before, through a whole new town I never been in before. An all I recognise is the wild flowers like knapweed an ox-eye daisies an bedstraw wha I seen in pictures but never have seen in this town, never before in this place, an it make it even more frightenin that I dont know these things exist so close to the walls I know well. Cos thats how it is as the rain ease off an stop an the wind pick up right in my face an make Scrubs common feel as big as a country.

The hours to 6 half 6 dont die quiet. They pressure me.
They pressure me in Harlesden with all the fuckup I see,
all them busted mechanics an skanky weed merchants an
out-of-work burglars. All them geezers, builders, penny-
a-dozen subcontractors, plumbers, roofers, Situsec crews,
chippies, lekkies, humpers, glaziers, cowboys, bodgers an
odd-jobbers buildin an repairin whole towns. Geezers in
vans, up ladders. Geezers with metal an wood an brick,
carryin timber, scaffoldin. Geezers gruntin, shoutin, cussin.
Geezers with paint in their hair. Geezers readin the *Sun*,
drinkin cans of Coke. Geezers havin a smoke 6 floors up
with their legs danglin off of planks. Geezers reversin
trucks, trailin chain, hookin skips. Geezers who look up
at the passin streets, who look up at other people, who

look up at other geezers an wonder if them geezers have got it better. An they envy them geezers. An them geezers wha is envied is same time envyin other geezers. An all them geezers wha find themself on one or other side of envy is just basic geezers, just basic geezers wha work all day long with other geezers, geezers they clock on with an knock off with, geezers they drink with, geezers they compete for bints with. Geezers they suspect of everythin, envyin their everythin, half-inchin their screwdrivers, tellin porkies behind their backs, stitchin them up. An then half them geezers go home to their wife thinkin which of them geezers shagged her while he was out. An other half go home to just groan all night on their lonesome. An while buildins come an go, appearin an disappearin, them geezers is still there. Cos at the end the day, theres geezers everywhere, more an more of them, lots more of them, geezers everywhere wha groan wherever they are, up a ladder or down, in a van or out, geezers wha groan out every stinkin corner this stinkin city. Thats wha I see.

Then I'm pressured in Notting Hill with all the gear shinin out the yuppie flats like mini department stores. I'm pressured on every street where theres busy people who got somethin to do even if its shoppin, specially if its shoppin, bein as how I want to be shoppin too. An then time pressure me more as I pass 100 phone boxes to call all the people I know, Josh, Delroy, Steve K, Steve R, Damon, Charlie, Jez an so forth, to call my mates an tell them. To call the bitch an really fuckin tell her. To tell them all. Really fuckin tell them all the same one thing: *J is back. J is fuckin back.*

But I dont give in to none of it. Then it start pissin again, pissin so hard the rain go straight through my shoes. It bounce up off of the pavement an pour out the gutters above an force people into Burger King. It force me into some Half Moon or other with a half-pint. Some geezers swear the pubs the first place youll find them. But none thems gonna dream about this gaff. Scrubbed pine an la-di-da paintins on the walls courtesy of new management. 2 chin-strokers proppin up the bar. Swedish student bint chalkin *spaghetti vongole with baby clams £6.88* on the menu board. The stanky diehard regular in the corner dont look right suppin bitter next to all that. Like he aint got the message. Like he cant hear the speed garage they got pumpin out. Which in a way is why I come in here. For the peace an quiet in the noise.

But then the bint change all that. Cos when shes finish with the chalkin in red an yellow she serve me like I was pesterin her. Like I was a nonce queuin for spuds in Scrubs canteen. Like I was nothin. So course I wanna break the place up. Rip off her brewery t-shirt an tight black stretchy trousers an fuck her in the arse.

But that feelin dont really stir me for long. Mainly cos the first sip of the lager brain me. Few secs later I'm starin like a fuckwit at the stains on the bar an wonderin why wipin the bar always leave more stain on it than before. You can tell the way this bars been wiped, down then across, 3 down an 2 across like she was fillin the *Sun* crossword same time.

Then as I'm tryin to think this all out for I dont know how long, a very weird thing happen. Somethin that never happen to me ever. I start to see a whole map of the Harringay ladder mergin out the wipes on the bar. First I cant believe it. First I think I'm bein distorted by the overhead bulbs. Only I have to believe it when I see Wightman Road an Green Lanes runnin parallel. Then all the cross-roads of the ladder one after the other. Their names start comin back in order an theys all like the names of crusty generals in black-an-white films, twats who send their boys out to get their heads blowed off. Names like Effingham Fairfax Falkland an Frobisher. Between them I see the wistaria spreadin out. The way it creep through the ladder, in an out the gardens. By now my heart is goin. Its the only thing wha make any sense. That small item is like as not still there an maybe it really is useful like Uncle say. Maybe it has answers I need. Its like sometime you can stare for hours before you see wha was there all along. I leave most of my drink an head back out in the rain.

Take me the best part of an hour to get up Harringay. Even though the walkin knacker me an walkin through the rain knacker me double wha feel good is just coverin distance. An anyway, rain cool my boil. It cool it all the way into the ladder where I forget about it totally cos I realise I dont have a fuckin clue where the garden is, even the street.

Make me feel like The Ugly out *The Good The Bad* an so forth. The bit where he find himself in a cemetery lookin for the treasure in the grave of the unknown soldier. Only tough titty the graves is all unknown soldiers. But unlike The Ugly I try an be methodical, go to one end the long alley that cut right through the middle the ladder. An I start walkin down, checkin for signs like wistaria an other climbin plants.

But today look different from that night. Today the alley is puddle up an drippin, smellin cack, rain smearin cack, cack marked with pram wheel, cack marked with shoe print, cack overlay with more cack. An Dog Shit Alley dont give up its secret. It just allow people to tiptoe up an down it, people who keep their eyes fix on the ground scannin for trouble, people who dont look up long enough to notice wha the alley cut through, which is to say everythin, through rich an poor streets, along a barbed-up wall protectin the well-tended pride an joy of its owner, then along a busted fence tryin to stop the wild course nature take.

I merge out the alley. The ladder streets wave downhill to Green Lanes, into traffic, business, fruit an veg, people with life management goin on. I dive back in along the cobbles, step over the cack, wall an fence closin me down, barbed wire left, razor wire right, follow by puttied-in broken glass, spike rails an stuck-on warnings about dogs. Like anyone need tellin. An it just go on an on an on like this, with all the charm of a corridor in Scrubs. Only I dont recognise nothin. Group of 3 kids go past kickin a football against the sides. Another trail them on a stunt bike. Little superstar look right at me as he wheelie past.

I close my eyes an try an smell for wistaria. Rain ease off to a mist an the heat is comin up again off of the ground. But I'm all snotted up. I lean over, blow my nose out on the floor an wipe off on a fence thinkin wha the fuck I'm doin here. Then another weird thing happen, a second thing, another thing that never happen to me ever. The sound of me blowin my nose come right back at me from a ways off. Which is to say its like I get an echo off of my own nose. Only it aint no echo. That noseblow I heard before an it trigger memory. Its that same bunged-up grocer I just know it with the same bunged-up snout he always must of had. That he must of been born with. That is like the trademark of his personality.

The grocers nose give me a bearin an it renew my hope. Which is a lot more than you can ask from any nose. So then I connect my mind back to me & Duane, to the moment when we heard the noseblow, to the walls an fences we was scramblin at that point that night. We cut ourself many little time. But not that time. That wall where Duane got snare didnt have no barbs or nothin. It just had wistaria an wire. It was just a regular wood fence, not busted up, not new. I'm walkin down the alley fast now, feelin like the clues is addin up. Couple Muslim mothers trundle past in their flowin robes an veils with 4 holy warrin kids an rag dolls an untold bags of shoppin. When they gone I snap round. It could be I just seen the fence, that fence. Look both ways. Other people comin down but too far off to pinpoint me. Walk back a few steps to give it proper surveillance. When I'm satisfied it be the one I grab a hold, look both ways again as well as up in the sky for passin helicopters an leap right in, still sprite as fuck, hopin for the best.

Other side the gorse an weeds an grass is 9 month longer

an stronger an the bramble scratch up my legs. 9 month growth innit. An look at me. This is me I'm lookin at in the bramble. 9 month on then 9 month back to fuckin where? I mean I'm rippin my hands in the undergrowth lookin for wha? Like a skanky dog with half a memory of a skanky bone. Half a memory of a life once lived. I mean it just dont compare to wha is true-life entertainment or to anythin I use to like doin. It dont compare to nothin. I'm pawin the ground in angry patterns.

I been warned many time about angry patterns. Like this type of negative thought pattern. It was one the screw counsellors who identify my patterns. She force me on a positive thinkin course. To test up my ability to be positive she ask me stuff like: *What would you think if your wife had an affair with another man while you were inside?* Some other con had already told me the right answer: *Accept them for who they are then move on.* Unfortunately I forgot this at the time an I said: Wait till I got out then stab the cunt. I thought that would shut her up but she go: *By the use of that word are you referring to your wife or the other man?* So I said: Why, is it more positive to kill one or the other of them? That did shut her up.

Same time it made me even more negative. I mean after that the question of Monica havin an affair with another man make my patterns rage like a boil. An it could be one the factors wha brung the boil on first place. An here I am, me, my boil an my patterns. An my already damp garms mucky with wet mud.

So basically theres a mega feelin of depression even when

I find the box. Any case, its general appearance dont exactly shout Christmas. Its all mash up, rusty where the enamel flake off. But still in the same one piece an still locked. Shakin it rustle paper inside. Then come the realisation that I cant break it open here even if I had somethin to do it with. An also I cant carry it about just like that under my arm.

I mean, negative patterns or no, has 9 month listenin to cons talk bollocks improved my ability to plan? The fuck. Just remind me all the stuff they said innit, all the stuff wha come out durin association with no pause for breath: *I dont know wha went wrong it wasnt the plannin it was just bad luck*. An everyone thinkin: *No its cos youre a total tosser*. An then carryin on thinkin: *I'm not a total tosser therefore next time I will not get caught*. Remind me also of wha the screw counsellors said: *On the outside you have to learn to recognise the daft chancer who is on a route leading right back inside*. Which everyone take to mean someone else, anyone else, anyone but you. Back over the wall with my jacket off coverin the box I look like a tooled-up blagger, a daft chancer mergin out an alley with his hooky goods. I can see myself on a *Crimebusters* video clip: . . . *And stay tuned because after the break we have amazing footage of a daft bastard who thought nobody could see him* . . .

Still, my old ways come back. Or maybe they sneak back along with the fear of bein alone out here without a car. So between bursts of cats an dogs I'm in Kentish Town Tyres and Retreads. I got an old mate there, mechanic name of Farooq. Hes in the pit under a car. A fully extended jack prop up a tv with oily fingerprints on the screen. They got a documentary about the North American moose, the largest member of the deer family. When Farooq come up for air he nod to me like I was expected any time this year. He drill open the box I show him, dont ask why or wha or where I been or where I'm goin or why I need a car or how I'm gonna sort him. All he do is make a call.

An just as the moose turn toward the spruce an pine forests of the south some kid turn up with keys. Farooq take me round the side an unveil the soaked tarp off of a recent MOT duckout thats mostly likely been cut an shut with a ringed an clocked scrapyard reject. The underseal compound to cover the joins aint even been painted over. The brakes a sponge an only one the wipers works. All in all the puddin with an engine go by the name Proton Persona. Farooq aint wordy but his sense of humour shine through. An he know I'm good when it come down to it. Generous good from way back.

—— Like they say Farooq, youre a diamond geezer.

—— Islam, he go, dont have geezers.

Which catch me totally off guard.

—— Yeah? Wha they got?

—— Mullers.

—— Yeah? I'm laughin. So youre a diamond muller.

He grin at me, throw a couple jump leads on the back seat.

—— Come in handy, never know . . .

He grin again through his cracked bearded face that tell a story, the whole fuckin history of raw hands an achin bones feelin spring after the freezin metal winter in a workshop where the sun dont shine. Which is to say Farooq rate in my top 10, an is almost a photo finish with Duane for IOU.

The Personas so hooky I decide to keep my licence on me as a first line of defence. But reality is, its the sort of car wha make me 2 time as invisible as before. From inside it all look more gloomier outside. Make it easier to blank the streets an shops an sheep. But not the women. They storm out every door an bus an up every street an side street busy as fuck the lot of them, stridin an struttin an stormin with big things on their minds, more fuckin important things than I could ever know.

An I'm comparin them, cant help it, to Monica. More fatter than her. Thinner. Leggier. Uglier. Hairier. I imagine her goin past with that fuckin important look on her face that make you want to look even more. Like women with important looks on their mugs dont need looks. Monica use to have both the looks *and* the look an I wonder if she still got them both. Because if she was here right now I'd rape that look off of her face for ever. *Yeah bitch, Daddy is home*. Still, a tosser in a Persona has to have fantasies.

Side street off of Kentish Town High Road past a mobile

soup stall for grizzly pissheads I park up to examine wha the box contain. Stack of papers is wha. An a red pocket Bible with the pages of the Book of Job turn down. Throw the whole lot on the passenger seat an the box into a dustbin in a front garden.

The papers is all sorts. Pink an yellow triplicate sheets off of invoices an suchlike. One from Avis for a 3.5-ton long-base Transit an another from A1A Wheels for a 7.5-tonner with a tail-lift. Then a big blue invoice from a Myerson & Son Butchers Sundriesman: 20 aprons @ £423.43; 300 rolls of heavy-duty packing tape @ £123.50; Epelsa dual-scale (lbs/kilos) digital scale @ £462.00. After that haulage receipts from Tilbury Electricals. A letter of credit. The tacho disc off of a truck with the speed an timin for some run or other. Clip to it is more receipts, some them foreign, for coffee, breakfast an all that. Then a bill of lading. Complicated. Then a letterhead page with a little aeroplane logo: *Escuela Lliriana de Vuelo Libre y Parapente*. Very fuckin complicated. Theres a list attach to it. Schedule statin some event or other takin place regular on the 14th, the 14th every month. Opposite theres a rota. 3 names over 12 months. Gunther Van Doude. Yuri Zamyatin. Joachim Hernandez. Between all this theres 2 transparent plastic sleeves, a 10,000-peseta bill in each.

From where I'm lookin all this is only a secretary short of the British Empire. Least a corner of it wha is forever Uncles. Which is to say its the sort of runnins his old man set up an he take over from his 2-up-2-down in Beckton. Could be anythin, smugglin, launderin, lorryjackin. Maybe the pesetas is fake samples. All I know is butchers sundriesmen an foreigners always get me confuse. Get me thinkin who we rob that night. Or try. Or why Uncle finger the gaff first place. Maybe it was his an hes creamin insurance. Or would of. Maybe the lockup belong to his enemy. Maybe. An now Uncles fucked, his plans revealed an his pear-shape knickers blowin across London. The papers I stash in the boot.

Me & Duane knew we was grassed. It was a feelin we had the both of us. Nothin make sense. An I aint even thunk about my domestic situation, how to deal with it. I look up, aware of the surgin High Road. 3.20 or so an the school rush hour is kickin in. From Camden Town to the shadow of Archway Tower theres a tidal wave of kids leggin an bikin it. Some of thems chuckin Tango off of the top deck gridlock buses. One girl about 14 with big red lips 2 feet in front of her stare right in the car. When I look back she laugh, flick her tongue at me. Behind her some other kids yellin at his enemy: *Tell your mum: the bitch is through.* Enemy come back with: *Yeah an next time you see yours get my pants back for me.*

Mums, bitches an pants: cant live with em, cant live without em. All round Archway, back of Junction Road an over Dartmouth Park Hill into my old street theres crowds of schoolkids who seem like theys havin more sex than me. An in among them theres plenty of horny mums wearin just-pickin-the-kids-up-from-school skimpy outfits an drivin about in cars like tinted bedrooms on wheels.

An course somewhere out there, out in the world of

plush bedrooms an horny mums, is Monica. Shes doin the school run in a pink Vitara. Shes checkin her nose in the rearview for specks of coke. As she stretch up to the mirror her silicone can be seen above the steerin wheel. Then shes drivin back from an undisclosed school to an undisclosed address to carry on with her undisclosed life. An if she thinks I'm not gonna stop her shes wrong. Because I fuckin will.

6 half 6 I'm drivin round Duane & Trudys tryin to keep the screen demisted with my sleeve. Muswell Hill is bubblin, gutters overflowin, drains under pools, the 7/11 like an island with people goin tiptoe round it. One way or other all the waters gushin down the steep slopes off of the Broadway toward Crouch End makin the tarmac shimmer. I went an cash up one the peseta bills in this bureau I know opposite the hospital on Praed Street, Paddington, land of whores an nurses. Moneyman look at me then look at it then consider the 242.29 on the rate board. Course he offer me well under which tell me wha I already know about the bill bein hooky. Whatever he give me I spend on sparkly an little presents for J & K.

Now I'm parked up outside Duane & Trudys on Hillfield

but I cant get out the car. Just cant. Cant move. Like I seize up. I'm nervous. I dont get nervous. Me I got nerves of steel. Nerves that dont never get nervous. I mean some burglars shit for 3 day before, the whole time durin an for 3 day after. Which is to say a lot of burglars spend their whole career shittin. So obviously theres more than an army of them who is inside on account of waste matters deposited at the scene. Which is to say dont work with a shitter. Me I never took no bogroll on a job. Never needed to. But here I am on a social, not even at work, my guts proper churnin an my bowels boilin.

From up here you can see the clouds clearin cross the whole town, driftin off south-east takin the rain in grey shadow over Canary Wharf an beyond. For some people rain then clearin skies mean somethin. They look up an say: its a sign. They say to themself the worst is over. But weather dont mean nothin. It dont say nothin about the worst bein over. Nerves shouldnt mean nothin neither. But if the 2 together mean somethin they mean I'm weak, weak an fucked up for all to see. I try grinnin into the mirror only it dont convince me. So I decide I'm gonna talk fast an be loud as I can. Clench unclench my fists. Get myself to the front door. Smooth my damp hair an take the deep one Trudy recommend. Knock a loud corny rhythm.

Few secs later Trudys standin there all swolled up. I launch right in with wha I hope is a mad shout of joy. Squeeze her shoulders. Give her a big kiss.

—— Ma God J, ma God, she go, grinnin, hair flappin in my face.

As I back off it occur to me, right there before I say actual words, that Trudy is 9 month pregnant. Like almost to the day. Which is to say this swolled-up womb I'm starin at is nothin more nothin less than Duanes Freedom Fuck. Then Duane come up behind her laughin.

—— Check him out: *he cometh forth like a flower* innit . . .

Then shoutin even louder so the street can hear:

—— JUBILATION IN THE NATION. *HAPPINACITY IN THE CITY.* THE MAN BE RELEASE FROM DA BEAST . . . *LI-BE-RA-TED* . . .

Me an Duane go into a clinch. Hes swolled up too, chunky round the belt an round the gills like he aint been jumpin fences.

—— Jesus yous both grown, I shout as I grab his cheeks. Look at all this lovely jubbly.

—— Couldnt let Tru eat all the ice cream an chips on her own innit.

—— Yeah but she been eatin for 2, I'm screamin. Then she go back to normal size.

—— J, this is my *noo* normal size, Duane shout back. An you better climatise your good self, you get me?

73

—— Oh yeah? How you gonna get through a toilet window lookin like that?

Duanes about to answer even louder but draw his breath an I catch a secret look, more like a supersonic blink between them, like I stumble on taboo subject.

—— Dont worry J, goes Trudy headin to the livin room with me & Duane followin. We'll soon feed you up.

—— Innit, Duane grin. Man need some meat an potato on him after wha he been tru.

Livin room is full of decor like brand-new IKEA show-room. Like its all been prepare by team of top-whack baby specialist. Livin room is where we proper look at each other the 3 of us. An wha is clear is the thing wha dont fit this scene. Which is to say my boil.

—— J, you look fierce man, goes Duane like he was buildin up to payback for his short lock. He look fierce innit Tru?

—— Yeah alrigh, I go.

—— No serious man. It look like a whole new face upon your face.

—— I cant fuckin help it can I.

—— No but—

—— Ive got something you can put on it, goes Trudy laughin, her cheeks all flush from the excitement.

—— Yeah? Like wha?

—— Forget it Tru, goes Duane. Aint nu'in you can put on that. Man need a surgeon.

—— Shut up. Wha you got?

—— Theyre medicated patches. They—

—— Aint gonna do nu'in.

—— Course they will. They draw out impurities without—

—— *Never in a million you gonna draw—*

—— Duane shut it. I'll take em.

Trudy wags a finger at Duane an goes off to fetch the patches.

—— Musta been tough innit . . . So tell me, how was it?

I grin cos I know hes takin the piss. Thats the one Q guaranteed to shut a con the fuck up. Otherwise every conversation, even if its North American moose an medicated patches, come back to the same thing: their time. But with that Q a con start to look dark an moody like its all too heavy to talk about.

—— I aint playin King Sob, I go just to reassure him. Sides your ears about to get proper bent listenin to Duane Junior.

—— The truth dont come clearer innit, goes Duane kissin Trudy as she come back an touchin her bump. We got time to burn one innit Tru?

—— Wouldnt be right if you didnt, she say smilin with her mouth but not her eyes. I left the patches by the bathroom sink.

—— Cheers Trudy.

Duane beckon me an we go past the big round dinner table laid for 5 with proper cutlery an serviettes an glasses an everythin on into the back garden.

—— Rules J, rules, goes Duane apologetic as he step out onto wha look like a fresh-laid patio.

He flourish his arms toward a silver salver on a plastic garden table.

—— Remember that?

—— Could I forget? Almost died for it.

—— Yeah well, life-threatenin graft been put to good use innit. *Check dis* . . .

He lift the cover to reveal 2 massive lines waitin to

happen like heart attacks. Next to them is 2 little shot glasses with wha must be Jack.

—— Case yous rusty on the basics 'low me to demonstrate the method of stimmin up, goes Duane stickin a bill up his nose an motorin down his line like a Formula 1 Hoover, shot to finish, face transformin into Evil Joker.

I grin ear to ear an my guts turn liquid just lookin at him. Follow the 3-step demo to the letter as Duane spark up a humongous spliff wha he prepare earlier too. Cloud of skunk puff out into the sunset. A 1,000 time when me & Duane pull one thing or other we would end up somewhere or other monged out, celebratin, chillin then passin out starin at textured ceilin. Ceilin with texture is a weed smokers best friend. Now, in the time it take a few drops or 10 to patter an scatter among the leaves above me I relive all that life. All of it. The smell of it. The taste of it. But my first big toke on the spliff is the last thing I remember. Cos next thing I'm comin round with my head in a toilet.

—— *Oh bwoy its movin*, go Duane laughin somewhere behind me. Thought you was gone. You been black out least 5 long ones. Thought you was lick up for ever.

—— Fuck me, I manage to groan, smell of puke risin up at me from the bowl. I'm still black out.

—— Old days nu'in used to blitter you. Need to work on that tolerance level innit.

I'm about to answer but I cant. Cos suddenly I'm blubbin. Which is to say tears overtake me, streamin out my eyes with snot an all sorts hangin off of my nose an I just cant stop. When I try an stop it force its way out. Duane goes quiet, pats my back, hands me tissue. But I just carry on. Sobbin is wha. King Sobbin. Cant even focus on him for all the stuff comin out of me. All the words the jumbled words.

—— Shes a fuckin bitch innit, I'm sobbin. Tell me: is she a bitch? Tell me. Shes a bitch innit D? Shes a fuckin bitch for wha she done. Tell—

—— Easy, easy. Relax. Here wipe—

—— You know, when I think of her I sometimes think *Monica* an sometimes *bitch*. You understand? So when I say summin like *Monica is a bitch* . . . You know? Then its confusin an I dont know who she is. Monica bitch or Bitch bitch? Yeah? Wha is she? I mean wha is she? You get me? You get me? I mean—

—— Fuck you on about? Come on man, take a shower or summin. Its just your nose talkin. Na mean. Shower make you—

—— Tell you wha I'm on about. I'm on about why she done wha she done. You know? Wha Trudy say? Wha she say? She seen her innit? She been—

—— Ah man, come on, goes Duane wipin my face with a towel.

—— Why she do it to me? I go, grabbin the towel off of him. Why she do it to me? I love her. I still love her an all that. I do. Sposin I had a son . . . Wha if I had a son? You got everythin. You got it all. Look at you. 9 month an you got it all. Look at you. Plush home, everythin. Family, everythin. Name it you got it. Everythin—

—— Ah man . . .

—— Why she do it? Why the bitch fuckin do it? Why she—

—— Cos man . . .

—— Why? Why she do it? Wha I done? Wha bad I done? I'm lookin. Why she—

—— Cos man . . .

—— Cos fuckin wha? Wha? I done everythin innit. For the woman I love an all that.

—— Yeah but—

—— But wha? Wha I done? Wha bad I done? Say it. Wha?

—— Come on man . . .

—— Wha? Say it. Wha?

—— Wha? You wanna know wha? You slap her silly is wha.

—— Wha? Wha you sayin? Aint like that. You know it aint.

Not the way she make out. Not the way she make out. I done everythin. Everythin.

—— Yeah man . . .

—— You know wha I done. You seen it. You know wha I done.

—— Yeah man I seen it.

—— Everythin. *Everythin*. Innit. Innit.

—— Yeah man yeah, you done everythin cept layin off . . .

—— Wha you sayin? Wha—

—— You got a streak man. You know it. Is all I'm say—

Theres a big knock at the door an Trudys voice hollerin.

—— *Duane you getting it?*

—— *Yeah Tru* . . . Forget it now J. Forget it. No point thinkin them things now. New chapter innit . . . Freedom innit. You done the tariff. You done it. New leaf an all that razz. Come on man . . . Heres them patches for your . . . for your whatever the fuck you call it.

Duane grin. Cant help himself. Set me off too. Then I feel the gak again drainin down the back of my throat an I bust out laughin like a maniac. Hysterical.

—— Hes back. J is back. Y'alrigh?

—— Yeah yeah.

—— Back with the livin?

—— Yeah man yeah. Gis one them tissues . . . cheers . . .

—— You sure youre—

—— Yeah yeah get the door man. I'm ok . . . I'm ok. I'll be there . . .

The laughin stop. Everythin go quiet in me. Only sound the water bubblin out the tap as I wash up. Then I put the patch on my boil without lookin myself in the eye. Then I make myself look myself in the eye. I try to see myself but all I see is a geezer with a patch. Then I see the shame in my face for lettin go like that. It sober me, sober me enough so I can start all over. Forget it all. Forget it now. I done the tariff I know. Only its like the punishment aint even proper begun.

Outside I can hear Duane greetin Sensi & Fran, them askin about me, Duane makin some daft gag about a burglar on a big job. Sensi & Fran laughin. They got the same deep gulpin laugh. Probably cos they done the same steroids. Actually you can only tell them apart when both thems in Lycra. Which aint too frequent as it goes. But even in regular garms their muscle ripple with a life of their own. Fran bein a ex-Olympic discus-thrower who once won a bronze on tele but was disqualified after the drug test. Sensi bein a ex-army boxer an ju-jitsu champion whose ears look like they was squeezed out his brain by someone who had him in headlock. A grin come back on my face an I storm out the bathroom.

—— BIG CHIEF FLYIN HEADBUTT, I yell which is wha Sensi mean in Japanese.

—— *Hold me tight dont let me go*, he yell back as he bearhug the air out of me.

—— Fran the Man, I whisper.

—— *My baby*, she cry as she wring the piss out of me.

The wringin turn to suffocation by chest. I hang on to the belief that I'm the only one wha can call her Fran the Man an live. When the 2 them finish usin me for bagpipe I realise they look more bigger an healthier than ever. An that me I shrunk by comparison.

Trudys callin us to the table. The 4 of us shadow-box our way there. Or more like Sensi & Fran do. They never understood their whole lives that normal people cant take too much rib-crushin. But with the old crew more less reunited it all start to go fast, faster than 9 month, mad fast. Trudy serve everythin perfect: caviar an sparkly, veal escalopes an green beans an roast potato an salad an French stick an butter wash down with fruity red then chocoloate gateau, coffee, brandy an all that. A feast let me say. An the whole time we just go through all the old stories.

The time Sensi (when he was 17 an still called Ron) went down the library to mug up on burglary only course all the burglary books was missing from stock. Only similar one in stock was *Buggleboots*, kids story about a boy called Buggles who finds a pair of magic boots. Course Sensi couldnt leave the library empty-handed.

The time me & Duane grab a antique vase with a fantastic curly design all round it only to discover the vase was original Poundstretchers an all the curly bits was pubes stuck on by the owner with wha must of been true love.

The first thing Duane recall stealin was his neighbours alarm clock radio while she was sleepin next to it. Neighbour woke up. Duane tell her in lovely soothin tones its alright hes just come to repair the clock. Neighbour mumble ok an go back to sleep. Duane leave the clock. Just as well cos next day the neighbour she tell Duanes mum this dream she had about the alarm clock an the repairman.

An I tell about the first time I got nicked age 14 which was on account of 1 witness. An 1 print off of my big toe. Why? Cos I took my shoes off so as to be totally silent. Then to avoid fingerprints I took my socks off an put them on my hands.

After a few drink flush her, Fran tell about the time she nobble her rivals discus at a regional athletics meet. She coat the discus with thin layer of lead causin it to fly out of control into a police horse. Knock the animal cold. Fran paint the picture of the muffs face as he start sinkin to the ground still tryin to canter.

Before she know it Trudys pitchin in with the time her & Monica let us all into the bastard hairdressers they was workin in. With Sensi & Fran an me & Duane an Trudy & Monica workin like a chain we got everythin out that night: 4 hairdressin basins; 2 double-sided 5-foot mirrors; blow-driers; stylers an combs; 4 hydraulic chairs; footstools; 1 trolley; 1 sunbed; the 6-foot chrome reception desk, an course most the black marble tilin. Trudy & Monica was in business 2 mile away within a week.

Then out the blue Duane go:

—— I'm done with all that. Heres to the future . . .

So we all toast an everythin only it confuse me.

—— Wha you sayin youre done?

—— What can it mean after a lifetime of doing? Fran go in a deep slow voice causin everyone to stop an think.

—— It mean I'm done with wha I been doin. I'm goin hydroponic.

—— Goin who?

Duane glance at Trudy. Shes already movin, pickin up plates an glasses, avoidin eyes, my eyes for sure. An then course Frans helpin her like a button just been pushed. The women. The men. As they go off with the first load of plates, Fran askin about the baby room an all that, Duane say:

—— I'm businessin J. Its my noo career. Hydroponics is in

demand. Bigtime. Way I see it everyones gonna be growin their own supply homeside. Specially after they go legalise the product. So thats where Duanes Lighting Systems come in. I'm gonna provide a guaranteed quality low-cost yield you get me?

—— *Quality low-cost yield?* You changed newspapers?

—— Yeah Sensi, I get the *Daily Reality*. So no more *mix an blend* innit. No more Dastardley & Muttley.

—— Duane I cant— Can you believe this? I cant fuckin believe this. I mean look at me. I'm gonna need support just to get my crutches back.

—— Crutches I aint got but I'll do you some armbands to tide you cos—

—— Fuck that man.

—— No serious, listen to wha this is J. This is opportunity for you man. Come in with me on this one.

—— Like I'm takin orders?

—— Whos orderin? I'm sayin partners. Partners is wha.

—— Nah man . . .

—— Wha no? Why no?

—— Because, go Sensi before he plunge a brandy, bang his glass down an start to fill us all up. Because *he whos got the craft, graft*. An theres plenty of graft out there. I mean look at him: the man is *ripe*. I mean examine the patient. Look at him. His circulations cryin out for circuit-trainin an his arse is itchin for the off.

—— Dunno about no circuits, go Duane laughin, swallowin, bangin down his glass.

—— Me neither, I go, followin suit.

—— Itchy arse fits though, says Sensi fillin up again. Hes ready for action. Look at him.

—— Revenge more like, Duane say as he look at me long an hard before he swallow an bang down the glass. House of cards J, I'm tellin you. Thats wha revenge is.

—— House of cards stacked up on a slanty table, goes Sensi sinkin his next.

—— By a pisshead, I go, gulpin, who is lick up on brandy . . .

—— An blind in one eye, go Duane as I fill us up.

—— With a nervous tick he inherit from his gran . . .

—— Who was a diabetic crackhead anyway . . .

—— An blind in the other eye . . .

—— Which cause her panic attack . . .

—— Which run in the family . . .

An so on an so on an so on. Then I more less achieve

blackout a second time. Duane an Sensi carryin me to bed is wha I remember. An Fran an Trudy floatin by. An Duanes last words: *Porridge 6.30 a.m.* An me callin him names. An the boil ragin soon as I lie down, an the walls, the thin walls, with Duane an Trudy on the other side like a mum an a dad, me like a child tryin to sleep, fresh sheet, fresh pillow, 10 by 6 or so, me like a child tryin to sleep like I been told, only I cant sleep like I been told because the sleep I sleep is more deeper than ever, full of bad dreams wha dont make no sense, wha I cant stop. Because its a proper sleep, a proper deep sleep wha fall on me like a smell, the smell of me rottin, rottin away.

Wake up fuck knows wha time, afternoon, stingin grey light comin through a yellow curtain with green red an blue farmyard animals on it. I know straight away I dreamed bad dreams cos I feel like the geezer in this story a teacher read out in school one time. Geezer wake up one day an suddenly realise hes a fuckin insect. On his back. Legs in the air. Couldnt get out his bed. Totally mess up his plans. Me I got it worse I swear. Hangover pound my head an white saliva stick round my mouth.

Outside its dead quiet. Note an keys on the kitchen table. Help myself an all that. My stuff in the wash. Back later an all that. Note add that Sensi expect me down the gym for a workout. Like fuck. Make tea. Take a bath. Try an relax. But my heart start to go mental in the hot water. After that my hands shakin too much to shave. Besides shavin would magnify the boil. Fact I decide not to shave again. Trudy leave instruction for a 3-step routine: scrub, cleanse an a new patch. I skip the scrub an wish I done the same with the cleanser cos it practically burn a hole in my face. Wake me up to normality though.

Before I know it I'm scannin round for Trudys address book which I know she got somewhere. Its been in the back my mind the whole time, from the first time I talk to her. Soon I'm not just scannin I'm huntin. By the phones. On bedside tables. Under phone books. On shelvin. I leave no trace. I replace everythin the way it was. Not long before the address book appear in the obvious place, which is to say in the kitchen drawer people keep for them things, things like papers, gas bills, postcards, microwave instruction manual, spare plugs an old half-use packets of plastic forks from summer barbies I never attended. This is the place where I meet up with Monica again. In a drawer, in her best friends address book, address like a strangers, new phone number, new mobile. At first I wonder if its the right Monica. Like maybe Trudy know all sorts of Monicas, penny-a-dozen Monicas who is all most likely ex-hairdressers tradin up to beauty therapists.

The phone on the wall next to the drawer is beggin me. I know Monica: she wait for the number to display before she answer. Bet even her home phone got display function as standard. She'll see Trudys number, its ringin now, an pick up for sure. What if Jade or Kylie answer? Wha do I say? I aint ready for them. No way I'm ready for them. So I hang up an dial the mobi instead. Few rings an her voice come blastin through like breakfast DJ.

—— How you doin babes alright . . . ? Tru . . . ? Oh Truuudy, its breaking up girl . . . Tru . . . Hello . . . Helloo . . . Trudy . . . ?

So I start singin *We cant go on together with suspicious minds* by Harold Melvin an The Bluenotes. Cos thats how we met, in a karaoke bar durin a friends weddin reception. Thats wha I was singin. I look her right in the eye. She use to say thats wha did it for her. The emotion. Now I try an make it a bit lighthearted. But my voice crack an I lose the time. It come out dreadful. Truly dreadful. Cant hold the notes. Get to *go on* an it all turn to aerosol mousse. Should keep goin through the chorus but even the well-known words go dim. Silence. Like for 2 whole secs she dont respond nothin. I say *Mon*— then she hang up. Which I guess dont surprise me. She use to like my singin. She use to say I got a good voice, specially with all-round bathroom acoustic an a showerhead for a microphone.

I stare at the phone for pointless time before I hang up too. I feel so ashame I go round the flat 2 more time just to make sure Duane & Trudy is really out. An that all the windows is well close to the street. Only it still feel like someone must of heard me, like someones in here watchin me, hearin everythin. I try an put it all together, to make sense of the me I think I am, the karaoke star I was an the Persona driver I become.

Course its only a matter of 3 mins before I dial all over again. Start to leave a message on her mobi then blow it out. Then I breathe deep an phone back an this time leave a message, a sort of *baby Ive changed it can be different this time* sort of message only without them words. Cos even though I changed its not because of me that I had to change. Only I dont say them words neither cos they would all come out bad, which is to say negative. I aint repeatin wha words I use.

Then I try her home phone. I just do, feelin theys all gonna be there, all of them, Jade & Kylie. Her. I try an imagine them. I try an imagine wha new toys an clothes an words J & K got now, wha new things they discover. I try an imagine who is really with them. Someone else is there too, some cunt playin dad to my girls. The nose man. Some cunt who watches, waits, the whole time schemin up other geezers wife. When I phone back it turn out I'm right. An who does this schemin cunt turn out to be? BTs one an only *Mr Answerphone* is who, talkin at me smooth an confident like he been livin with Monica quite some time. *Your call cannot be answered right now* . . . Fuckin bastard. *Please leave a message after—* So I do. I let it be known that we is gonna talk for def because I know where she live. Only I dont use them words. I aint repeatin the words I use. *I know where you live* is most likely how it sound though. Which is pretty strange, I mean sayin to your wife that you know where she live.

After that I phone the mobi again but its engaged. So it diverts to the message system. So I leave a message tellin her not to worry cos I aint into messin her round an all that, cos I aint intimidatin nobody despite of everythin, cos all I wants a chat. So I tell her not to worry about nothin. Then I tell her that I totally accept whats happen. Because I moved on now. But even so, even though I moved on an everythin, I still care about the future of my children.

Then I phone her mobi again. Its still engaged so I leave another message to let it be known that I mean wha I say. Then I phone her mobi again but she is still talkin because of course its good to talk. So I leave a message just to say that Tru never give me no numbers. Cos I dont want no bad blood comin between the 2 best friends an all that. Then I have to phone again to tell her where she can reach me, which is to say round Duane & Trudys, for the time bein till I get sorted. Then I phone her 2 more time, one time at home to tell her to pick up the phone, to please pick it up, to pick it up right now, all the time swallowin the *fucks* an coughin through the *bitches* an generally chokin on the words I cannot say. Words I cannot say to my home answerphone cos J & K could easily hear them. An they shouldnt have to hear them words.

Then I make the second one, to the home phone again, cos by now the mobi is well switched off. I'm more calmer. So I know I can say wha I want to say in a responsible manner. I phone really just to let her know that she can just phone me whenever she want, like in her own time, which is to say when shes ready, when she aint pressured, when she aint surprise an all that. Which is to say after shes took some time, long as she want, to think it all through. An then, only when shes totally ready, she can call. Which is to say that at the end day, after all is said an done, shes in control. Shes makin the decisions. I add to her that basically I'm leavin the ball in her court. Its down to her. Cos its the best way. An all that. It really is.

Jesus do I breathe easy after this long ordeal been completed. Then I get dress up in a pair Duanes joggers an one his t-shirts. Then I get in the car an go straight round to see Monica an the kids.

Laughter come out the neighbours house from a game show. *Theres a lot riding on this answer Jackie . . .* Nothin but Yale lock on their front door. Not like Monicas door. Down the street theres a Situsec van. 2 builders with fluorescent stripes sittin on a wall by open drain eatin rolls an listenin to Capital Gold. I drift by one time. Obvious shes out. Maybe she was never in.

Either way. Capital Gold an game show dont suit the area. Which is to say a secret des res village off of Hendon Lane with its own village green an its own stone monument honourin the reses wha decease in the wars. *Their name liveth for ever more.* Yeah well, maybe I'm gonna add my tag to the list of people they aint never gonna forget. Corner the green pick out a bench. From there 32 Village Road is clear.

An me I'm hidden from her gaff by bushes. Plenty bushes. Plenty wildlife. I got all day. Sensi could live here all year. Survive off of berries an beetle grub like that US pilot they shot down behind enemy lines. He use survival tactics. Eat woodlice full of protein an carbs. Liveth for ever till his tooled-up commando mates come rescue him in helicopter. Trouble bein I aint Sensi an I prefer my woodlice cooked.

Other hand gettin in to see Monica is gonna need more than commandos in helicopter. Gonna need front door keys. Like 6 of them. Cos if I teach the bitch one thing its coverin security lapses. She got barrel, Chubb, window locks an grilles. Alarm even. All this mean she spend a wedge. Either she got a rich dad she never acquaint me with or she got a sugar dad she keep secret. But it aint her wha pay for all this. An it stand out a mile even among gaffs wha got electric gateway.

Either way. She'll be back. She will be. To her armour-plated village hideout. Hour, hour an half. Round half 3, 4. Jade an Kylie. Just matter of waitin. All I need do is nothin. Which is difficult when you got nothin to do. Not like the Situsec boys who probably got jobs stack up till next year. They do nothin like it was nothin doin nothin. Just sit there learnin daft lyrics off of the radio an eatin endless supply of cheese rolls.

A little rain come an go. The wind too. Even come an go once twice together, the wind an rain. An all type cloud float an rush on different levels in opposite direction. Onyx bin crew work the street. An all type people come an go, fixin this, plumbin that, deliverin boxes, goin to the shops, comin home, sweepin the path, takin the rubbish out, havin a chat, walkin the dog round the streets. An it carry on like that for hour, hour an half.

Its partly cos I'm waitin for a pink Vitara that I dont recognise Monica straight away. Even when I do, after I seen the Audi she got, even then I dont. Stuck out one the back window is a palm. Can feel wha the air feel like against it, fresh, heavy, then numbin. Even when I attach the palm to Jades face it dont quite look like her. Shes gigglin over some joke with Kylie who look almost as big as her. An it aint like Jade stood still 9 month. Fact Kylie start school only 2 month after I get done an the first years the most crucial. Cant help it but it hurt me to think the girls is gigglin an please with life without me. Must be half-term, most likely the last day of it aside the weekend. Add insult to injury, Monicas chirpin away on her mobi as she park up, her life rollin on an on, things to do, *busy busy*, busy as fuck without me.

They all get out. They all got new hairstyle. Monica gone celebrity blonde. Plus she got Florida tan. Fact they all got them. That an new styles. They look like lost tribe of curly-hair people strugglin against dead straight hairdos. Its like I only recognise them from photos in my memory. Even her chest is cover which always use to be out an about, on show, even in dead winter, cos she was proud, now its gone, cover up in stylish garms, *celeb discreet*, like it was for certain eye only an all that. Which is to say not mine.

Point is 9 month on the fuckin bitch aint even turn ugly. On the contrary dear Watson. She been on holiday. She taken good care herself. She got lists of friends to blab with. Lisha an Rach an Sooz an Carm an course Trudy. She got everyone new styles for a laugh. Cos she felt like it. Just like she never felt like sendin me letter. Never wrote nothin. But she got everythin. She got my goods. Cos they was hers, in her name. She was never even there on alibi night. She plan it all. *Bitch is plottin* is wha Duane say an he aint usually realistic. This time he was too realistic cos the bitch not only plot but succeed also. Matter fact she taken over a country, a whole fuckin country, my country, an all its people, my people, an control it all like she built it, like she own it, like she got it all herself from Homebase, like she pay for it, like she work for it.

They clamber out an all that, with shoppin an all that, bags an bags of it, bitch lookin round the whole time, up the street an down, nerves in her eyes. They was never home. She aint heard them other messages. She wont now. I'll rip the fuckin phones out the walls. I'm gonna burn it down. I wait till she start on the locks, keys janglin, load of keys for load of prop that she cant get into fast enough. Greedy fuckin bitch. Thats all she ever want out her husband. Gravy train. Fuckin slag. Gravy train slag with a Florida tan. An blonde like a bitch. Like she was livin the life, largin it like a dancehall queen.

She get to wha look like the last of them, the last the locks, which is wha I'm waitin for. Cos I'm out the bushes by then an walkin up behind an I cant see Jade an Kylie no more. Theys there but blurred, gone blurred. All I see is the slag thief, the sly bitch overdue for payback. All I see is her loaded down with gear, hooky gear handled by her, cos thats wha she is, a gravy-stinkin slag handler of goods wha she steal out my pocket, out my mouth, wha she rob, she rob me blind, 7 years she rob me blind.

Whole time my feet squeak across wet mowed grass. Shes openin the front door, pickin up bags. An I'm there, close enough to smell how slack she is, how her perfume trail the air, how sugary she is. An I feel someone inside, the BT man, there but not there, a feelin I cant put my finger on of her bein shagged all over the shop, stuffed floor to ceilin, wheelbarrowed along the hall an back, seen to upstairs, downstairs an over my ladys chamber pot. Cos thats how you make a place your own, by shaggin all over it. Thats wha I feel, standin as I am for a good 3, 4 secs, just standin there lookin at her back like it was cell wall. An her back become full of detail, creases an marks in her black leather jacket. More you look more you see. Just like on a cell wall. Then the 3 thems goin in. I'm waitin for her to turn, hopin the kids is goin in first so that when she turn for that last bag of shoppin she'll be alone for a moment. Just me an her after all this time. Then I can punch her in the face.

But it dont happen that way. Instead wha happen is a word, a word is wha come out, one I never would say, would never think of sayin, wha a nonce an only a nonce would say. An even a nonce would regret it. Word I say is *hello*. Then it ring in my head 3 time for each them in my family. An all 3 them turn round together like trained cabaret act with pleasant surprise on their faces till they see I aint no chippy neighbour come to discuss the foulin of the footpath. Monica glance open door. Kylie she dont so much as recognise me. Jade speak first. She say *Daddy*. Thats when I remember the little presents I got them. Been in the boot all night an all day. 2 type furry animal. I think I must sort of sink to my knees an take her hand. The nails is painted like she experiment with Monicas polish. When she was born her nails was blue an her fingers wrinkly like an old mans. Then her nails turn red like henna an then normal all in a few hours of bein born. Next thing shes paintin them. I try an hug her only she pull away like never before. Then she go:

—— Mummy you said he was dead.

—— Wha? I go standin up. Wha you tell em?

Monica focus on the boil patch, practically make her squirm, then she shrug with her eyebrows wha have been in a perfect state of pluck since 1994. She go:

—— It was a white lie.

—— Yeah? Wha would you call—

—— Dont start J.

—— Jade, I go leanin down, Jade honey, say hello to—

—— Jade, go inside now an take your sister . . . Go on . . . Now . . .

Worst thing is Jade dont seem too bothered one way or other, see her dad or no it dont make a difference to her. She look at Monica, see shes serious. Then she take her sister by the hand, an they go in. I cant make her say hello. I cant make her stay. I'm a stranger tryin to give her a sweet. Wha can I do? I look at Monica an wha I got on my mind must be in my face. Cos she know, she know maybe even before me, that I'm about to do it. But wha she say come out in a voice like a growlin demon. She go:

—— Touch me you will be dead.

She say *touch me you will be dead*. Threat she never use before. Threat wha proper shut me up cos I know there an then she got back-up. She got power. She got commandos an helicopters. She got shoppin an a hairdo. Clear wha the bitch is tryin to do. Which is to say intimidate me.

—— Who you been seein?

—— Nobody.

—— Bollocks.

—— What difference does it make? Its over J an my life is—

—— I dont give a fuck wha your life is wha about mine? Where was you on the night?

—— Tellin you now J, you gave them an *undertaking*. Remember? End of. You harass me, stalk me—

—— Stalk? Dont make me—

—— Its a crime now. End of. Understand? You do any of that, interfere in any—

—— Quack quack.

—— I mean it—

—— Quack quack.

—— J, I'm tellin you—

—— Bollocks I care.

—— I'm serious. Only reason I dont go for the divorce is to save you shellin out. Thats how—

—— Bollocks. Only reason is cos you already got some miscellaneous cunt shellin out. Innit. Cos you—

—— Yeah right J. Tell me, whos the expert on miscellaneous cunts?

—— Who is he? Whos the nose man?

—— The who?

—— You know who. Some fuckin gram-a-day merchant wha you—

—— Least I aint scared goin to bed at night. Least he— You—

—— Yeah yeah—

—— Dont fuckin *yeah yeah*. Everythings violent with you—

—— Bollocks.

—— Your idea of washing up was to throw everything out the window. *Oh honey Ive done the dishes* . . .

—— I got the fuckin dishes first place. Top china. Villeroy an Boch. Retail £17 a plate. We went through 3 alarm systems to get them an you—

—— Dont start all the caveman stuff—

—— The wha?

—— Its not even the point.

—— Well wha the fuck is?

—— Point is I'm not havin Kylie growin up askin what Jade asked me one time . . .

Oh yeah oh great. Here it come. Shes settin me up. Its a way with her. Gettin you to ask a question that she got the ready answer to. *Wha did Jade ask you one time?* Aint fallin for it. Say nothin. Only this feelin start to grab me, edge of my vision start to blur or nearly, sort of start to blur till I find I'm starin through her, just right through.

—— She said: *Mummy* . . .

—— Quack quack.

—— . . . *whats a bitch?* You—

—— She could of heard that anyfuckinwhere.

—— Yeah right J. Course she did. Anyfuckinwhere in her own home any fuckin night any day of the week any week of the year for years, for years every time I . . . and every time I . . . and every time I . . . and when you . . . and when I . . . and every time we . . . and then when . . . and I always . . . and you never . . . and I never . . . and you always . . . and and and and and . . .

And quack quack quack quack quack. The village green. Quack double quack. Barrel locks, 9 month. 18-century cheveret. Panasonic video recorder. Butchers sundriesman. Fuel injection. Sony widescreen. Monicas chest is cover but above it her skin is deep brown an theres a new gold neckchain with a new gold lizard on it, a new gold lizard like a special little gold lizard for a special little lovers in-joke. That kind of gold lizard. Kenwood stack system. Audi Quattro. Hewlett Packard. Tilbury Electricals. ABS. JVC. Alcantara super-suede sofa. 10,000 pesetas. Finally she run out of times an places I call her bitch. So then its my turn.

—— Why you fuckin do it? I lean in her face. I can smell the cream she got on her face. Why you fuckin do it? Why you fuckin do it?

Just like that. *Why you fuckin do it?* An so on till I ask it

100 time. Then 2 or maybe 3 or maybe 10 or 12 or more secs or even more or even more longer time than that, a whole time go by before I realise that I have Monica up against the wall by somewhere round her throat. It take all that time or more or even longer than that before I am myself again, before I can judge distance an so on. Before it all unblur. When her face come back in focus I feel relief. Which is to say when I see her an know I done her no harm I feel relief. Only her chain aint there no more. Marks instead wha wasnt there before.

She bend down, pick the chain off of the floor. She aint cryin or nothin. I guess she look disgusted. She try an stay compose, examinin the links for damage. Then she start breathin heavy. First I think I really must of done somethin. Thats when she slap me so hard my boil sting an my eyes water. Then shes breathin even more heavier like she was expectin one to come right back at her. Then she lax up when she see it aint. Me I'm rooted, lookin down at my feet. Its all slippin out of control. When she feel shes in the clear an there aint gonna be comeback she go:

—— Didnt you use to joke about how you liked women who hit back? Yeah . . . Yeah thats right J . . . You changed your mind now?

Truth be told I'm more stun by this than the slap. Cant think of nothin to say. Cant walk away. Cant crack her back. Because. Because it aint the practical way. Thats wha the screw counsellor repeat: *Theres always a practical way to resolve the issues*. Besides the little fuckin village is crawlin with busybodies an theys all community vigilante types with their index fingers glue to the 9 button. Only thing I can think of to say. *Theres always a practical way to resolve the issues*. Only course I dont fuckin say that. Still got some self-respect. So ask her again. Wha else? Keep my voice down, right down to a whisper, cos thats wha it is now, my voice, just a whisper, an I ask her again the same old chestnut, why she done it, why she fuckin done it to me, all of it.

—— I just told you, she say. I just said it didnt I. I just told you.

—— Wha?

—— I said I was scared. I did it cos I was scared.

—— Of me?

—— Dont start.

—— I change.

—— Dont start.

—— But you done it before innit.

—— Done what?

—— You left me before innit.

—— So?

—— You come back.

—— So?

—— Wha you mean so? So why—

—— Because I was scared you stupid pig . . . Yeah work it out. Work it out J. Think about it. Bitch leaves cos shes scared. Bitch comes back cos shes scared. Think about it. You ever thought about it? Dont answer. All you think is the world owes you everything and that you deserve it all your way. And that, as you would put it, is bollocks. Period. End of. Its—

—— I got rights.

She say nothin. Pout. Fold her arms, look at the sky an all that an shake her head. Which is to say the silent treatment.

—— I said I got—

—— An I said its over. Since time, since—

—— Since you grass me.

—— Dont start.

—— Since you grass me innit . . . Did you grass me? You did didnt you, you—

—— Could I look Trudy in the face if I had?

—— That aint no answer. Sides, Duane got off.

—— He was lucky.

—— He had Trudy.

—— Ever occur to you that sometimes they know things, the police. No? Cos that what—

—— Where the fuck you go that night?

—— Out.

—— Leavin the kids?

—— J, its water under the bridge—

—— Fuckin aint. Where you go? You was most likely too coked up to go to the school play.

—— If you must know, I was. I'm not perfect. But that wasnt—

—— No? Well wha the fuck—

—— I was looking for a place . . .

—— Wha you on about? Lookin for wha place?

—— For me an the girls you stupid pig. Only time I could do it without you askin questions. You get it now? Its over. End of. Finished. You want access, write a letter. Anything else, tellin you now, I'm ready this time.

—— Yeah sugar dad gonna sassinate me innit . . . Get it done £700.

—— 650 if you haggle.

—— Bet you ask an everythin didnt you?

—— Didnt need to, she go, reachin inside her jacket. Ive got what I need . . .

Mini tape recorder is wha she produce the sly bitch. Instinct make me think of snatchin it, stampin on it. But people watchin. Like the whole Net Curtain Village. An wha the point? No point. No point nothin. She got me. She did. She manoeuvre me. Time was when she count on me an me alone. For everythin. You do stuff like I done for someone you dont think of not trustin them. You think you know them but you dont. After years you think you know them like you know yourself. But you dont. You dont know wha they really feel when they brush their teeth, chew their food, blow their nose. Which is to say it take years for you not to know someone.

An shes still quackin at me, tellin me she mean it an all that. Tellin me shes serious an all that. Take them licks like Duane say. The practical way. No point fuck all else. Only Duanes sittin pretty. They all is. All of them. But I'm gonna come back for him, for sugar dad, for mister gram-a-day nobody. Thats wha I tell myself. Thats the practical way. Come back for the cunt. An write the letter like she tell me. Meanwhile go like she tell me. Walk on like a well-train dog feelin her watch me go. Walk on like a nonce feelin the whole world of geezers watch me go.

Dont even see my babies. Dont even proper greet them. They grown up an forgotten. Me I forgot their presents in the boot. Just as well cos they got no more use for no furry animal. They got all they need. So I go, door shuttin behind like it was shuttin on my old life, like I aint got the smart words to open it, not like the BT cunt, the gram-a-day nobody sittin pretty an hole up in there instead of me.

All I got is the green in front which seem to grow more bigger just walkin through it. Seem like everywheres growed too big. They say bein inside do that to you. Make everythin bigger than wha you remember. Bigger than wha you imagine. Thats wha they say.

When terror take a hold

Next thing I know I'm outside Sensis gym in Hornsey. Only place you can batter someone without gettin pulled. Drove here like a cunt pickin argument with vannies. Come to nothin. None of us really want to scrap in the rain. The gym is different. Sensi been done for organisin bare-knuckle contest. Then he got into Total Fightin, which is to say only murder is bar. Now he steer clear both them activity. Do business by the book. But course batterin is still expected. Thats cos the mugs who turn up got sponge for brain, sponge for soakin up punishment, sponge for the blood wha slop round their gummy gobs an sponge for not carin one way or other about it. Which is to say the spongebrains is either crap bouncers or crap boxers. Sensi he train both type. He train the crap bouncers to box an he train the crap boxers to bounce.

First thing I know I'm bein batter all over. By the aroma. Cos everythin stink in a gym. Sweatin bodies, bad air comin out bodies, all that mix in with industrial-strength toilet cleaner, antiseptic an all that, plus bits of other bodies, balls, arseholes, chests, armpits, feet, hands. Take a proper chef to put all that in a human casserole, which at the end the day is wha a gym is. Jade an Kylie use to love runnin up an down the stairs soon as they learn how. In the ring a couple frighten geezers spar. Which is to say tiptoe round each other much as they can, like the ring was a maze an they got trouble findin each other, specially when Sensis not lookin. Jades voice come at me as she run downstairs: *Whats for Christmas?* I bin them, the furry animals. Thats one the first things she learn to say. *Whats for Christmas?* Nothin now. No furry animal. Nothin. Just the smell in the middle all this place of my girls, of J & K runnin up an down the stairs, a trail of them in the middle all this. It flood back like the smell was always there an always with me. Anyway.

Over the far end the hall Sensis doin some pad an bag work with a moron called Mickey. Hes light heavy for def but he can only move like a bulldozer, backward an forward. Make my way. Sensis explainin him through a new move.

—— Its a simple combo Mickey . . . See? Hook right to the head yeah?

—— Yeah . . .

—— Slip left yeah?

—— Yeah . . .

—— Hook left to the liver. Ok?

—— Ok . . .

Sensi catch eyes with me, give me a daft grin, signal 1 min, then turn back to Mickey whos trottin on the spot, sweat drippin off of his nose, waitin for orders.

—— Ok lets go again . . .

Mickey roll his shoulders, tap his mitts together, fill his lungs an give it his best.

—— Yeah Mickey yeah *no* . . . No no . . . See its hook *right* to the head, slip left . . . Ok?

—— Uh . . .

—— Again . . . Hook right, slip— No, left . . .

—— Left . . .

—— Yeah Mickey yeah . . . Again . . . Hook . . . No *left left left*. *Your* fuckin left . . .

—— My left?

—— Course your fuckin left otherwise youre wide open to

left uppers an right crosses an full tins of brew from your own diehard fans, you with me?

—— I havent really built up my fan base yet boss.

—— It was a jest Mickey . . . Lets try one more time, real slow. Remember: boom, shimmy, boom. Alright?

—— Ok boss, Mickey go, rollin his shoulders an the rest.

—— So . . . Hook right, thats it, slip left, *beeyewtif*— NOOO Mickey NO, its a fuckin hook to the fuckin liver.

—— I know boss . . .

—— Yeah? So what fuckin organ are you aimin at?

—— Well . . .

—— Wheres the fuckin liver? Dont answer. You wanna be Iron Mike Tyson its the combos. The combos is everythin. When his trainer shout 13, Iron Mike come back with combo number 13. BAM BOOM BAM then BOOM BAM BOOM. You with me?

—— Yeah boss, BOOM—

—— Yeah alright Mickey alright, knock off.

—— Alright boss, Mickey go, passin his practice mitts to Sensi. Same time tomorrow . . .

As he lumber out Sensi whisper:

—— Couldnt beat a punchbag. Luckily in his case it dont matter. Hes got a hard head an hes gonna use it in round 3. Just have to figure a way of keepin him upright till then . . .

Sensi swerve round to check the activity or lack in the ring.

—— Oi . . . When the 2 you ballerinas finish *Swan Lake* you can go cos I'm closin . . .

The 2 ballerinas look well relieve to hear that, settle for a points draw an follow Mickey to the cupboard wha is the dressin room.

—— Here, Sensi go, passin me the mitts, stick these on . . .

—— Jesus H. They stink to fuck.

—— Supposed to.

—— Yeah?

—— Yeah. Bit of revulsion makes you hit harder.

So he hold the bag while I hold my stomach cos the mitts aint only stinkin inside theys soakin too. I proper lay into it with Sensi shoutin encouragement. Still, my effort is more BIM BIM than BAM BOOM. Even so after 10 secs the sweats pourin off of me. After 20 I cant breathe. After 30 I want A & E. Only Sensi keep me goin. *Jab, cross, jab cross, left an right*

to the head, left an right to the body, jab, cross, jab, cross . . .
An so on an so on.

—— Feel good yeah?

Throw the mitts off an squat down to revive my breath.
I'm like:

—— Oh man . . . Yeah, yeah well, in a way, oh fuck, in a
way it do . . . It feel good yeah, you know, fuck, workin
off the revenge an all that . . . innit . . .

Sensi shake his head an pull me up.

—— Aint fuck all gonna work that off J, cept the revenge
itself.

—— Yeah well, I go, bit taken back. Yeah . . .

—— Course you want revenge. Course you do. Only
natural. Someone get one over on you you wanna have
em first chance. Only natural. Course it is. *You go'a do what
you go'a do.* Only natural. But like I tell Mickey every time
he get beat: wantin revenge is one thing but what really
counts is how you go about gettin it.

—— Yeah course.

—— You say yeah course J, but I seen plenty wannabes
come an go with revenge cloudin their vision an no technique.

—— So wha you sayin?

—— Sayin the obvious innit. Look at the futality of your situation.

—— Aint been doin nothin but. I lost everythin. Ev—

—— I know, I know but—

—— Step at a time Sensi . . . Chill round Duanes while I figure it all out.

—— Bollocks . . .

Sensi start unhookin the bag, shoulderin it to the corner the gym an layin it down. An I'm waitin for him, kind of stumm up by his words like he slap me too. On his way back he pull off his sweatshirt revealin 2 tatts: a Japanese dragon on one arm an a woman discus-thrower on the other. Wouldnt want either of them round for tea.

—— Wha you sayin bollocks? Step at a time. Other ways just the same old.

—— From what I hear the same olds still fresh an well pissed off.

—— I just seen Monica. We talk an all that. Thats my—

—— Aint about Monica.

—— So say it then.

—— From what I hear J its Uncle—

—— Thats also down to me. I'm dealin—

—— J forget it, forget it. All I'm sayins your visions all wuzzy. Dont get me wrong, I aint blamin you for it, I'm just sayin . . .

—— Wha?

—— Well look at it. I mean for starters it aint gonna work round Duanes.

—— Youre talkin riddles. Aint start to work yet. Aint had the chance. 9 month man. I only just—

—— Nah, even that aint that simple . . . Its . . . Look, lets go down for a swift pint . . .

I dont mind. So Sensi lock up an we step out into wha is light heavy rain. Which is to say each few drop feel like glass of water on my head. We walk fast through it, up past cars an houses, more cars, past a Situsec van with steam-up windows, toward some high street or other.

Lord Montagues fillin up with after-work drinkers. More suits than geezers, shirts creasy, ties loose, moanin about Tube tunnels, goin oh ya ya about mortgages an pay rises, laughin office laughs about some fuckin Herbert in marketin. Place smell of pie an perfume. Sensi order me one the pies an a Guinness while I sit at a table starin at this office bint. Shes talkin with 3 suits. Same time shes tryin discreetly an all that to pull her knickers out her crack. Shes pickin at them through her skirt with her long purple nails but you can tell the knickers is well an truly up there under her twisty black tights after a long 9 to 5 in front of a screen. You never catch Monica doin that public. Pickin at her knickers like that. Never in a lifetime. Even though its a very horny thing to do.

—— Its the whole couple thing, go Sensi out the blue as he plant the pints down.

—— Wha? Sensi, respect an all that, but my couple business is my—

—— J, aint that. I'm— No, come on dont shake your head. Listen—

—— No man, I aint no Mickey.

—— Just hear me out right . . . Yeah? Ok? Ok?

It aint but.

—— All I'm sayin is, I'm sayin when couples is couples they get to know other couples. With me?

—— So far . . .

—— So when couples split up its gonna impact on all the couples *that* couple know yeah? Yeah?

—— Yeah spose . . .

—— So the couples what stay together sort of have to choose between the 2 people what split.

—— Choose?

—— Yeah right, too fuckin right they have to choose. Dont work otherwise. Couple cant be friends no more with both the 2 people in a couple whats split. With me?

Truth be told I'm about as with him as Mickey. Least the pie an Guinness fill the hole.

—— So cut to the chase. Youre sayin—

—— I'm sayin its the tale of the tape. 2 fighters in the ring an you measure up, accordin to what you feel, what you know, accordin to the stats. Then you choose. An Duane & Trudy, well, they sort of chosen innit. Between you & Monica. An sorry but theres only one way of puttin this: it aint really you they chosen. An the reality— No no wait wait . . . The reality mean theres fuck all you can do. Aint your fault. Come to that aint really theirs. Way it is. You with me?

—— Fuckin bollocks. You dont know the score.

—— I'm tellin you the score. Its hard I know. Course it is. Only natural. Course it is. But the only thing whats bollocks is step-by-step bollocks. Its obvious you cant stay round there no more. Yeah?

—— Course I can.

—— J, the vibes is already there innit. Come on, I mean, you must of—

—— Vibes is just vibes.

—— Vibes dont stop J they dont. They—

—— Vibes can carry the fuck on. So wha?

—— You can live with that? Stay round Duanes with them vibes goin on? After what I just told you?

Aint got no smart answer. I'm eatin pie.

—— I mean—

—— Yeah yeah yeah . . . So wha then?

—— Well, I been thinkin, goes Sensi washin down half his pint. My cuz is away a few weeks. You can stay round his. Give you a breather.

—— More way than one . . .

—— Exactamento. Is all I'm sayin. Plot your moves from there. Serious moves. You know? Meantime I'll wedge you up. Even sort you out some new garms for kick-off.

—— Yeah?

—— Yeah . . .

Suddenly the pie chew like wood.

—— Oh man . . .

—— Wha *oh man*?

—— Duanes my—

—— Bollocks. Be a relief for him. Probably wanted you out the picture in the first place.

—— Youre off your fuckin tree talkin to me like that about him.

—— I dont mean it the way it come out but—

—— Then dont fuckin say it.

—— You tellin me you aint a shade bitter about all hes got?

My mouth open but my eyes drop in my pie.

—— Yeah course . . . Natural . . . I mean, look at it J, just look at it. No no listen . . . Look at it . . . Everythin I just say is from me, *Sensible Sensi*. Plus look at the rest. Look at it. Duane got the oochie-coochie in the pipeline. Plus Trudy got him folded an wrapped for a full-on LTR. With me? Plus his daft-bollock business. I mean, fucks that all about? *Lightin systems?* . . . I mean, gimme a break . . . You know? I mean, since when did Duane have a fuckin clue about business. Hes a black man with dreadlocks innit.

—— Wha?

—— I aint racialist or nothin you know that. But—

—— Oh man . . . I dont fuckin know . . .

—— Thats why I'm walkin you through it point by point. Sides . . .

—— Wha?

—— Theres graft out there an I know you. Aint like youre gonna be workin over the jump in the Old Pratt an Tosser. Or security guard on 3 sobs an hour in a fuckin all-night parkup. Or site work. 5 a.m. turnout when its 10 below. You with me?

—— Yeah yeah . . . Fuck . . .

—— Top of which things aint too clever for me neither. Frans got serious hip trouble – maybe you already noticed maybe not . . .

I shake my head.

—— Well anyway, its her bones. Shes gonna need all sorts. Probably for the rest of her life. Drugs shes on sprout hairs round her nipples. Yeah really. Cant tear em out fast enough . . .

—— Heavy . . .

—— Plus theres the rest. Council want to close me down.

—— Kiddin.

—— Nah no joke. Complaints about drugs an youth an the rest. Such as my previous. You know? Couldnt handle no fine, never mind closedown. Not now. Debted up to my fuckin hairspray. You know? So I need to get busy. An truth is I'm sick of the whole fuckin routine, the trainin, the reps, the dawn workouts, the trainin, the workouts an more reps. Its all in the reps. Every fighter knows that. Like my first judo teacher told me: *a head-diving uchi mata doesnt push your limits . . . what pushes your limits is the repetition of the head-divin uchi mata . . .* Respect an all that. Deep words. I live by them words. But the years go innit. An Ive learnt life aint about reps. It just aint. An it aint about endin up as a cutman for a chimpanzee like Mickey. You know?

Yeah I know. But wha now? Sensi finish off his pint like he was pressurin me to do same. So I do.

—— Well?

—— Well wha? Wha can I say? Like you said, things aint too clever right now. I know you got a situation but I cant just—

—— Why not?

—— I'll think about it. I dont know . . . I'll think about it . . .

—— Sooner the better . . . Lets chip . . .

So I leave the rest the pie which truth be told aint goin down too good anyway. Follow him out. We stand a sec lookin at Hornsey in the rain. Just cars an houses. All just cars an houses. Hardly no point gracin the gaff with a name.

—— Come down tomorrow for a proper workout an I'll sort you with keys to my cuzs flat same time. Hows that?

—— Yeah maybe, I tell him just wantin to get away by now.

—— No maybe. *The man who chooses never loses*. An when you come down the gym bring your own bandages.

—— My own wha?

Sensi bust out laughin.

—— For your wrists, J, for your wrists . . . Under the gloves yeah? Otherwise its a fiver.

—— Wha?

—— It was a jest J. Wheres your fuckin humour? I'll throw in the fuckin bandages just haul your arse down there an get some focus back for fucks sake. Tomorrow yeah?

In the end I nod, say ok. Sensi grin, vice my shoulders together with one arm, which for him is a friendly gesture. Then he turn off up the street, another geezer with keys swingin as he disappear among cars an houses. Cos thats wha you need to be a proper geezer, a car an a house an a set of keys. An out there it aint nothin but cars an houses, an geezers with keys.

Whole world turnin on its heads how it look to me. Me I turn the other way, another geezer with car keys swingin, head down, head down walkin to his car. In the rain. In Hornsey. An it could be like this now for ever. Forever walkin to my car. In the perfect grey. Everythin driftin round me in the rain, same speed, no more faster or slower than before but always gettin worse, just slightly worse, a little worse, every second, worse. Places to stay I cant stay no more. Friends who aint friends. Wife who aint a wife. Kids who keep growin up an forget their dad. Me as anon as all them anon geezers.

An all us anon geezers dream one thing. We dream to be flash cunts. We dream to be flash an smart an wedge up an totally the king the hill without even askin, without even tryin, without liftin a pinkie. Because all the anon geezers is like all them anon slappers who dream to be pluck out the crowd an splash over magazine covers with the words

supermodel discovered in Hornsey

writ under them in red. Monica use to always be greedy for that, for bein hairdresser turn page 3 supertart.

An thing is, when I was the flash an smart an wedge-up king the hill it was me wha done the pluckin. Which is to say I had the power to pluck. I had the gear. I had the hat *and* the cattle. I had the LS. Which is to say I discover her an pluck her out the crowd. No more power now. Cattle went stray. Hat blew off in a gust. An me I sunk back in the anon geezerhood I come from. Least lookin round I'm in plenty company.

Only walkin to my car it begin to dawn that despite of all the anon geezers on all the anon streets theres certain among them anon geezers wha seem so much like the anon geezers I already seen that I start rulin out coincidence. Which is to say when your mind is well fuckin blank you start brimmin it up with para ideas. Either that or I still got instinct. Which is to say whys there a Situsec van every time I look up? They was in their steamy little van when we went in the Montagues. Still there now. Steamin away. Maybe the 2 thems eatin rolls an callin in shouts to their favourite radio show. Maybe theys on the overtime skank. The *u* is half rub out of Situsec. I make a mental note. The Personas park further up just past a Renault 205 an a 5-series BMW. Then a Transco van. *Piping gas for you*.

Look about. Situsec dont move. Nothin move nowhere.

Nothin except the rain. Stroll up. Press the key in the door wonderin wha connect me to Situsec, wonderin wha Uncle got to do with it, wonderin how Monicas sassin go about his business for £650. Tellin myself its none them things, that if anythin its just one them vannies I piss off. Then tellin myself its nothin, nothin at all, just my imagination an all that. Food for my blank mind. Sometime even self-defence is too depressin. So I stand there good few secs not knowin whether to get in or not, go somewhere or not, do anythin or not. To be or not to be an all that bollocks.

Eventually course I open the door. Wha else? Live for the moment. As I do the Transco van clank from inside. Then it start rockin an everythin. First thing I imagine 2 Transco geezers inside shaggin the arse off of each other. *Pipin it for you* an all that. But paranoia get the better. Neck hairs standin, I'm lookin all over the street. Specially, this is weird thing, specially at the Situsec van. Cos as I'm lookin at the van wha aint doin fuck all except steamin, the rear cargo doors of the van wha is rockin an wha I should be lookin at bust open.

2 fat geezers in black leather jackets an balas instead of blue Transco boilers try an come out same time. I look round for the bank they plan to rob. Only they aint goin nowhere, rubbin an shovin each other like it was competition to see who get to the pavement first. In the end none them win cos they fall out together on the boot the Persona. Then slide down an disappear in the hole between the Persona an the van. But for 2 Big Macs they gather themself together faster than fast food,

arrangin their balas as they come toward me. An still I dont really twig, mainly cos of them lookin an actin like Ealin comedians.

Next thing I know I'm backin off, car keys still in the door, lookin at them, starin at them, heart in mouth. One them come one way round the car. Other the other. One them got a hood in hand. Other got wha look like a cosh wrap in a newspaper. All this goin on split secs. They try an surround me, closin off the pavement. Garden wall left, park car right. Which is to say, no more comedy. Then the one with the hood order the other:

—— DO THE CUNT. DO THE CUNT *NOW*.

Other with the cosh an a bunged nose come back with:

—— HOOD THE CUNT. HOOD HIM FIRST.

So the 3 of us is dancin about, them orderin each other an makin grabs, me fendin them away like it was matin ritual for American mooses. So I'm thinkin to take my chance when it come. When the one with the hood open himself up for a lunge I go for it an punch him in the gut. Maybe Sensi would slag off my style an all that but he wouldnt say nothin when my fist disappear in the geezers garms, then disappear in his fat, an by the time it reach his gut most of my arms in there. Which is to say the punch just run out of impact. Which is to say I make the wrong move.

Next thing is the most simplest thing of all. Next thing I'm dyin. Crumplin to the wet floor. Down to the wet floor dyin. I been killed. I know it. I know it. It been done. Blow to the head wha done it. Oh Jesus an all that goin through my mind. *Oh Jesus*, last thing I most likely say. Last thing I most likely see is my hand in a puddle like a family of 5 by the sea. Or 4 an a dog call Benjy. Benjy wasnt just for Xmas. It come on holiday with us to the sea an everythin. Then hood go over me. Black me out. Black everythin. Black blackness out. Even black Hornsey out. Black fall like deep sleep. I suppose it fall like death.

But thing is my life dont flash like they say. It carry me away instead. I'm carried off. 2 or more them now. Cant tell. My legs an arms reachin up like the insect an all that. No voices. Dump in van. My head make metal sound on the metal door or roof or floor. Cant tell which. Least the sound mean I'm alive. Least I'm dyin slow I'm thinkin. Then shout of *GO GO GO*. Like police. Only it aint no muff wha boot my rib, tie my arms behind, tie my leg too when I move an stick a foot on my dizzy head. Least the foot orient me to wha is up. Then van engine start up, driver wrench it in reverse, follow by mega crunch. There go the Persona. One call the other a cunt.

After that the driver push hard, like the insult hit home, rollin an swervin about, brakin hard like he was tryin to make every no-chance traffic light. Apart from the engine, silence. None them say nothin. Which is wha proper shit me, not the dyin, not the feelin of me goin black. Its the knowin wha is to come, the silence bein the silence of the pro, the killer, the sassin an all that. Which is to say soon as I realise this, fear take hold, wakin fear wha start to turn my guts an bring the puke up. But I keep it down. Pukin would be daft in a hood.

Didnt Monica once learn me out some magazine that when you get adrenaline goin the pain an fear is somethin you dont feel no more. Everyone sort of know that. But you really know it for def tied like a pork joint in a Transco van. So I try to be like one them spongebrain who dont care about kick in the rib or blow to the head or wha it mean. Anyway. After that I dont move or even try or make a sound or even try. Just stay still in pitch quiet. In my dark place. The silence of the victim, a pro victim, a true pro victim silent to the end.

Maybe we drive a long way.

Maybe I'm black out a long time.

Maybe the world change an all that.

Maybe it give up an die cos when it all come in focus again nothin look real. Head pound like a road drill. Only it aint a road drill. Fact is my head pound like it pound. Like it would after I been cosh. Cos it never happen before so it dont feel like anythin except like wha it is. Which is bad. Blow leave metal taste in my mouth an throat. Dont feel myself. Dont know where I am no more. Instead I see myself. I see myself tie in a chair in a damp brick place. I see pipes round the walls. Rusty paint drums in a corner. I see one light bulb cable in from outside. The whole place is half a cell minus decor, trimmins an air. Ropes pressure my lungs. I feel myself not breathin like I use to. Place like this is a cupboard even the skeleton wouldnt get in. Like the last place, last place anywhere.

If all this is Uncles work its already more than he ever done to me. Already a step beyond. An if it aint him, if Hood & Cosh is their own firm then they gone way too far to whip off their balas an jackets an reveal Joke of the Week t-shirts.

Radio start to seep in from the same direction the light cable go. Sound increase like it was comin my way. DJ cackle. Follow by a jingle. Ads. *If youre thinkin of going skiing this Easter forget Aspen, forget Val d'Isère* . . . Door open behind me. Scrape over the grit an brick dust. I try an turn to see but the steps go round me the other way. *. . . is the place to go . . . So go on, just get your skis on and go* . . . Radio click off as I turn back.

—— Ever been up Beckton Alp J?

The devil I know look down at me. Hes got a face like he fell out his tree an hit all the branches on the way down. Plus scars on his shave head from ancient bottlins. Anyway, que sera sera an all that but at least it bein Uncle lax me. He slip a little radio back inside his coat, black coat wha he must of took a long time matchin with his black shirt, black trousers, black shoes an black everythin like he was really someone.

He already disgust me with his big thinkin mans question. Like hes gonna tell me great memories, memories wha made him wise an all that, older than his years an all that. Cos thats wha I hate about him most if I think about him, his age. Which is only 20. But fuck that. I aint gonna let him in on how I feel. Disgust pull me together. Give a cunt like that the benefit no fuckin way. Business, ok. Rest he can eat off of the floor, him an all his comedy nonces.

Enter Arno on cue. His breathin suction whatever air there is out the place. He shuff-shuff round, brick an grit, scratch the grey fuzz wha sprout off of his chin an give me the gloatin once over. Eyes like currants in a doughball. Accordin to Duane. When hes done gloatin he go:

—— How you . . . been keepin J?

—— Could do with a holiday.

—— You just had . . . one. Cheapest an—

—— Yeah alright.

Arno cough which is the nearest his asthma get to a laugh.

—— Oi Arno.

—— I'm . . . going boss . . . Just came to . . . say hello for o . . . old times.

—— You said it. Go watch them goons.

—— Going . . . boss going . . . going . . . gone . . .

—— Yeah . . . So where was we?

—— Beckton Alps.

—— Oh yeah . . . But its *Alp*, J. Cos theres only one. People often fink it should be *Alps* but it aint like theres a load of em. Its unique. You ever—

—— Nah.

—— Should do.

—— Yeah?

—— Yeah. Wicked view. Ma old man use to take us all up there, me an ma bruvvers, when we was kids. For skiin. You—

—— Nah.

—— You should.

—— Yeah?

—— Yeah. Dunno what youre missin. Wicked buzz, wicked.

—— Really?

—— Yeah really. First time though, nuvver story innit. First time is always about facin your fear. Dad use to say that when terror take a hold is when you start to live. Y'unnerstan? He use to say, like he use to ask each of us *whats the worst fing can happen when you ski down the slope?* So we all fought about it an come up wiv different answers.

All sorts. You know? Like broken leg wiv the bone stickin out. Or fence post froo the gut cos you cant stop. Or ski stick froo the eyeball. Bit of a laugh. Bit of a giggle. Cos all sorts is possible when you start imaginin yeah?

—— Yeah. So?

—— Well, I mean. Look at your situation here.

—— I'm lookin.

—— Wha d'you make of it?

—— Well maybe if I could get up an take a stroll I could look better.

Uncle sort of smile to himself. He brush fluff off of his coat, fluff wha I suppose his fruity imagination make possible. He can play any role he want any way he want now. He got the time an he know it. He stare down at me. Me I have to look up or look away an neither make me feel good.

—— *Maybe*, he go real slow, *maybe if you could get up an take a stroll . . . you could look better . . .* J, are you gettin lippy?

—— Well I mean, come on. Whats this all about then?

—— *Well I mean come on whats this all about then?*

—— Yeah.

—— Its about you imaginin stuff. Its about you sayin to

yourself, *Well, this is the first time I am in a room where I aint never been, tie to a chair sos I cant move nuffink an basically I got no control no more* . . . Yeah?

—— I'm with you so far.

—— Good. Well then next, say to yourself, just ask yourself, in your own time, *Wha is the very fuckin worst fing wha I can imagine happenin to me while I am tie up in a chair in this room.* Yeah?

—— So?

—— You imagine summink?

—— Get to the point.

—— This is the fuckin point. So wha you imagine?

—— Wha you wanna know for? Wha you doin this for? This aint gonna get us nowhere.

—— No?

—— Nah.

—— Tell me the fing.

—— Why?

—— Tell me the fing.

—— I been cosh over the head. I cant fuckin think shit never mind imagine shit.

—— Still. Have a go. Have a stab . . .

—— Um . . . ooh um lets see now, no . . . no . . . nope . . . hmm nothin. Nothin at all. Nothin seem to be comin through. My imagination must of turn grey in stir. Way it is. Sorry.

—— Well since you aint gonna respect me by tryin J, supposin I do summink to you wha make you tell me the fing. An after that supposin I go ahead an do the fing as well . . .

Fuckin cunt. Fuckin total cunt. This aint the holiday I could do with.

—— J, you there? I said—

—— Yeah I hear.

—— So wha is the fing wha you imagine?

—— Havin a cardiac before I make a million. That usually scare the warts off of my dick that does.

—— J, yous startin to get on ma tits, sittin there all tie up an tryina sound like you got NVQ in metalwork—

—— That an algebra.

—— ARNO . . . Tellin you, room aint big enough for 2 smart cunts.

—— So tell us wha the fuck its about an I'll be on my way. Thats—

—— ARNO.

—— So wha is the deal here?

—— ARNO.

—— Coming. Coming. Come, Arno go as he cough.

So then Uncle— fuck that. His names Philip Burnside, product of his dad Rays sploshers miscarriage, grown up a bog-ordinary prat who just happen to be takin bog-ordinary pliers out his coat an handin them to his well-confuse sidekick.

—— What, he gasp, are these . . . for boss?

—— Fuck d'you fink? Torturin him.

—— But—

—— Take em . . . Go on, take em . . .

Arno wipe his hands on his trousers like he was a surgeon receivin a special tool an hygiene really made all the fuckin difference.

—— So wha the fucks this to do with?

—— Soons Arnos got you moody for love we shall talk again.

—— Boss . . . I dont . . . know if I'm the right m . . . man for the job.

141

—— Arno you wouldnt be right for any job. You was a whores cleaner when I come across ya, ha fuckin ha, an she was about to fire you anyway for jackin off over her knickers. So for you this is the opportunity an challenge you been lookin for all your miserable fuckin life innit. Right?

—— Yeah . . . boss but . . . how—

—— Arno sunshine, he go as he put his arm round him, one day I'm gonna miss you. Y'unnerstan? I really will. So be useful while youre still with us . . .

—— But boss I . . . dont—

Uncle snatch the pliers back.

—— Its a bit of an art is torture. But its simple really. Just imagine the worst you can fink of happenin to you ok? Then you do that fing to him. But in case you get stuck, heres a quick demo . . . Number 1: clip his ear or some uvver dangly bit or a tit or a toof or his little toe. The choice is yours. Number 2: squeeze fuckin hard. Number 3: twist, cos thats really wha torture mean, twistin. 4: observe the result. 4 is seriously fuckin important cos uvverwise yous workin for nuffink, y'unnerstan? Last 5. 5 is: check the patient.

But the patients lost. For good 10 secs I dont know where I am. Just dont know. Heat an pain blot me. Make me scream out. Never knew I could. Never knew I had this ability. Only once it start you cant stop it. Make everythin go distant. Like theres nothin to my body except my ear. Whole of me an ear. Pentium processor, DVD, Motorola V3688, Black and Decker 48-bit drill set, Bosch dishwasher, Bosch microwave, Allegra Starck chrome tap. Uncle slap the pliers back in Arnos hand.

—— Remember them 5 points. I'm gonna get the Thermos an make a coupla calls but I'll be back. Meantime, I wanna hear him Arno. Y'unnerstan? Broadcast the cunt.

Then he leave. Me an Arno is there like 2 noncey panto stars who dont know their lines an the curtains just gone up. He look more frighten than me. Embarrass too. Dont know where to put himself. So I scream loud as I can. Which wake the dead an freak the fuck even more out of Arno. Then he catch on an start to cough like he laugh. Then I scream again. An he cough again. We both know this aint gonna work in the long run. Truth be told it dont even work in the short.

He come back, blabbin on his phone but wavin Arno to carry on, tappin under his eye to show hes gonna shufty till the jobs done. Arnos hand start shakin. His breathin get more heavier like he got asthma attack on the way. Uncle wave him on again, finish his call with a *bell ya back in 5*, an as he slip the phone in his pocket Arnos hands reachin toward me.

I'm hopin least Arnos gonna clip the other ear. But he aint got the initiative. He probably think hes doin me a favour. It dont take much second time round. The lobe split an I scream for real. More better an louder than the first time. Arno stagger off an puke in the corner by the drum. Uncles disgusted with the pair of us. Start askin me about the night in question, about wha we got, whisperin in my ear, like a bitch, feel his breath, then slappin me. Like Monica. Like a woman. A womans slap from a man. Turn my stomach worse than anythin. *Wha you get?* Slap. *Who was wiv ya?* Slap. *You touch summink din ya?* Slap. *Where you hide it?* Slap. *Where is it?* Slap. An so on.

Me I say nothin. Too late now to admit anythin. Stick to the story J, I tell myself. Dont pass out. Dont give him nothin. But he know. He know I'm holdin out. Only thing slowin him up is watchin Arno hunch in the corner tryin to pull his own tongue out his throat.

—— Its good practice Arno, bit of throttlin, for when I sell your arse to that fag S an M club in Bermondsey. Which could be any day now . . .

Arno look like hes gonna die. He seem to stop breathin 2 whole secs. But he survive. Uncle pat his back an tell me:

—— Arno got a way of livin innee . . . So one last time J, he go as he carry on pattin, I wanna know wha you took out my lockup. Yeah . . . it was my lockup you mug. I always use mugs or aint you figured that out yet. No? Well now you know . . .

He stop nursin Arno an turn his attention back on me, his voice changin from sick sweet to sick fuck.

—— I wanna know, he shout in my ear, wha you got. Cos whats missin is very fuckin important to me . . . Y'unnerstan?

—— Didnt get nothin . . .

—— Then where the fuck is it?

Slap.

—— Wha?

—— Where the fuck is it?

Slap.

—— I said where the fuck is it?

Slap.

—— I dont—

Slap.

—— Where the fuck is it J? You know what I'm talkin about. A box. An boxes dont just go walkies. An whats in that box is my lucky number. An its such a lucky number that its still lucky after your 9-month stretch. 9 month I been pickin bogeys waitin for you. So—

—— I dont—

Slap. Then he look down at me a couple secs, examinin the patient an all that.

—— J, J, J, mugsy old J . . . This aint workin is it. Oh well. New approach . . . Like my old man use to say: *Vary the approach an youll find a way* . . . So, J, you seen the Marathon Man? . . . I said—

—— Yeah . . .

—— Well youre Dustin Jewboy an me I'm Big Larry Olivier innit . . .

Then the cunt go behind me, pull my head back by pinchin under my nose. I have to breathe through my mouth. Then he stick the pliers in my mouth. I start strugglin an all that course I do but in the end you cant. I mean in the end I know wha hes gonna do. In my head I cry for Mum. But it change nothin. He clip a tooth, a bottom tooth. It dont break straight away. Only second time. All I hears Arno retchin all over again in the corner. Blood all over me an all that an I cant even put my hand up to it. Then he ask me again 2, 3 time. Me I aint in my body no more. It leave me behind. Or I leave it. Whichever. I sort of hear myself say an keep sayin wha I already say to him. After a bit he grin:

—— Ok J, I believe you. You never lie before. Not to me anyway.

So then he untie me like nothin happen. Send Arno for tissue an all that. Brush dust off of my shoulders. Examine the ear like it look worse than it is. An it all end just like that, no trumpets, no tea. Just my face lock up with pain.

—— Now listen to what I'm gonna tell you . . .

An he keep tellin me next 10, 15 mins non-stop. He tell me I'm gonna drive a truck. Just like old times. Drivin for the man. Only this time the man is him an not his dad. An this time the truck is travellin from more farther away than Tilbury. Arno come back with tissues which he divide between me an him. When I wipe off some the blood an all that, Uncle offer me a smoke. My hands shake as I take one. Cant stop that either.

—— I got plans, big plans J, an my old mans backin me. I'm expandin an I'm gonna carry on expandin. This is one of my moves. An youre useful when you put your mind to it. Y'unnerstan? Youre gonna go on a little trip for me . . . Open road. Youll love it . . . On exes you ugly cunt. An I aint even gonna ask you to kiss my dick. All youre gonna do is drive a truck. Just like you done for my dad way back in the days before they took your HGV off of you. Ha fuckin ha. So—

—— Where to?

—— *Where to* he says. I tell you where to: to a destination you will know in good time. See J, this is a *need to know* sort of operation. An you will do my instructions to the fuckin letter. Cos I know you. I know you got schemes goin on in that lumpy bonce. No dont shake your fuckin head. Fact dont say nuffink . . .

He reach in his pocket, pull out a photo an give it me. Its a blur snap an it wouldnt make the mantelpiece. But the 2 faces on it is unmistakable.

—— Jade an Kylie innit. You might be ugly but your girls aint. Well fit the pair. An see, thing is J, Dad learn me one lesson more important than all the uvvers. He tell me you should only ever freaten someone wiv summink they really value. Get me? Uvver words, I can turn them spunky little bitches into movie stars. Y'unnerstan? 2 little bitches in a 3-wank video. Nice. Well nice . . . You unnerstan innit. You can run but they cant hide. Say no more ha fuckin ha. Nuff said, as they say, nuff said . . . So, let us all join hands an be friends. Fact I'm gonna intro up my crew, bein as how you is all togevver now. OI CUNTS . . . IN HERE . . .

So then Cosh an Hood come in an they turn out to be Martin an Geoff, 2 sub-postoffice blaggers from Ruislip an Harrow on the Hill. Geoff mumble *no hard feelins mate* an all that. Make a daft crack: *You should change your dentist mate.* Martin laugh an wipe his nose the whole time with a wet ball of tissue. An everyones havin a fine time. An all that. Then Uncle put his arm round me an he start walkin me to the door, grit an brick dust crunchin under our feet. He

walk me outside where its night an where its cold. Didnt
notice the cold before. Now it chill me through. Theres no
buildins except the one we been in. Theres no lights except
a long way off. Nothin look familiar. It dont even look like
town. A sign say SAND BALLAST. Another say FAIRLOP
PLAIN BOATING LAKE.

—— Want a lift to the Tube?

Shake my head.

—— Fair enough. You need to stretch your legs. Call us
tomorrows. No . . . day after. You got the mobi number innit.

I nod. He signal Arno an walk to his Merc. Arno do as
hes told, dont say nothin, never even look up, then he sit
in the passenger seat, eyes on his lonely lap. Behinds the
van, turnin over, Geoff at the wheel unwrappin the foil
off of a KitKat, Martin wipin his nose in the same soggy
tissue. Merc pull out first, van follow. Martin nod at me
like a mate, like we just done work together. Then they
turn on the road, red tail-lights flickin among the silent
black hedgerows for 2, 3 secs. Then the van an car is out
sight an all there is is me an the night an the cold an the
sand ballast on Fairlop Plain. An the only light I got left
is the end of my smoke.

Hours later I'm sittin in Sensis cuzs flat on Mortimer Road. I'm watchin the wallpaper curl off of the walls an the rain churn the muddy garden. Someone once took care this place, this garden. Celery, chive, fennel an all them still poke out the weed an nettle. I been watchin the rain for 2 hour or more as the anaesthetic wear off. End the garden is the railway embankment. Its overgrown so I cant see the railway. But every few mins I can feel the intercity go past shudderin the plates an cups in the kitchen. Distant view take in the houses of Kensal Green opposite, Trellick Tower farther west on the left an the gaswork on the right. I put the tv on for the noise.

They got some documentary about how Caesar build a bridge across the Rhine river inside of a week. They got army engineers donkeyin an Caesar experts figurin an a whole bunch other geezers stickin their oar in an wha they is doin is remakin the whole bridge an everythin out wood an rope, down to the last plank an nail of wha Caesar himself done, just to find out how he done it. An I'm sittin here in Sensis cuzs flat in Sensis cuzs armchair watchin Sensis cuzs tv in between watchin Sensis cuzs garden an I got 2 stitch in my ear an a big chunk of silver metal instead my tooth an a serious fuckin headache wha all the paracetamol I been swallowin dont ease. An I'm thinkin how fuckin pointless it is to build a bridge wha has been an gone when theres so many new ones need buildin. Which is to say bridges for geezers like me. Cos mine is all burn to shit. An all I want is to kill someone. An all that. Him. Stick a ski stick through his eyeball an all that. A million ways go through my head. A million an then one.

Least the henry of skunk Duane give me as a kiss-off help a bit. When he see wha happen he was more shock for himself than for me. Told him I'd been bouncin off of the walls, pissed as a fart. He didnt buy it. He was too shock for himself, for his life an Trudys life an the baby they got comins life an all his lightin systems an big ideas about the market an all that flash before him in a split sec. An with the words *check me if you need anythin man* he say goodbye to me an the old days both. I know it. Not to mention hintin bigtime that I aint in Trudys good book after pilferin through her drawer. So they was glad, after all, like Sensi say, to see my back. An Duane & Trudy they aint alone feelin that. Monica feel the same. She slap my face an that flood back now more than the toothache, the earache an the headache.

I hit her. I did. More than once. I hit her more than once. But that dont amount to no streak. I aint evil. An if I was I aint no more. I done wha I done. But the good I done must come into it. Wha good I done cancel the bad an leave me in credit. Anyone measure it, anyone count it up, anyone crunch the numbers I'd be way out ahead, bustin the ribbon an doin interviews while they was still superglue to their blocks. I would be. Fact is anyone can fuck up an most do. But this I never deserve. All wha been heap on me. All wha been done. 2 wrong dont make one right an I got 10 or a dozen or more wrong weighin my way. All them wrongs nobody deserve except maybe the worst. An I aint that cos I just spent hard time in the company of that, the worst, a person, a geezer, a fuckin animal, a total fuckin animal who would not know right if it came round his gaff an sat in his favourite chair, who would exploitate my girls in some nonces film done in some nonces basement for a nonces own pleasure. Me I'm wha come between my girls an the person who would do that to my girls. An this is the shit wha tour my head while I wait.

Anyway. I got the Persona back, rear wing an brake light mash up by the Transco van but the keys still in the door all this time later, just like I left them. It warm me how honest people is. Only thing I lost is my drivin licence, the one piece ID I could do with drivin that wreck, the one piece ID wha is gonna boomerang back on me I just know it.

Anyway. Now I'm waitin for Sensi to turn up with

Warren. They been down some steam baths havin a tough time. When I told Sensi wha happen to me he just wanna go round an crush ribs an all that. He call it a security measure. Which for def it would be. But when he say them words I know the whole things dead on its feet round 1. Uncles way too connected. We both know the obvious, that goin round all hothead could backfire. An theres no way I'm gonna risk my girls an thats that.

I almost phone Monica again. I mean I want to an all that but I dont know wha to say, how to say it. She aint never gonna believe no amazin out-the-blue reason for talkin to me. All she'd tell me is I'm sick. That I need professional help. That counsellin is the way forward. For me. Alone. No 50/50 from her. No give an take. An she would be right in a way. An showin her wha I look like is just gonna prove her side even more. Anyway. Truth be told I am sick, sick with hate. Hate her for starters. Hate wha she done to J & K. Like she done genetics on them, make them look exactly like her an act exactly like her an do exactly wha she tell them an believe exactly wha she say. An really the only thing wha keep the fear an the pain an all that under control is the hate for wha been done. Hate is better than all the anaesthetic, weed an paracetamol put together in a fuckoff cocktail by the name Suicide Express.

Anyway. About 9 they turn up glowin like headlamps after their steam. Frans with them, full supermarket placky in hand. She mother me an all that. Check the war wounds. Laugh an tell me I look like Freddie Kruger. For the first time I notice she dont move round too clever. Limp about as she prepare a meal. Meantime I'm meetin Sensis friend who smell like a slappers inside pocket but is suppose to be *well useful when it come to ways* an *totally unflappable when it come to means*. Thats why Sensis givin him the full MC intro.

—— J, hes goin, this mans the greatest benefit worker I ever met. Hes been everythin from a disabled Falklands war hero to a single mum with special needs kids to a family of 6 refugees from Kosovo. He reads papers. He understands the fine points of the law. He got fantastic eye for forms. An if the Queen had ever bother to talent scout she'da made him Minister for Social Security.

—— Unfortunately there were no vacancies, Warren go, adjustin his round gold specs an revealin his perfect smilin teeth. But in any case, I prefer to work behind the scenes.

We do a round of know-wha-you-mean looks an Sensi intros me while I take in Warrens appearance which is thin an tall, least 3 inch above Sensis 6 foot. Top of that hes one them super-smooth geezers you would believe if they told you they was Falklands war hero. Even though there wasnt too many black geezers with gold specs, iron white shirt an red silk cravat on Goose Green. Fact it come to light that Warren Abrahams hail from Ghana but his grandmother on his fathers side connect him to Golders Green an the traditional community of the Mount Sinai District Reform Synagogue. From there it was a short step to becomin the *fifth-ever black Jew at Eton*.

After that Warren bring us up to speed with his *areas of interest*. Apart from gettin Sensi buildin permission for his gym, he is a fully train-up accountant, immigration adviser, benefit expert, legal consultant, shippin operative, company director, translator, currency trader an a importer/exporter of precious metals. Course hes also property developer, luxury car dealer, former diplomatic whatever-the-fuck to the overseas development department of the government of wherever-the-fuck. Finally hes a father of 1 or 2 but he lost count. He aint the only one. After his list reach its grand finale an hes presented me with his gold italic business card I'm just a bit wide-eye. To say the least. Till I realise wha need addin: Warren Abrahams is a know-it-all, do-it-all behind-the-scenes fucker of anyone he come across. In a word: dodgy. In 2 words: well dodgy. In 3: just the man.

Because in the end wha this meet is really about is the *bollix lickle boxy*. Sensi reckon the papers all mean somethin. An 9 month didnt mess with their meanin otherwise Uncle wouldnt of done wha he done an so forth. Logic like this lead Sensi to bring Warren in to do some sums. Warren take the papers over to the table in the main room. He clear a space among Sensis cuzs gear which is mostly weights an weight trainin gear an stacks of mags with name like *Soldier of Fortune* an *Combat an Survival* an books with name like *The Death Dealers Manual*. He sit there castin his expertise on the dots an crosses on every item I give him.

Meantime Fran cook. She aint exactly got Trudys touch for cuisine. Fact she cook like she throw discus. Which is to say she bang, she cuss, she stir, she taste. Then she cuss, bang, stir, cuss, bang, stir, taste then cuss again, stir again, bang again an again an again. Even unflappable Warren start to get concern. Eventually everythin stop but the stirrin. Then she serve it up. Sensi call it *a fine old rip-arse chilli*. Which it is. Least it blank the headache a few mins an remind me I still got feelins. We dont say much just glance over at Warren every so often while he toke on his little cigars an take an make the odd call. After about an hour Warren join us for a drink an a spliff. When the 2 click in he clear his throat, adjust his specs an all that, position his dick an all that, an begin wha he call his *analysis of the situation*.

—— My prima facie presumption is of course that this documentation was together when found and that there is a definite link between the individualistic items. Furthermore I'm assuming that other items – if found – would flesh out so to speak the rest of the development . . .

Confuse aint the word. I look at Sensi but he nod back at me like it was all crystal. An Warren he has a way of smilin at the end of every statement but without changin his expression, just by openin his squinty eyes a bit more.

—— So, Warren continue when he figure we is all in agreement, my overall legalistic impression is that we have the fundamental ingredients for fraud. This particular activity subdivides into myriad complexities. To proffer an example: diversion fraud. The kernel of diversion fraud is when a party which we shall henceforth call X has goods directed from Point A to Point B but the goods do not arrive as per the prearranged documentation.

—— They get ripped off, Sensi go, mainly to put me back in the picture.

—— A vernacular way of putting it and not incorrect. Additionally goods may be misdescribed on what is known as the Bill of Lading. Or they have other cargo loaded with the listed cargo. Or Importer A uses a Letter of Credit that has been forged or the same from a non-existent bank or one which exists but which has no foreknowledge of the LoC and/or its intended use or one which has an insider so to speak in its midst. Then one cannot rule out that the ED, the Export Declaration providing assurance to a bank that a cargo exists and to enable its pre-delivery payment, may be falsified. Thus, you see, Importer A may accrue goods. The goods may then be appropriated through misdirection or misdescription. More specifically, the, um, *Spanish connection* implied in the documentation could be the source of a particular cargo. Tilbury Electricals could be the misdescription and Myersons the destination, real or diverted. Or, of course, it could be an altogether different combination. The tachograph could tell you a great deal if you knew how to read it. I mean whether the truck travelled at motorway speed, if it stopped, when it stopped, for how long and so forth. A pattern might give away what happened on a particular run. The point is, shipping operatives, stevedores, drivers and hauliers can all be involved at some level depending on the OC. Thats, er, *organisational complexity*. Its the old yellow brick road, and everyones on it. After all, the permutations of such activity, as you can imagine, are multifarious and known to many, both big and small. What seems clear enough is that these documents do relate to an organised activity, a regular long-term activity that may well be active even after all this time. Of course, ultimately I would need more relevant and shall we say *proactive* detail for the interrelations to become translucent . . .

Me an Sensi is both a bit flabbered by all the toffology to react straight off. Warren look at us an laugh, which is a laugh without sound, just his eyes widenin an his gapless teeth sort of peepin. Then he go serious.

—— But one question gentlemen: whodunnit?

—— Well thats what J heres gonna be findin out.

—— Me? I dunno wha the fucks goin on. Whole new world out there . . .

—— Of course, Warren smile, but how does this mysteriously titled Man from Uncle come into it?

I look at Sensi a bit surprise.

—— Its alright I told Warren about him cos hes got someone in the Regional Crime Squad out in Essex. Apparently

Uncles bein watched cos of all the weird bollocks goin off every other day round Tilbury.

—— Thats all we fuckin need. Uncle bein sniffed by a hooky muff an us puttin ourself in the middle.

—— The officer in question is certainly not hooky, go Warren like I insult him.

—— Well wha would you call him?

—— I would call him absolutely and very enthusiastically corrupt.

Sensi give a good chuckle at that one. Me I discover when I try an laugh all the aches an pains I didnt know was there.

—— Thats how its all gonna come together, Sensis goin. I feel it J. I really do. We all want it an we can do it, proper work it out an then proper do the cunt. I fuckin guarantee it.

—— So who is he exactly? I mean the one, go Warren doin comma fingers in the air, *we shall be doing*?

—— A geezer what need doin, Sensi reply.

—— Would you be so kind as to elaborate?

I want to say hes the geezer wha threaten me an mine, wha threaten my family. I want to say that but the word *my* stick in me. So Sensi go ahead an fill him in on Phil Burnside, his now sick old dad Ray, the haulage business, pawnbrokin, fencin, bodies with no hands or heads washin up in the Thames estuary every so often, people like me with no teeth queuin for emergency dental work, an course he tell how the Burnside family in general contribute in a absolute an very enthusiastic way to the tradition of this great land.

—— So, Warren go, adjustin his specs as he turn to me, youll be calling him soon will you?

I look back at Warren, wonderin who the fuck he is, how come he just walk in my life an get handed a menu an information an make request for phone calls like he was a *for real bruvver* an all that. But my headache turn my vision grey an I cant even string the right words.

—— I suppose I will. I have to . . .

The 2 them look at me an I realise they mean now. They want me to make the call right now. Problem bein I just aint quite ready to do this, to deal with all this now, to talk to the cunt while I can still smell him on me an taste blood in my mouth. Fear creep back. Worse fears. New fears, like a grey pressure behind the eyes. An here I am gettin even more pressure from 2 more sides like I had no end of sides to keep pressurin. Bottom line is this: Sensi he figure he cant be beat. An Warren he figure he cant be outwitted. Which is to say if Sensis brawn then Warrens brain. So where the fuck that leave me? It bring back wha Duane use to rap down Willesden Sport Centre in the old days: *Brawn an brain need raw prawn for dem game*. An here I am all use up an raw like a fuckin prawn in a game. Only the stake is highest for me. I lose everythin an yet I still got more to lose in whole new ways I never imagine. An it dont fuckin help that its 20 to 12 an I dont have a girlfriend. Not even a 4-leg friend to shag. Them 2 is still waitin. An I glance at the pair in turn.

Oh yeah I'm a hard man innit. Oh yeah I done time innit. An oh yeah I'm thick as a thief. So I take out Uncles mobile number. I dial 141. I make the call. It ring. It connect. He dont speak. For a second I dont speak. I could hang up, make an excuse, aint talkin to voicemail, aint leavin a message. Theys all waitin.

—— Its J . . .

—— Yeah? Well wha fuckin time you call this? You musta just woke up you dozy wanker.

—— Never slept. All the excitement keep me awake.

—— Still all mouf innit . . . but I bet you aint grinnin ha fuckin ha . . . *Nil by mouf* innit . . . You still there . . . ? Oi, you—

—— Yeah . . .

—— Meet us up top Beckton Alp 11 tomorrow night. I'll fuckin show you the sights . . .

Hang up. An then wha? Warren suggest we *reconvene* after my meet. An then wha? They go. Sensi leave me some shells for new threads an stuff an then I'm on my arse again with a half bottle of Bells. I leaf *Soldier of Fortune* but the story of Billy Joe from Arkansas who went an join the Contras with no military experience an got shot by another Billy Joe from Texas fightin for the other side just depress me. So I drink an stare at the night lights through the trees beyond the railway with new patterns mergin in my head, new patterns settin in for the long season. Which is to say night an drink an self-pity fall in that order night after night. An after that the intercity go by.

The Millennium Dome, the Beckton sewage works, the North Circ, excavations, bulldozers, the A13 an a few other sights of our times all take the eye off of the Alp which you would otherwise see for wha it is. Which is to say a sad fuckin nipple of landfill risin out the waste. Even the halogen light an the toxic drizzle dont help hide nothin. Just make it more grimmer. Theres nobody round the place, no Merc park up with Uncle waitin. No Martin & Geoff with the tools their trade.

All there is is a path. It zigzag up the Alp like they was tryin make the route scenic. But it look a scar instead. Still I aint here for the view, whatever Uncle say. I'm here to listen to the cunt, take orders from the cunt, so that I can find out how to really take the cunt when the time come. *Focus*, Sensi keep tellin me. But focus only come through thought of pleasure or pain. I forgotten pleasure. I done the pain. An however much I want to kill Uncle I cant. He'll be watchin me, waitin for that. So I aint really focusin on nothin. I'm just blank as the snow I imagine.

Top the Alp theres benches. Ski lift go down the other side. Pylon shadow crisscross my own. Whole things a sad fuckin joke, an Alp in this place, to come skiin in this place, without snow, up a landfill. Or to even come up for the view. Its just a extra bit of discount world to give to the same people wha get artificial trees for Christmas, people wha dont know the difference. Still, here I am in my new jeans an shirt, trainers an a kagool. On time. Thats wha matters. Not that I dont expect Uncle to be late. Even well late, like out-of-order late just to wind me up, show me whos boss an all that.

Which is wha I'm thinkin when I catch a shine off of the back Arnos bald head, his 3 strand black hair plaster down on his scalp by the rain. Hes maybe 20 foot off, sittin on one the benches goin down the opposite side. Look like hes floatin. Like he was some wise guru waitin for his people. I glance about for the gurus boss. But its just me an him. Make me para. Get me thinkin trap. I go over anyway. I have to.

—— So where the fuck is he?

—— Hello ... J, he go without turnin like he know everythin or dont care about nothin. How are—

—— Never mind that. Where is he?

—— Busy . . . J. Just you an . . . me. Take a pew . . .

—— Nah. Wha he get me up here for?

—— He thought it . . . would be a laugh, go Arno with a half-smile. Me an you up . . . here. The 2 gimps—

Arno dont get another word out cos I punch him in the ear hard enough to knock him off of the bench into the slime where he belong.

—— J dont please J . . .

Then I kick the fuckin toad in his bollocks but this dont connect nearly hard enough. So I go round the front to his head.

—— He said youd kill me, hes moanin, wrigglin, tryin to turn his head away.

—— Yeah? So why you fuckin come then?

—— Cos he said he'd kill me if I didnt. Said between you an him an the climb I'd be dead. I'm here to die J. Here to die . . .

Amazin how fear clear up Arnos windpipe an get him warblin like a movie star. Amazin too how wha Uncle want or expect get me doin the exact opposite. I back off. Take

a deep one. Fact I practically want to make it my business
here an now to save Arnos life for the rest his life. To make
him Judge Dredd invincible, immortal even. Least outlive
his master. If it was in my power right now I really would,
I'd make him immortal just to fuck Uncle up. As it is wha
can I do? I pull him off of the floor an back on the bench.
Pat him. Pat him twice. His trousers is all fucked up. Back
of his old jackets all muddy.

—— Thanks . . . J, he go, all double up, no colour in his
mug like a death mask. Thanks. I—

—— Shut up.

   I point in his face.

—— I tell you now you ever mention wha happen out there,
you ever mention it or anythin like it again I'll fuckin kill
you I swear. I will I fuckin will . . .

—— Course J. Alright. Ok . . . J . . . I'm . . . just a—

—— I know who you fuckin are. I know. Dont ever compare
me an you. Dont ever. Cos you aint nothin. Youre the
fuckin scrapins is wha you are. Youre the fuckin hole in
the arse. You get me? You get me? There aint nobody
lower. Nobody.

   Arno nod. I sit down next to him. Pat his back. Just like
Uncle. Pat it twice. I almost tell him to take deep breaths

but in his case that would be like addin insult to injury.
Instead, while I calm down I let him talk, which course
most people dont.

—— I could have . . . been good at business, hes goin. Got
a head for . . . it J. I have. But my health is what it is. My . . .
chest, my legs and everything. Youre lucky to . . . have that,
your health J. Very . . . valuable. People respect you . . . if
youve got that more than if you got . . . money. More than if
youve got women. I used to have women. My boss back . . .
then brought them over. I should say *bought* . . . Russian,
Czech, Thai you . . . name it. Shouldve settled . . . down
then but . . . never did. Too . . . many to choose . . . from
I suppose . . . I . . .

He quack on. Then my headache crowd in an I see Monica
front of me lookin at me an it sicken me, the way she look at
me, the way shes like the law inside me, lookin at everythin
I do. To get her back if I want her back I have to stop bein
violent. An all that. An here I am, here I am with Arno. She
wouldnt understand. She never has. Age 14 I siphon petrol,
steal bicycles. Age 20 I shortload an overload, filch an dip an
half-inch, workin the depots, the factories, the warehouses.
Age 26 I was haulin an storin an generally shiftin for a phone
book of people. An all nights, any nights, nights like this, I
would be out workin. Daytime lookin, night-time workin.
Or night-time lookin, daytime workin. She never understand.
How she ever? But she accustom herself to the life it bring.
That she done. Anyway. Arnos still quackin.

—— Youre . . . lucky with that as well, he go as he peer at me out the corner his eye. Wife . . . Kids . . .

—— Wha you mean by that?

—— Nothing . . . J. Nothing. Just you got . . . a life when it—

—— Wha he say about my kids?

—— Nothing. Nothing more. I—

—— Lot of nothins innit.

—— Well—

—— Wha he get me up here for?

—— Well I . . . He . . . He wants you . . . to do something.

—— Yeah he said. Wha?

—— He wants . . . you to . . . touch a load outside of . . . Tilbury.

—— Meanin wha?

—— Meaning hijack . . . it J. Steal it. You have . . . to memorise the details—

—— Aint fuckin stealin a truck.

—— Its all . . . the rage, Arno cough or laugh. The boss

showed me one . . . of his cuttings. Lorryjackings are on the increase. Mainly cos of him, Arno cough or laugh. Essex Bill've even got . . . a *lorry desk* . . .

—— Bollocks. I dont steal trucks. I dont steal handbags an I dont steal trucks. Thats the way it is with me. Understand? I do . . . I dont . . . I do . . . I dont . . . I do . . .

Etc. etc. etc. Arno just sit there. Course he do. Me I'm talkin for my own benefit, like the wind, the east wind fillin me up, him lettin it, him lettin me blab an blab like the east wind. Blowin an huffin an puffin. Cos I know, I fear, that if I work one more time for Uncle he will have me for all time. J & K is gonna live a long an full lifespan an the longer it is the more time Uncle will have to threaten me. But right now I aint got no choice. All I got is the east wind. Eventually even that stop. Which is to say I stop tellin Arno wha I do do an wha I dont do.

—— So gis the detail then . . .

—— The cargos supposed . . . to leave Tilbury the 14th. As soon—

—— In 3 day from now? Youre sayin 3 day from now?

—— Yes. On the 14th.

—— Yeah but fucks sake . . . in 3 day? The 14th? 3 day from now?

—— 2 an . . . a half, go Arno shruggin cos it dont make no

difference to him an he carry on sittin there like he was the most patient man on earth.

—— Wha time?

—— Round 8, 9 p.m. if the . . . sched is accurate. A1089 up . . . to the A13. Its a Merc youll . . . be pleased to know. 30-, 40-tonner. T-O-R on the reg . . . plate. You plan . . . it. You take it. Boxes. Inside. 4 of them with aeroplane pictures stamped . . . on them like a logo or something. Thats what . . . you want. Then—

—— Hang on, hang on . . . Youre sayin theres 4 box in a 40-tonner? Thats like 4 needle in a huge fuckin haystack.

—— Theyre near . . . the rear. Ok?—

—— Fuck . . . Nothin about this is ok . . .

—— Whatever. Find them. Then ditch the . . . truck. After that transfer the . . . gear to a safe house. Call in once its done an . . . youll be told wha to . . . do.

—— Wha the cargo?

—— Dunno. Listed as . . . flowers from Barcelona. Perishable.

—— Wha about the driver?

—— Also perishable.

—— Dont fuckin give me that.

—— Its what . . . he said.

—— He wants me to—

—— Up to you . . . he said. Driver stays . . . overnight in Tilbury. Continental B & B. Least 4-hour rest. 8 more like if his rigs been on . . . the skid all night being checked. You never know. Drivers a Yuri Zam-ya-tin. Russian. Or something. So . . . you decide . . .

Yuri Zamyatin. Sure. One the names out the box. Which is to say its why Uncle wanted the box so bad, para all the names, the *associated nominals*, people wha is *known but not wanted*, was gonna fall in the wrong hand. Mess up the whole schedule. The 14th every month. An its also why he want me an nobody else to do it, in case I'm lyin, in case hes been compromise. See wha happen. An after its done, succeed or fail, hes gonna proper deal with me.

—— Wha else?

—— Nothing . . . Well, there could be . . . a police escort . . .

—— For flowers?

—— For anything. These days they—

—— An I'm suppose to take care that too?

He shrug again. I just give him a look like I'm gonna start on him all over.

—— Wha they really got in there?

He hesitate a sec. But he know full well hes got to give me somethin, even if its a lie.

—— Chips. Computer processors. Pentium. Stuff like . . . that. 80k's worth. Maybe 100. Or more. 4 boxes. More or less the latest. Up to . . . 300 quid a unit. Worth . . . a lot J a . . . lot.

—— Wha about exes? He said—

—— Um . . . well, he go, hand movin to his pocket. He said . . . to give you this for . . . exes . . .

Then he pass me a £20 note while he watch my eyes. One. Just one 20 all on its lonesome.

—— J . . . please. I— J please I have to give it to you.

—— Fuckin joker.

—— He said—

—— Shut up.

—— J—

—— Zip it, I go, snatchin the 20 an stickin it back in his pocket. For dry cleanin.

I put a smoke in my mouth an fish round for my lighter as I get up to go.

—— J . . . J . . .

—— Wha?

—— He wanted . . . a number. Somewhere he can reach . . . you . . .

I shrug an give him the number the Scotland Yard property shop which I know by heart. Why the fuck not. Then I spark up my cigarette, ready to leave.

—— J . . .

—— Wha now?

—— J, are you . . . gonna kill him one day?

Question floor me. Which is to say it make me sit back down. Cos its the sort of Q I cant help askin myself. An cant answer. Old Arno aint the sharpest tool in the box an all that but he know wha is in my mind. He know probably better than most wha is in every losers mind. But that dont mean he got the right to ask. It dont mean anywhere near. Maybe hes workin me, usin me, like for his own reasons. But lookin at him, the way white saliva coat his dry scared lips, wet mud on his trousers, the whole of him fucked an gibberin shit only a moment ago, I forget it, put the bigthinkin brainwave out my mind.

—— Cos . . . Cos if, hes mumblin, cos I— if . . . I mean if—

—— Then wha?

—— Then well . . . I mean . . . I . . . know where . . . I know where . . . hes gonna be . . . on a certain . . . on a certain night . . . the 14th. Just him . . . on—

—— Shut it Arno. Forget it. Go back to bed . . .

Only he don't go back to bed. Instead he press a tiny folded square of paper in my pocket, folded 20 time an then some like neurogami practice. He push it in the pocket with a dirty finger, with the words *look at . . . it when youre ready*. But lookin at it now or later dont matter cos suddenly fear rush through me, uncharted land with no A–Z to see me through. I'm farther from my life than ever an travellin more farther away. Ma god. Ma god. So I just sit there a moment, up Beckton Alp, in the drizzle, just me an a asthmatic gimp. An we just sit there a moment, 2 gimps, silent as oldtimers relaxin of an evenin, takin in the view an all that, the sights, the great sights of our time. An plottin murder.

Breakin jaws an
pluckin spoil

Sensis shoutin the address against a background of music an gruntin an squealin. I try an tell him I aint in the mood for a party but cant get a word in. An anyway his mobi eats my change like its been fastin all month. Phone box off of the rollercoaster ramps an flyovers of the A13 is the last place I want to be.

Traffic revvin past. Trucks headin east to Tilbury. Crews of garmed-up clubbers headin west to the bright lights. Its Sat night. Big night out. I stare at a water drop trickle this way an that down the glass of the box. Then another. An another. My head start to pound again. 4 laughin Indian waiters run out the Indian takeaway an into a massage parlour across the street.

Then someone knuckle the door. Geezer in a parka, hood

hangin over his face, bareleg slapper behind him in high shoes with her toes out. Pushin open the door I look at her feet, her perfect red rained-on toes trottin through all the puddles in her black trotty shoes. Get my wood achin. Monica had whole range them shoes. She like to wear them an make her feet somethin to look at an think about. Even when she wasnt wearin black trotty shoes an her feet was inside somethin else like trainers I would still get horny just thinkin about her manicure feet inside her trainers, her black trotty shoes inside her armoire-cupboard.

I drive most the way to the party with my mind fixated on her toes. An needless to say my woods achin most the way. Like a reminder of how I use to feel, Sat night, 1 a.m., big night out, headin up the West End. Me I'm headin up some yellow street in Hornsey to some chip-paint open-door short-let semi with a trio of square-jaw hard-drinkin Aussie nurses checkin in the invites an the not so invites.

Name of Sensi get me through into a crowd of geezers wearin the same jeans an shirts an trainers as me. Empty beer tins on the floor, piss-warm 12-packs in a corner, people shakin on the thin carpet to some old Madonna comin out cheap stack, others burnin spliff holes in the landlords furniture, pukin in the back garden. Middle-age beard in a jacket tryin to cop off with a mix-race bint half his age who is more or less collapse in a armchair. Woman nearer his age sweatin under the brown wha hide her lines with some plukeface teenagers hand up her front. Its the sort of party wha happen every Sat night in every shitarse burb with whoevers left standin in the local at chuck-out.

Like a roundup of all them drinkers whose lives is rule
by licensin hours.

One the Aussie nurses, who turn out to be waitress from
New Zealand, ask the other Aussie nurse, who turn out to
be cage dancer from South Africa, where Sensi is. She dont
know. But the third Aussie nurse, who turn out to be for
real Aussie nurse, tell me Sensis upstairs in the chill-out
room. Chill-out rooms lit with candle, red cloth over the
bulb, chilli light round the window, *Ambient Club Trance
Remix Volume 3* on the cd. Geezer snorin on the sofa.
Couple rubbin faces in a corner. Sensis pissed an gibberin
to a group of 4. One them I recognise straight off by the
way her purple nails fiddle with her knickers. Which is
to say its the knicker bint from the Lord Montagues.

—— Armani? Sensi ask when he catch sight my outfit.

—— Marksio an Spensari.

I look down an see for the first time the mud on my
jeans. Theys all too blittered an laughin to notice. Sensis
slappin my back an doin intros. All 3 girls he intro as
Orla. An the 1 geezer he intro as Susan. Me he intro in
the followin way:

—— Me an him is gonna pull off one of the biggest blags
in the history of crime. Innit J . . .

Truth be told I'm a bit shock hearin Sensi slur on like

this an for a sec I wonder whether to give a fuck about it. Then I say:

—— We *is* the history of crime . . .

Ha fuckin ha. Big joke. Get a laugh all round. Knicker bint carry on smilin at me long after the joke is over. Its a coke smile wha pins the edges of her mouth to her eyebrows. When it stop I see she got square glasses an no lips. But she is the one wha is really call Orla. She tell me she love criminals, the underworld an all that. *Its so exciting. Not like 9 to 5. Have you got any stories?*

Susan give me a triple vodka orange like he was handin me a prize. One the other Orlas chalk me up a line. I tell them about the Wealdstone corner shop blag of '94, the biggest confectionery haul of the last millennium. It was well sweet. Ha fuckin ha. Then Orla tell me she dont date. Wha she actually say is: *I'm not available for dating at the moment.* Not like I ask her. Still. I tell her its ok because I totally respect that. Then she say: *But I will shag you now.* Then before I can make my own decision one way or other, she grab me round the head an force her tongue in my mouth.

After a bit of that she take me to another room, bedroom with coats on the bed, an we fall on it an it all happen on the coats, with keys an change an mobiles crunchin round under us as she grab an grab an scratch an scratch with her long purple nails, the nails she use to finger her knickers. An me I pull her tights right off an her shoes come with them an a button come flyin off of my shirt an her glasses fall on the floor. From wha I see her bony body is as bony as mine but office bony, an office chair commuter body from a different world. The only thing wha really bring us together is the condom in her bag. She comment on my muscle. She make me out to be tough an rough an a bit dangerous. I'm her Saturday night story for her Monday mornin coffee break.

Whatever happen happen fast. So fast my dick dont even get hard enough before its over. The coke kick in, make it soft, softer quicker. She even tell me to stop playin with her nipples. Like I had no technique. Still. It amount to a shag. But it almost disgust me, the way theres no buildup, the way theres no karaoke, no Harold Melvin an no Bluenotes. Straight away it make me feel guilty. Miscellaneous cunts when I had wife an 2 kids an a home an all that never did. Now I feel like a 2-timer cos I'm just provin to Monica wha I'm like, like shes standin there with the words *I told you so* on her lips. Not that she use them words. She got a special look instead. A look wha say youre guilty, the whole of you in general for everythin you ever done. Meantime Orlas nose is talkin, as Duane would say.

—— I used to do loads of coke in the office. All the girls was in and out of the toilets the whole time. You never even had to buy your own just go in the loo an youd just find all these crumbs all over the top of the toilet, you know, the cistern thing? If youre on a budget, well I mean, you just chop what you find dont you. But we was all paranoid the whole time thinking the boss was gonna find out. Then course one the girls, Liz from customer services I think it was, caught him doing it in his office. Caught him with his nose down, tee hee hee, on the glass in the photocopier. He'd been doing it for years like the rest of the department. It was the same bloke it was, mums the word, I mean who was dealing to everyone. But in the end me myself I had to stop doing it. Youll never guess why. Go on. No? I'll tell you anyway. It was cos it just totally shrunk my tits. Seriously. Trust me. I went down 2 whole sizes. Cost me a fortune in bras I swear. Still if thats what coke does to you you shouldnt be doing it should you. Makes everything shrink in the end. Thats what they say. And we're living proof. In the end its priorities isnt it? You have to sort out your priorities. Coke or tits. Coke or willy . . .

I try an grin cos thats wha shes still doin ear to ear but it feel like my prowess is gone an I just want to get the fuck out.

—— You dont say much do you?

Thems her famous last words an all that cos I'm gettin up an I'm mumblin, packin myself up an mumblin an excuse, excuse bein one wha dont often spring to mind. *I'm married*. Thats wha I'm mumblin. *I'm married*. Thats how I leave Orla, half naked, on the coats, squintin without her specs an tryin to get her tights outside in.

Go back an grab Sensi whos all over one the other Orlas. He see I aint gonna let go so he give up his gropin.

—— Fuckin shit man I was well in there J, hes sayin back out on the street. Well in. I cant believe—

—— Yeah well how come you aint home with Fran startin a tribe?

Sensi go silent.

—— Cant man. All them steroids I done play havoc with my count.

—— Yeah? I didnt know . . .

—— You didnt have to. You already done the daddy routine. But truth is mens sperm count is goin down all over Europe anyway. Was on tv.

—— So is the fuckin brain cell count. Wha you sayin all that stuff to them Orlas for? Army trainin tell you nothin about loose talk an all that?

—— I didnt say nothing. Wha d'I say? It wasnt nothin. Fuck. Just havin a laugh. Take it easy. Forget it . . . Jesus . . . Just tryin to have a good time. Have a go one day, you might like it . . . Jesus . . . We might as well get goin now. Tell us what happen up Beckton on the way . . .

On the way meanin on the way to the pool hall in

Hackney where he arrange to meet Warren. Sensi is the first passenger Ive had in the car an it feel like I'm lock in a small place all over again with someone who only see things his way. I open the window hopin the damp airs gonna sober him to reality but once I been through it with him hes like: *Computer chips, yeah man yeah, technologys where its all headin, even the coke barons are turnin to it . . . its big in the States an its catchin on over here . . . yeah man, cos course its easier to rip off a truck like that than actually smuggle gear . . . an if youre done the tariff aint gonna be as bad . . . 100k man . . . or more . . . probably a lot more . . . thats just what hes tellin you . . .*

Which is to say his eyes is full of £££ an streetlights an more £££. The big opportunity hes been waitin for an all that. *A one-off cleanup heres to the future sort of operation innit J.* Hes so buzzed he even point out the bit of the Grand Union canal where they threw Jack the Hat McVities car keys after they done him. Like suddenly he was really up there with the Twins. Which is to say by the time we get down the Haggerston end of Mare Street youd have to say the geezer was exuberatin, so much so he fail to see the biggest problem of all: we only got 3 day to plan an organise an execute the bollocks. Daft an dafter. Or wha.

Pool hall you wouldnt know was there. Shutter like a shop. 4 aerosol tags in different colours over the front like the place was bein fought over by local crews. JAX. cc KRU. HedZ. MoMo. You stand in the oil patch. You choose one the 5, 6 scabby bells. You press it. You wait

for black ring eyes to appear in a slit. They blink at
Sensi. Shutter rattle up halfway. We duck in. Pirate radio
comin from somewhere. *Hello live caller whass grindin in
the manor . . . ?*

Sensi intro me to a scar up 20somethin Turk name
Hikmet. We shake.

—— Alright friend? he go to Sensi. Long time no see.

—— Busy busy. Hows tricks?

Hikmet shrug.

—— Spots an stripes innit . . .

They chat about boxin an some 21-year-old Turk wel-
terweight whos comin through an who they both want to
see on an amateur card up Barking Town Hall. Anyway,
its obvious Warren aint here. Would of sniffed his eau de
Superdrug from outside. An inside theres only 3 tables.
Only one is bein use by a couple ashface doleboys,
unlicense cabbers, shifters on the drum, even their cues
look hooky. They keep their eyes on the spots an stripes,
check us out with their ears. Back past thems a tv with
some older Turks smokin stinkin cigarettes an watchin
documentary in Turk about the antarctic penguin. Most
likely its one their daughters asleep on cushions behind
a little coffee bar. Hikmet offers us coffees an we take
a table.

—— Choose your weapon, Sensi go as he grab a cue an rack up.

Its the last thing he say for some time cos after I choose a cue I beat his high spirit senseless, which is to say 5 time in a row an all the way till Warren show. By then the doleboys is gone an most the Turks is out scoutin fares. Hikmets in a corner takin a long sexy phone call judgin by his grinnin an whisperin.

Wha get to me about Warren when he stroll up to the table is he dont make nearly enough eye contact. He dont look at me. Joke instead with Sensi. Like he got other stuff on his mind. Like it aint me hes got on his mind. Or like it is but not in a positive thinkin sort of way. Like I'm his employee is all. Like him an Sensi is doin the talkin. Like I'm Arno an cant talk the way he can. Stress get my boil goin. An the other thing wha get to me is the way he take on board all I'm eventually tellin him with wha is the total opposite of exuberation. The opposite bein more less cold as fuck. *Unflappable* as Sensi say. Like *oh the 14th let me just check my Filo, yes I think we could fit that in* . . .

Sensi stand aside for Warren to play the winner an I beat him in silence just chewin on the grit out the Turk coffee. Warrens tellin Sensi: *Hes good . . . he certainly is good . . .* After I pot black I go:

—— Warren, let me ask you a thing. Wha make *you* so ready to do it so fast?

—— J, he go, leanin his cue, I'm not much of a poolroom hustler as youve probably surmised. But I am a business-man. And I have the following rule of thumb: make your move fast, make your money fast. Otherwise perhaps one should consider joining a lottery syndicate.

—— Dont give me the high hat. Its a straight fuckin Q I'm—

—— Easy J easy, whos the one in a jam?

—— You tell me.

—— Wha you sayin now? Youve got to go through with it. You said so yourself. But to your advantage. Thats the point. Come out ahead without Uncle breathin down your neck. You know? Take the goods an deal with the cunt later when—

—— Excuse me gentlemen but I really do not wish to listen—

—— I know Warren, I know, go Sensi. That aint your end.

—— Thats wha I'm sayin. Theres more at stake for me than—

—— There always is, go Warren smug as fuck.

—— Not a return ticket to Scrubs, Warren old boy. Not for you.

—— Quite. But lets be rational about this. We all have

our reasons. I'm putting up the operational funds, so to speak. And youre working out the operational details. With correctly applied effort, it can be done. Starting, may I suggest, with a recce of the target area ASAP.

—— Roger.

—— J, fucks sake . . .

—— Well wha is this? This aint Enid Blyton. *Recce ASAP* an all that. Sensible shoes at dawn. Bandits at 3 a.m. captain.

—— Well what the fuck else you plannin. He's right J. We have to go shufty.

—— May I also suggest picking a spot where the target may be stopped easily and without arousing suspicion . . . ?

Sensis noddin, course he is, sober but pissed, hard man but excited like a kid by secret confabs about targets an all that, thinkin how hes gonna be the smartest on the block, the king the hill an all that.

—— Meanwhile I can make enquiries as to the nature of the escort, if any. Perhaps this Uncle of yours could find himself arrested when he comes to collect. That may be the best solution no?

—— Maybe the only solution, go Sensi noddin.

—— I can have a discreet chat with my contact on Monday. Obviously he'll need to be looked after, as it were.

—— Aint goin 4-way with no muff.

—— J, none of us want that. Do we Warren?

—— Of course not. But he'll want something up front. Or points. Or both . . . Anyway, to continue, it seems to me the key issues are as follows: transaction, transportation, containment, distribution, division, contingency. TTCDDC. Undergraduate business studies.

—— The first 3 is us. Wheels an lockups is J's middle name.

Ha fuckin ha.

—— Double-barrelled, I go.

—— Speaking of which, thats another thing we need to sort out innit.

—— Wha? You must be fuckin jokin. I—

—— I am J, I am. Smile. Candid camera. It was a joke . . . Jesus . . .

—— May I continue? . . . I'll continue. Distribution, division, 3 *ways*, minus investment and sundries of course, and contingency: theyre my department. We can meet on Tuesday to finalise details. Quite frankly the less we meet the better. As for the rest, its outside my operational parameters—

—— So to speak.

—— Quite, J, quite. Well, I'll call my contact . . .

—— Now? Dont pigs sleep?

—— No Sensi, they fly, especially at night when no one can see them.

Sensi laugh as Warren stroll over to a corner. Then under his breath he start havin a serious go at me. The word *respect* crop up 10 time every sentence, how I aint got none, how I should get some, how I owe him some, how nobody is gonna have it for me unless I have it for them. Quack quack. Whatever. This aint me & Duane no more. This aint the old days.

My ears is tune into Warren. First hes cagey, turnin about in case sound is carryin. But he like his audience too much. So hes struttin about, cool as a tv penguin. An he cant help a sound or 2 escape. *First thing . . . tennish . . . Chester . . .* Or maybe *Dorchester*. Or somethin. Aint even wha he say but the way he say it. I wonder wha type muff he got in the Regional Crime Squad. *Mugsy* aint the answer. All I know is I wouldnt turn my back on Warren, not for a sec.

One by one they finish, Warren his performance, Sensi his quackin an Hikmet his heavy breathin down the phone. By the time the 3 thems sayin their au revoirs I'm starin into the distance, way off, far as I can in a shutter 3-table pool room in Haggerston. But my instinct to do the right thing an to find the right way must of die with the old days. Cos all I see is wha there is. Which is to say spots an stripes.

Sunday aint the best day to panic. Not because its quiet an theres nothin open an nobody to help you. Its cos you cant move for the traffic. 12-hour gridlock all the way. The weekly stockpile traffic, the grandma traffic, the army of Christ traffic, the granddaughter on her way to grandma traffic, the DIY traffic, the Sunday league traffic, the special occasion traffic, the market traffic, the stupid cunts on a charity cycle traffic, the geezer an his best mate on a cruise traffic, an course the 2.2 kids to the park traffic.

Monica use to love the whole thing. Prepare to sit in traffic 2 hour. Sit in traffic 2 hour. Bicker. Kids bicker. Bicker with the kids. Park up. Unload. 500 families all racin it. On with the coats. Round a park. Up a hill. Pat a dog. Down a slide. Munchies. 1 in 4 tread in somethin. Back in the car.

Smell follow. Sit in traffic 2 hour. Bicker with each other. Bicker with the kids. Get home. Park up. Unload. Off with the coats. Off with the shitty shoe. Prepare dinner. Bicker. Eat dinner. Bicker. Watch tv. Kids to bed. Drink an spliff. More tv. Shag if youre lucky. Bicker. Drink an spliff. More tv. Pass out. Sleep a sleep. Once a week, every week. An they say switchin to Saturday is mad. Still, theres nothin now I'd go back to more than all that.

But thats a house of cards on a slanty table an this is Sunday, the day of proper panic. I'm drivin up to see Farooq on a hunch, head full of paracetamol, dark clouds swarmin, rain by nightfall, truck tacho on the passenger seat an Farooq under instruction to get someone who know how to read one, cos I never did, who know about Tilbury, who is God an know everythin in general.

Meantime Sensis suppose to be sortin a lockup off of the A13 an Warren hes workin on the distribution the hooky chips an so forth. Which is to say with the 3 us graftin wha could possibly go wrong? Only thing wha really make sense is the monkey Warren give me for *operational accessories*. Whatever. First thing I do is give Farooq somethin off of the top. Truth be told I give him a choice: 150 now or 50 an a part-ex on the Persona. Course he take the 150. The 350 shells wha is left is just gonna have to go the distance.

We drive up an industrial estate in Edmonton. Jam in Finsbury Park. Traffic lights out Manor House. Accident on the North Circ. Tailback round Fore Street after a tunnel closure. We head to wha Farooq tell me is a haulage yard. Turn out to be a right arselick description for a shed sinkin in mud an diesel, a Portaloo, a mini forklift with a flat back tyre, a gate with no fence, all crown with handpainted sign: H & H Transport. Like H & H was goin somewhere. Which maybe they is, bein as how they is *Frieght Specialists & WasteTransfer NIGEIRA–GARNER–SA–ROTTERDAM.*

—— Come meet one the H's, go Farooq crackin a smile.

—— Yeah? Which one?

—— The living one . . .

The living H is in the shed, armchair behind a desk, hankie in his hand, another up the sleeve, 2 electric heater by his feet, a stain old tea mug an not a lot of paperwork. Hes one them relics with a face more dump on than a buildin-site wheelbarrow. He toil his life till all he can do is nurse colds an flus all year round. Extra VAT on fuel would kill him stone dead. Probably wha kill the other H. Which is to say he cant exactly stump up for lifes quality gear, like a red carpet for me an Farooq. Wipe his nose. Stare at me. I stare back. No names. Farooq sort of mumble about me being the person he mention, about H workin for Customs up Tilbury.

—— It was a tally clerk.

—— Yeah? Well whatever. I was told you could read a tacho.

—— An experienced man could read one.

—— I was told you was experience man.

—— I am and I could read one.

Its like he smell the notes in Farooqs pocket. Like he can nose a crisp 20 even with all the snot in his snout. Farooq know the score an hes bowin out, steppin back in the yard for a smoke with the words *talk your talk*. So I take the chair opposite him an I put a tenner on the desk with the tacho.

—— Whats that for?

—— Wha can you say about it?

—— For a drink an a half not a lot.

—— Its a drink an a half more than you had innit.

—— Really? You ever hear the one about peanuts and monkeys?

—— You ever hear of a family of monkeys name Burnside? Course you have. Well the peanuts is from them.

That shut him up. An out his silence come a sort of de-icin of his attitude, a sort of mental rollin out of the big red 2-grand kilim carpet.

—— Moody tacho, he mumble, can get a man in a lot of bother . . .

I shrug, spark a Bensons, makin sure he look at the lighter flame, like it was the fire he aint gonna be playin with, not sittin like he is in a puddle of diesel. Still. You cant rush him. He blow his nose good an hard. He make sure all the gluey bits is soak up in his bog roll. Mumble about chicken flu, about how its the chicken flu season, about how the Chinks brung it over an spread it through takeaways. Only then do he draw the tenner an the round paper tacho disc over toward him.

—— P-O-T . . . Port of Tilbury. Point of origin . . .

—— How far it go?

—— The vehicle? he ask like it wasnt obvious. Well, it says 158 km . . .

—— But?

—— Well . . . I dunno. I mean, looking at it, youd have to add up all the peaks.

—— Wha peaks?

—— See them, he go, pointin at markins like on a graph. Every peak in the inner circle equals 10 km.

—— Theres only one there.

—— Not even. Thats what I'm trying to say. It says 158 totalled up, 158 solo to Luton, but the peaks show less than 10. Arguments sake call it 8. Travelling at . . . 50, 60 kmph, say 30 to 40 miles an hour. Then, see there? In the middle . . . You see them? The 3 styli—

—— The 3 who?

—— For distance, time an speed. Its what the tacho records. The odometer? No? You have your speed, and course your time on the 24-hour clock – thats the thick line round the outside – to show—

—— Yeah but whats all that mean?

—— Well thats what I'm saying. Its strange because . . . I mean, where did you get—

—— You know better than to ask that . . . Strange because why?

—— Well cos the tacho was obviously on for a long time. Goes all the way round 24 hours non-stop. Illegal for a start. They have to have regular breaks. Its the EU and all that. Some of the Tilbury drivers arrive in the afternoon, rest, do the overnight. Might take their statutory in a B & B. I mean, do 4, 5 hours, take 45 minutes. Daily rest, 11 hours in 24 and 6—

—— Yeah but youre sayin wha?

—— Well, first place, driver only went down the road. Second, he stopped but he never switched off his tacho. You stop, you switch off.

—— So he forgot.

—— Not if hes professional. Everything depends on it in a way. Job, everything. Its all regulated. Its one of the most reg—

—— So maybe he took a long sandwich break.

—— Maybe.

—— Well wha you sayin?

—— I dunno . . . Things go missing.

—— So this youre sayin went—

—— It might have. I dont know.

—— Which is to say it did.

—— Maybe, maybe not. But things do. Thats all I'm saying. One time a 40-foot container did a hey presto. Clerical error. Bit of confusion over the seal numbers. Another time a 40k tractor unit went walkabout. Turns out a certain tally clerk told a certain barman from the Flying Angel Club to let a certain docker know where the keys were. Like left overnight behind the reg plate. It happens. Even with the cameras, dogs, surveillance, full turnout inspections, you name it, it still happens. Even with all the paperwork, ships manifests, gate passes, an all the clearance they require. So it couldve been cake on a plate ready for eating. Trouble is, theres still the mug shots as you leave. You have to hide your face. See, thats how they got the docker. Who turned in the barman. Who turned in the—

—— Let me guess: tally clerk.

—— . . . who pointed them to the tractor unit on a certain stretch of the 227. You work for an increase in your lifestyle, then you work for a reduction in your sentence.

—— Manual for Grasses, page 1.

—— Manual for Survival, introduction.

—— Wha you tellin me?

—— Well I'm not trying to put you off your tea. Just that getting anything out of Tilbury takes nous. Even stowaways prefer Felixstowe.

—— Who says I'm tryin to get anythin?

—— Well you aint exporting food to the third world . . . I'm just saying maybe an insider got nous. But not for peanuts. Even family Burnside peanuts.

—— The nuts depend on wha youre sellin.

—— Gate pass could be useful. Not as useful as the drivers own docs of course. Thats what you really want, a full set of drivers documents. But that takes time. Gate pass'll still get you in though. You know? Look around a depot maybe. Once-over a loading bay, warehouse, whatever. Just to make sure what youre looking for – *if* youre looking – is there . . .

I dont react. So he reach under him, somewhere or other where he got his secret stash hole. Fiddle about, come up with a laminate pass which he hand me.

—— This'll get me in?

—— It'll get you in.

—— How much?

—— Oner.

—— Half a oner.

—— Split the difference. Plus a money-back guarantee.

He give a nervous chuckle, knowin the last thing he want is comeback. I nod, give him the peas for a pass I dont even know I got use for. Then I'm turnin to leave the tally clerk turn con turn pure an simple H, like his name an his life was cut off of him letter by letter, I'm turnin when somethin jump in my mind.

—— They got flowers goin through Tilbury? I mean—

—— Flowers? Oh sure. Sure they have. Theres an all-night bus-stop service from Rotterdam bringing the tulips an daily feeder vessels from Cork bringing the shamrocks and of course—

—— You takin the piss?

—— Are you? They got all sorts coming through Tilbury. Sunflower seed, rape seed, butter, lamb, plywood from Charleston, Virg—

—— Yeah alright.

—— Grain silos, shifting 2,000 tonnes an hour.

—— Yeah alright.

—— Word of advice: whatever youre gonna do, do like

the drivers. Other words touch nothing on the inside. You can never know who opened and closed the unit last so you can never be sure whats being freighted. And even if you are sure, use gloves and burn what you wear. Come to that, burn the truck. Theyve got smart paint and smart water and top of that theyre all smart. And you might think youre just as smart as all that, just as smart as they are . . . But flowers, he start chucklin, flowers . . .

Back outside them storm clouds is gone. But its rainin anyway. I drive Farooq back to Kentish Town like everythin was AA1A Positive plc. Which it aint. Like I was a mover an a shaker. Which course I aint. Which is to say this is all too big for me. One step too far an all that. Too big an too far. An no floor for my feet. Burglars need floors. The DSS should be told. The DSS would most likely tell me stealin a truck was a challenge an a opportunity. Shore up my rusty skill. Keep my hand in. No employment gaps an all that.

Crime is many things to many people, a deep con once said. Everyone look at him, waitin for the rest, waitin for the second half the sayin, the bit with the but. Only there wasnt none an everyone look at him confuse an call him a cunt. But me I was young an I just thought yeah, crime is, so therefore I can do wha I want, do who I want, cos theres worlds out there, excitin worlds wha can buzz you to the max. Now I'm like, so fuckin wha? Life in general is many things to many people. But be it crime or life or life of crime shit is shit. An this is shit. Employment gaps or no, come Friday I'm signin on.

Meantime between paracetamols it weigh on me that I cant let nothin happen to J & K, that I must go through with this whether I understand or no. An I understand fuck all. Wha you dont understand can hurt you. Maybe its wha the deep con should of said. Only he was too busy passin on the same shit he heard once upon a time, his first time, when some other deep con sat there soundin off. An he was young then an he believe. An now hes old an he has to believe. Thats all I know.

Call Sensi an fill him in on the detail, the flower truck, its driver stoppin over at the B & B, the pass. Only thing I dont tell is how to ID the crates with the hooky chips. Meantime hes made headway with the lockup. Better than a lockup he got an empty sublet in a lowrise opposite Rathbone market. Keys left in a hole in the brick outside the door. Between the lowrise an the market is the flyover of the A13 like a streak of slurry. Canning Town is where I pick Sensi up. Hes carryin a book, *SAS – The Real Story*, an a sport bag which he place a bit too careful in the boot. So course I ask him wha he got in it. He come back with a wink an a nod.

—— You tell me. Take a guess? Or phone a friend? Who wants to be a millionaire? You wanna be a millionaire . . . ?

Arsehole make me panic even more, like it might be me directin the car east to Tilbury but hes the one with his feet on the pedals. He even has to verbal some squeegee refugee, some sad fuck who wipe a stain on the screen for 10p.

—— What you givin him anythin for? Cant believe how they all come over an all of them get social an housin an fuckin handouts left right an centre for them, their 6 wives an their best friends for doin what? Sayin they been tortured is what. I could say that. Kick in the arse is what I'd get. Fuck man, *you* could say that. You actually *been* tortured an what the fuck they gonna give you?

I concentrate on the drive. The Persona clud along past Beckton Alp, ski lift shuntin skiers, then the silverlit factories of the Dagenham works, then the matchin 3 grey red tower blocks wha stand out a mile on the flat land like they was the only buildins left after the Blitz. After that the 13 more less head down the river an dont stop till it hit the coast round Southend. All the way theres pylons an chimneys slicin the skyline. Which is to say London dont really stop. It just roll on till the sea stop it. But between the West End an Southend they maintain a grey field with a grey cow in it for a bit of country heritage an all that. An the rest the view is undercoated, topcoated an weatherproofed in soot grey an petrol blue.

Only thing fightin against it is Sensis mood. Hes on a mega bubble, prattlin on about the future, crackin crap one-liners an tellin all about his cuz who phone him from

Marbella where they got him in custody on a charge of air rage.

—— Charge bein the operative word, hes goin, cos they had to divert the plane: 75 grand. Then park at the new airport: 50 grand. Refuel: 15 grand. An course the fine: 85 grand. So he told me after that he cant even afford goin clubbin tonight . . .

Sensi bust out laughin, expectin me to do the same. Support your mates stories an all that. But I dont. Cos the rearviews fillin up with vans, BT, Hainault Aggregates, Thames Water, Eurocar, Parcel Force. An in among them an other vehicles is a Situsec van. Its still too far back to make out the driver or his mate but its the only van tryin to close up the 8-, 10-vehicle gap.

—— Fuckin hell, J, Sensis goin, just chill out. Youve got to get some—

—— Yeah, focus back . . .

—— Well we aint gonna pull off nothin with your attitude. Tellin you right, tomorrow, first thing, after the recce an everythin, just go down Porchester baths an lax yourself up a few hours. I'll sort the transport an the contingency. You done plenty already. Plenty. You have to chill otherwise your nerves is gonna fuck it up for sure.

—— Yeah ok, I go, ok . . . Sorry man . . .

But by now theres new things shuntin up an down my dumb landfill head. Like for instance *Porchester* is wha I heard Warren sayin on the phone back in the pool hall. Must be where hes hookin up with his contact, somethin Sensi couldnt know or he wouldnt of said it.

—— Forget it, forget it, Sensis goin. Water under, hes goin. All forgott— Whoa, J whoa pull over . . . pull over . . .

Sensis spotted a sign for a layby 200 or so yard ahead. *Wild Flowers @ £7 for 3 bunches*.

—— I aint superstitious but come on man . . . Good-luck flowers for the flower blaggers . . .

Manage a grin an get ready to pull in but without warnin, without slowin or indicatin, just to see wha Situsec do. Ahead in the laybys a Luton, geezer next to it with a trestle table floggin grey bunches of nothin you could put a proper name to. How long Situsec been back there I dont know. Feel like too long. The 13 is a long straight one an there aint nothin but streams of vans. Only maybe I seen them already round Kentish Town, carvin up the 134 in the bus lane. Or maybe up Manor House, pushin their way cross the box junction where the lights was out. Or maybe they was rushin the red to keep up past Bow Creek. Or maybe it was them overtakin on a zebra near Canning Tube. Maybe. An lookin at it, the half-rub-out *u* in Situsec I seen somewhere before.

Only one way to make sure. When the layby come up I pull in sharp more less flingin the cussin Sensi through the windscreen, then stop right there at the front end givin Situsec no chance to pull in. Sensi actually enjoy the cheap thrill an hes grinnin as he jump out, already reachin for his money. Me I turn back an stare right at the van. Its still steamin at 50 plus, too fast an too late to manoeuvre. One way or other it has to pass.

An sure enough, as big grinnin Sensis gettin flowered up with bargain good-luck bunches, the driver an his mate tool past. An this time my instinct come through for me cos the driver an his mate is none other than Martin the Cosh an Geoff the Hood, the cunts, both them pretendin not to look, like cheatin kids playin hide an seek. You can just hear the war of words kickin off inside their new van. *Dont fuckin look dont look. I'm not fuckin lookin I'm not. Pull over pull over. I cant fuckin pull over I cant. He saw us he fuckin saw us. No fuckin way he saw us no fuckin way*. The cunts.

Suddenly I'm gladder than glad Sensis here, a ex-squaddie boxer, a ribcrusher, a skullcracker, a hard an desperate man with a sport bag. He jump back in, blabbin how the flowers is a sign, theyve got to be, a good sign like an omen an he keep tellin me, 3 time, 4 time, a good sign, an omen, a good sign, an omen, over an over like prophecy was speakin through him. Then we get back on the road, Martin an Geoff way up ahead, sittin there with their KitKats an hankies, wonderin if they been revealed, figurin out how to switch back, how to unfuck the new situation.

Me I'm wonderin whether to tell Sensi about them. Most

likely he'd want to chase them all the way down the 13. Run them off the road into a 60,000-volt pylon. Kill kill faster faster an all that. So I hold off, just watch them, let them make a move, knowin this is a full-on problem wha is gonna need proper sortin. Cos after all theys either here to watch me do business or to take my business once I done it. An neither them possibility is good.

Eventually the Tilbury turnoffs start appearin. The 1306, the 1012, the 1089. Martin & Geoff is up ahead an they know they got a decision to make. Course theys gonna opt for hard-shoulderin the van before the turnoffs, hopin they can sneak back behind. Whatever happen its obvious I cant let them know I know. So I drive on, pass them as they idle on the shoulder like it was nothin, an let them ease back into their comfort zone a half-dozen cars back. Then we get on the 1089 headed for the dock. Sensi sus me checkin the rearview once too often.

—— You know em?

I nod.

—— Theyre the ones innit. The ones who—

Nod number 2. Save Sensi twistin round an givin the game away I describe them for him. He smile, come back with: *Shouldnt tempt fate like that should they. I mean, thats our transport sorted innit. Aint like theyre gonna report the van stolen. Cos it probably already is. Am I right?* He aint wrong.

An this for def is the all-too-plain solution to the problem, the very solution wha would occur to anyone, wha occur to me too more less straight away. Sensis goin:

—— We drive about, recce, set an ambush, rope em in. Rest depend on how the target react . . .

I dont give him nod number 3 or even look at him, knowin his face is gonna reveal to me wha I got writ large all over mine. Which is to say he dont need no push toward revenge. An me I been push enough already. Still, gettin a hold Martin & Geoffs van aint just the all-too-plain solution to a problem. An it aint just them temptin fate. Its me plottin against Uncle like I was ready for suicide. Its also me & Sensi makin the sort of choice wha call up destiny like it was a 24-hour emergency hotline. Who know how destinys gonna reply but the 1089 lead us an them to Tilbury, to the docks, a place we dont know an aint never been.

Road clear up as the traffic branch other ways, to the M25, Bluewater, Southend. With no cover Martin & Geoff is force to drop back. Ahead over the low hills the cranes of Tilbury is loomin. Heavy gusts push black clouds over the fields an farm buildins. Roundabout. Sensi choose Tilbury Town. I follow his instinct. Dont want no messy situation developin near the port. We take Dock Road through the sad scatter of shopfront wha is Tilbury. Shippin agents, haulage contractors, the Thurrock Irish Association social club, a mission, a fish fryer, the Continental B & B, an then scavengers livin off of the business the port bring in, skip an scrap merchants, car breakers. Martin & Geoff hold back as the road curve once twice then peter into council ghetto. Finally the black cloud deliver. Rain slam down.

I know wha Sensi is lookin for when he tap me left into the carpark of a small block flats. We merge in. 2 burnt-out cars sit in the corners. A vandalise tractor unit stand in the middle next to a skip surround by twist of metal an damp-rot palettes. Through the rain over the other side the Tilbury railway is sea containers, scores them, stack up in tiers like mega tower blocks with no windows. Sensis noddin to himself.

—— Perfectamento . . . Lets go . . .

I park out sight behind the tractor unit. We got secs is all. Sensis grabbin somethin out the boot. I'm grabbin one the rusty twists of metal.

—— Wont need it mate . . . Take a butchers at this . . .

He display to me wha he got, an wha he got come as no small surprise. It come more as a shock. Which is to say it aint the obvious wha the back my mind suspect. Cos it aint no gun. Wha Sensi produce is a full-on medieval crossbow.

—— Beautiful innit. Panzer Pro with a 175-pound pull. Other words cant miss. Ive even made my own bolts so they cant trace nothin. Split a skull, tell you that.

213

—— Bit fuckin medical . . .

Sensi laugh, rain spatterin his head, only it wasnt no joke. He pull back the bow, slot in a bolt.

—— Case of *who killed cocky bastard?* innit.

—— Who did? I go, throat lumpin up.

—— *I did, said the barrow boy, with my bow an arrow boy, I killed cocky bastard* . . .

By then Martin & Geoffs van is pokin in. Sensi tap me toward the car as he conceal himself by the skip.

—— Block em off once they commit . . .

I duck back in the seat, engine still runnin, knowin this is Sensi & me an wishin it was me & Duane. Their wipers is on the delay, their faces appearin every 3 secs after the wipe, eyes lookin side to side cross the carpark. Seem Geoffs tellin Martin to back out but Martins creepin the van farther in. Dont need me to imagine the fresh war of words goin down between them. Sensis crouch, ready. Me I'm waitin for them to clear the entrance to the carpark by min 4 foot.

Moment they do I'm movin, clutchburnin the 20 foot to the back their van to cut them off. Glimpse them both an both them glimpse me. Theys all over the shop, dont know whether to come or go, mouths movin, new war of words.

Back it out back it the fuck out. Wont go in reverse wont fuckin go in. Which is to say the vans rockin with panic. First it kangaroo forward, then gear crunch in reverse but I'm there first, in the gap, my passenger door takin the brunt as they kangaroo back, me out the car an runnin round the front the van.

Sensis over the driver side. Crossbow ready at his shoulder. Linin up, aimin. Steady as a skip. Point fuckin blank. For the first time I believe hes really gonna do it. Martin & Geoff believe it too, both pressin back far as they can against their headrests, arms rotorin round to protect their faces, one them screamin *no no no*. Rain drown them. Engine cut them out. Everythin still as fuck a sec. Then his trigger finger twitch.

From that angle the bolt shatter through Martins side window, trim his nose hair, an bang in Geoffs headrest 2 inch behind his right ear. Might as well be stickin out his temple cos the effects the same. He sit there stun. They both do. Sensi already reloadin, slippin a second bolt in place, mutterin *I cant believe I fuckin missed.*

Thats the point I jump in the way. Have to. Pull open Martins door. Hes in his seat like a fuckin squirrel, little arms curl up by his chest. An judgin by the airwaves one the other has shit himself.

—— Just as well he miss innit Martin. Cos I wouldnt mind askin the 2 you some Qs. Ok?

Martins mouth try an answer but instead it just nibble

his tongue like it was chewin on a nut. Which I take to be a yes. Sensi he just shrug, just like that, dont mind if he kill them or no, like the soldier he was, back in uniform, on a mission, do or die, all the same. So he wave the bow at them, order them out the van, military style, on the floor, face down, legs spread, arms down the side, palms up, *one word youre shish kebab*.

The sub-postoffice blaggers from Ruislip an Harrow on the Hill aint arguin their lives away no more. Eyes down. *Moanin like bitches innit*, Sensi tell them. Whatever. Now they both been reduce to 2 well-meek scum who for def aint inheritin the earth. Sensi tell me to get some jump leads. I get the ones Farooq throw in for free. Then Sensi tell me to cover them with the bow while he take the leads to them, askin them politely whether they would prefer to be tie with the red one or the black one, *pos or neg what'll it be?* The meek scum stay stumm.

Take some doin tyin a geezers arms behind him with just a jump lead, croc clips bitin somewhere near their flies, their heads bouncin once twice on the ground, blood leakin. *Payback*, Sensis goin as he take his time. *Think of it as payback.* Me I control my patterns cos God knows I want to mash them. Instead I tell him to hurry up. Sec later he hold the first one up in the air like a package, *look at that* he say, then one after the other he slamdunk them in the boot the Persona, transferrin out his sport bag to the van. Wha the fuck the idea is now who know.

Sensi ask me if I know where we can take them. Back up Fairlop Plain bein the obvious answer only its a right schlepp. Jump-leaded in a crate in Krypton Metals & Non-Ferrous Scrap bein the more closer option. So thats wha we go for. Heavy rain like a blessin to cover this madness. Everyone blinkin, squintin. Mud all over. Very messy. Least they aint bleedin too bad. Once the 2 thems nice an cushty in the crate an before Sensi stick the gags in, I ask my Qs.

Dont take nothin, no torture, no pliers, no nothin to get M & G to proper fess up their doins. Which is to say theys settin me up as a fall guy. Number 1: take my business. 2: leave me by the road, batter or dead, all the same, nothin personal, a job of work is all, thats all it is. The whores. Geoffs dumb enough to blab about how theres plenty others just like him & Martin that Uncle can call up any old time an that if he find out about this I can *kiss my kids on a video near you*. Which is to say he turn my stomach. Which is to say positive thinkin fly out the window an I hit him an gag him there an then.

After, I get a hold Martins mobi an I make him bell Uncle to tell him *the whole plans tickin like a antique godfather clock*. Uncle chuckle at that one. Then I get Martin to add that *J is well in the palm an he aint sus nothin*. An I also make him tell Uncle not to worry if he dont hear no more cos the mobi coverage round heres shockin an hes seriously thinkin to change networks. Uncle bein smug with his own brainpower love it all. *My dicks drippin with pre-cum*, I hear him say.

When the little confabs over Martins phone go straight in a puddle, a deep one. *Cant I phone my missis?* Sensi tell him he must be jokin, that its too late for that. Then his head an Geoffs head go well down in the crate. Sensi & me pile Krypton scrap an non-ferrous metal on top an a load other shit an get the fuck out, Sensi collectin the van, me up ahead in the Persona. The plan we got is simple: park up in Tilbury an get a bevvy.

Course we dont. Cheese sandwich an a Coke out the newsagent instead. For Sensi. Ibuprofen for me cos the paracetamols aint workin no more. Sit in the car near the roundabout, van behind, windows steamin, muddy, soakin, well away from Dock Road, well away from scrap merchants, well away from the Continental B & B.

—— You should get your head seen to, Sensi laugh. Sorry man, didnt mean it like that . . . Tell you whats good for migraine. My gran use to sort me out some marjoram. Essential oil. You get knocked out worse than Mickey, tell you that . . .

Then hes quackin on about M & G. *See their mugs? Did you see their mugs? Them mugs was a picture. Stink up the van baad. Did you smell it? Smell that? Fuck man that kind of stinkin shit come from one thing innit: fear. Total fear. Champion fuckin fear. Tellin you, Panzer crossbow, beautiful, tellin you man, it instil the fear just lookin at it. Dont it just? Dont it just shit you the fuck up?* Then hes playin with the bolt he had to chisel out the headrest. Me my skulls splittin.

—— So next, Sensis goin, we focus on the business, use the

pass, get in the port, recce the truck, figure out the route an the exact spot where we take the bastard innit.

—— We aint stoppin it.

—— What?

—— We aint stoppin it.

—— The fuck you talkin about? We have to stop—

—— Nah . . . Better idea . . .

—— Yeah? I'm holdin my breath . . .

—— The gate pass I gots useless. Bad feelin. Dont trust it. Aint the answers all I know.

—— Well what is?

—— Driver docs. Only the drivers docs is gonna get me in Tilbury an a 40-tonner out. So forget the hijack, the crossbow an the jump lead 2-step routine. Aint goin through all that bollocks another time.

—— Fuck J, that was a top buzz . . . I mean we got the transport *and* we mete some serious justice. So what the fuck you whingin out for?

—— Aint whingin out.

—— So whats with these driver documents? We aint got them an we aint got the time—

—— The Continental, you see it on the way through?

—— Dosshouse on the corner?

—— Thats where the driver stop over for his rest period. Notice the stairwell?

Sensi shake.

—— Open window top. Second floor. Buildins on a corner. Wall round the back for access. Like it was meant to be. Plus somethin tell me that windows always left open. Little window wha nobody really bother with. Open all year round, year in year out. Cos after all, nobodys gonna get through it—

—— Until . . .

—— Duane call a window like that the Eye of God, winkin at you. Any case, the fallbacks the other window, the one under it on the first. Its a simple catch is all. Piss it.

—— Yeah? What about the internals?

—— Well, my guess, the internals, I mean, dosshouse shithole like that, I mean, you dont exactly need no deluxe mechanical pick gun or 20 sticks dynamite.

—— Yeah, Sensi grin, flexible-friend the gaff while youre booked in the presidential suite. Out an in an out.

—— French farce it with a blindfold.

—— Usin toes an nose . . . The B & B, yeah, course, Sensi

go as my idea finish dawnin. Steal the papers off of him, the Russian. Yeah man, for def, yeah, yeah, jubblies, A1, a stroke of G. Not to mention wicked an cunning . . .

—— Easier than stoppin a truck anyway.

—— Easier than stoppin a truck . . . Mucho mucho easiermento . . . J . . .

—— Wha?

—— Dont bother gettin your head seen to, its workin fine. What times the driver show up?

—— Wont be till tomorrow some time. Late p.m. or so. Thats my guess anyway.

—— We'll come down early, recce the target. Plus if you got cold feet about the 2 ponces we can stick em somewhere else.

—— I aint got cold feet about them. They survive General Panzer an his homemade bolt point blank didnt they? Prove they got 9 lives. Any case, Mr Kryptons gonna save them. Other words, theyll survive bein bang up in a crate overnight. Wont they?

—— Ooh, dunno about that J, go Sensi strokin his chin. Dunno about that at all. Cramps a killer, a real fuckin killer . . .

Which dont make it sound any better. Until I think of Arno an his schemes. Suddenly cramp sound positive, like at least it isnt me doin the business, doin the killin, but someone else, somethin else, somethin natural.

We get goin, Sensi drivin the van, me up ahead in the Persona. Back on the 13 the lights fadin, the sunsets comin on, purple orange neon over Beckton, Dagenham, Canning. We head back home in the traffic like weekenders, like dayjobbers. An round us, all around, the town roll on. It pay no attention to nothin. It care about nothin. Fact it care less. For def it dont notice 2 geezers, one in a Situsec van, other in a Persona, rollin up the 13. An back there, back in Tilbury, it dont notice a crate in a scrapyard or 2 sub-postoffice blaggers dyin of cramp. Truth be told it dont notice nothin. It dont notice nothin cos it aint got the time. It just roll on. Thats all this town ever do. An I hate the way the town roll on an on. An then on.

It was a well-long evenin. An after that the whole night was even more longer with Sensi drinkin an quackin an drinkin, *cant wait for the off . . . itchin for the off*. He phone Warren back 2, 3 time just to confirm the sums. Which is to say Warren phone for the update an claim he know a buyer for the Pentium processors, as long as theys mint. He reckon he can get 50 squids a unit. He reckon his ends in the bag. He reckon hes ready an waitin. Up to us now.

Sensi love it, gulp it all down. Between drinkin an quackin an phonin Sensis addin an dividin, workin it all out, well happy doin accounts, any accounts, *this is my long-term thing J, this is it*. Trouble bein Warrens figures aint nowhere near Arnos. Arno told me theyd fetch wha? 300? Maybe £50 is the real tag. Or the fences P. Or it could

223

be just Warren doin his own personal arithmetic. Not that Sensi give one either way. He just quack an drink an quack, grindin me down with his phoney excitations, about how to leave no evidence, about H's advice to burn everythin, an he go on an on borin the years off of me, strippin them off like so many layers of damp wallpaper in his cuzs flat. Then course hes too lick up to drive home to Fran. So he fart an crash on the sofa. In secs hes snorin like a pig in love. With itself.

But all thats by the by. Me I didnt sleep. Me I lie awake, head throbbin an all that, throbbin sometime so bad I see things I didnt know was there, an I lie awake tryin to out-think the headache, focusin on Warren an his other half, his contact, focusin on wha I know already about them, which is to say not to trust the pair. The Q bein how much not to trust them.

Then soons the dawn was up I was out. Snuck right past Sensis rumblins, over his risin fallin chest, inch from his vice hands. Left a note sayin I'd catch him later on his mobi. Then I roll down the Harrow Road an over the Paddington basin with one thing on my mind, one thing aside the shadows of long animals wha start to follow me, springin out dens an kennels an holes. Every now an then I have to squeeze my eyes close to stop them. But the one thing aside them is Porchester baths.

Café opposite open early. Sit in there readin the paper, Sensis cuzs red Edmonton Oilers baseball cap coverin my face, a face I stop lookin at wha seem like a life ago. A Thames Water van, leak detection unit, stop up for tea.

Then a P & D duo, Dad & Son, come in for a full English. Me I eat eggs on toast. Read the items concernin little people an their daft lives, the sort of lives even scrap merchants wouldnt take off of you. Like theres the middle-age burglar they done cos he left his earprint on a window, listenin out before he enter, not thinkin his ear is unique like his finger. Next theres the 2 teenage boys they done, geezers of tomorrow, who was rumble as they try to buy sweets an crisps with homemade fake fivers. An under thems a 3-line item about a macaw with an attitude problem whose owner put it on Prozac to stop it devastatin the furniture.

I finish my eggs, my paper, tea an smokes an by then its comin up to 10 a.m., the baths is openin an a couple regs is already waitin. Then a couple others, an 1, 2 more. Any them people could be Warrens contact. Cos after all wha does a muff really look like? Fat, fatter? Suited up, casual? Crusty, smooth? Whatever. Another 15 mins an Warrens strollin up, pretendin to check his green shoulder bag while he check out the street, gardens behind, library right, café left. Then with his matchin green rain jacket an khaki strides an shiny shoes he stroll on in the entrance, thick lifestyle mag in his hand, the sort Monica use to get me to read way back, *for my own good* she said, some mag with stuff about why mens nipples get sore, some cruddy glossy with a title like *Zing for Geezers*.

So I figure give Warren 10. 2 mins to strip off, 2 to fold his careful schmutter, 4 to flex himself an fix his hair, last couple to leaf *Zing for Geezers*, then down the shower. Plus an extra 2 mins in case the mags got foldout 16-year-old eye candy to keep him busy. Then I follow, pay in. Course its mens day. Which is to say men lollin about, scratchin crotch, pickin ears, walrused on the sunbeds among the fancy columns in the tile hall. Theres an Arab squawkin in some broken lingo down his mobi with a few words poppin out every few secs . . . *semolina* . . . *ship-ment* . . . *fucky bastard* . . . Not far from him the ones an twos wha come in is now a group of blabbin regs . . . *It was the same cunt I pick up round Hyde Park only a week back an he says to me he says* . . . Other words, cabbies the lot. Old pruneface attendant old as the baths mop a corner.

Round the sides is the lockers. Head down I'm scopin round till I spot wha could be Warrens mag lyin on one the beds. So I pick a bed on the far side cover by one the columns. Strip off quick, quiet. Grab one the check wraps they give you an throw one the towels over my head like a boxer. Garms I just dump on the bed in case I have to scram. Arabs shoutin for breakfast. *Tea egg tossed ok?* Old pruneface nod an start movin.

The one time I been here you had to go down the steam rooms, one the Roman *ariums* or wha, to get any P & Q. Which is to say Warren an his girlfriend is gonna be somewhere down there. So thats where I head, have to, but adoptin a sort of slouch, draggin my feet cos a new walk is a good disguise an it concentrate me away from my pumpin heart. The tile stairway lead past the freezin plunge pool. From there a maze steamy corridors open up, everythin hissin, drippin, feet slappin in pools of water, tiles warm then cool, feet damp, boil damp, animal shadows, a stark man sleepin in a chair, water runnin off of a pipe above an drippin on his head. Picture Jade in my head, liftin her drippin an gigglin out the bath, water runnin off of her all over me.

Then 1, 2 polite shadows pass me, people I never even saw comin in, like they just been here since time, livin since time in the glowin fog. Them aside, the gaff aint exactly rammed. The hourglass is runnin down in the empty sauna. The Jacuzzis bubblin away by itself. A lone raw steaks slabbed out in the tepidarium.

Eventually only one place is left, the obvious one place in a way, which is to say the full-on steam room, where you cant see fuck, nothin except maybe the odd toe appearin on the floor as it cut the cloud on its journey. Cant help it. Cant help this, the feelin, a feelin like death is crowdin me, crowdin in on me, them animals, their shadows, my children, I half expect them out the steam, to come out the steam an hug me to them like they use to, an everythin would wind back to a perfect day once upon a time, once upon my time, our time. Instead I'm facin the plastic flaps. Other side them flaps is Warren, for sure, he must be, smooth as a silk cravat, bullshittin Baksheesh Bill.

From outside I try an catch a sound but theres nothin. So real gentle I chest through, treadin on a hose, rollin it over, cold water pressurin through. Stand dead a sec. Then a voice move round me like the scorchin steam as I feel for the edge, the wood bench, hopin I dont end up in Warrens lap or worse the muffs. The voice is low an slow an hissin, a voice wha is most likely always low an slow an hissin an nothin but.

—— Umar, the voice is goin, you arent telling me anything . . . What are you telling me . . . ? You cant give me names . . . ? My very hairy arse you cant . . . What do you take me for . . . ?

Ease down on the bench. Impossible to make out exactly how far they are. Close enough. Stretchin my leg would be like playin footsie. If I cant see them it stand to reason they cant see each other neither. An more steam belch in the whole time, suffocatin me under my towel with heat an fear, a well-ugly buzz wha aint like jumpin fences on summer nights up the Harringay ladder. The voice is hissin:

—— You ever go to a Cat C fixture back in the heady days of aggro? Saturday afternoon on the turnstiles? No? Thats where I got my gongs—

—— Quite but I dont think theyll be awarding you—

—— Dont get smart Umar. My point is: you will give me names. You will give me times and dates. You will give me whatever I want. Thats a thought isnt it? I know it . . . You know it . . . So talk to me . . .

Truth be told this voice proper shit me. Get right in me like one them tv hypnotists wha can make you eat onion while you taste apple. Feel like I'm givin in to it, the fear. An wha shit me even more, aside this voice, is wha I see when smart Umar, which is to say the for real Warren, wriggle an squirm, breathin heavier an heavier in his own personal hotspot. Cos every time he squirm the steam shift. An the shiftin steam reveal the dick wha belong to the voice. An the dick is very fuckin tiny. Really fuckin microscopic in fact. Like a white maggot in the grey steam. An it shit me cos it reveal the very thing wha even *Zing for Geezers* would never reveal. Which is to say it is well known that geezers equip with tiny dicks is well dangerous.

—— Well, the voice is goin, the meters running . . .

—— Sure, Warren go, clearin his throat. Of course. You see I cant—

—— I thought we were beyond the *cant* stage.

—— We are, we are. Its just that youre putting me in a rather invidious position.

  The voice go hm hm hm like a laugh.

—— I.e., Umar sunshine, i.e. you are well and truly fucked and plugged with a used 10-inch strap-on dildo purchased on the Internet off a trannie crackwhore based in Harlem . . . To put it more nicely, you may soon require many rolls of the finest toilet tissue for your rather sensitive—

—— At least—

—— I havent finished yet . . .

—— I just think that no escort would be best.

—— Oh you do?

—— Can you do that? Ensure theres no escort?

—— Umar, I'm gonna make very fucking sure there is an escort: me. So . . . talk to me . . . Tell me something . . . Because otherwise we both know its a one-way back to Wonko Wonko on the dawn banana boat and the only thing between you and the high seas is yours truly. Clear . . . ? Umar, I said is that—

—— Could we perhaps adjourn upstairs. Its somewhat—

—— Somewhat what Umar?

—— I'm merely point—

—— Shut up. Its far too late to *merely point*. I mean, do you know what youre looking at, I mean what youre lookin at with your little *please send your donations here* 419 scam, your little earners, money laundering, passport fraud etc. etc. etc. etc. . . . Do you know? 10 years plus. You wont be the first done for laundering but you will be one of them. One of the first examples . . . Maximum sentence *pour encourager les autres*, if you catch my drift. And once youre inside, and bunkbedded, and spanking the old monkey, I will personally let it be known what a tremendous help youve been to the men in blue. What an exemplary citizen youve turned out to be. I dare say I could even organise a fetching snap of you and me shaking hands over a pewter shield. Go down a treat in B-wing . . .

—— Quite. Look I—

—— I havent finished yet . . . You see Umar, registered informants, coppers narks, grasses, call them what you will . . . Point is, you are one. You will be used. So how long do you think youll—

—— I know that, I realise that but—

—— *But? Cant?*

—— Its a predicament—

—— It is.

—— . . . and I just have to—

—— *Just?*

—— I'm merely—

—— *Merely? Again?* Umar . . . you will get your cup of tea and a slice—

—— New ID . . .

—— Hm hm hm . . .

—— You said—

—— I said you will get what you get. Anything is cuffable. I told you that . . . Thats what I told you. Anything at all.

231

I should know shouldnt I? Right? Glimmer of reality back there? Hello? Right?

—— Yes right . . .

—— Meanwhile . . . names . . . dates . . . times . . . Not boring you am I? Not too repetitive for you I hope? Especially—

—— I just would—

—— *Especially* . . . I want to know where our number 1 friend will be on the night. Not just the dreamy light-weights in their bunny slippers and favourite jimjams . . . Clear? Right? Ok? So Umar, its really quite simple: you talk to me . . .

Umar talk. Course he do. Anyone would after 2 mins listenin to this fuck. But them talkin aint no longer the thing. The thing wha matter is wha the muff really want, who he really want. Maybe hes an all-or-nothin sort of muff. Other words, bein *enthusiastically corrupt*, he not only want a couple bangups under his little red balls, he want to ice it all off with his extra, his hooky chips, hooky whatever, whatevers goin will do him nicely. Thank you very much an all that.

Q is, whos he really after? Cos this is the only thing wha need concern me. Cos if its Uncle then I'm wonderin wha the fuck I done with the piece of paper, the one Arno give me. Wha he say? *I know where hes gonna be on a certain night* . . . I just push that fold-up scrap out my mind.

Now it could mean everythin, everythin I need right now, top the list bein a way out. No murderin. Just one call an Uncles out the picture. It could be that easy, that simple. No more worries. No need to take no truck. No need to worry about Sensis next move. An for def no need to be in this place no more.

Umars talkin. Course he is. Slow at first, like the hypnotist done the business on him. Each breath clear a hole in the steam, each hole glow like a light bulb, here, there, wherever he turn, wherever he breathe. But wha he really know, Warren? He dont know enough. Truth be told he dont know shit. I have to move. Shift my left leg close to the flaps, push my foot out. Then I stand an step through in one go, grippin the towel round my face, silent as fuck, only one person more silent. Heat make my head spin. Sweat pour off of me. On the way up I plunge in the freezin pool. Stop me dead. Close me up.

Back in the tile hall theres more people lollin, easier to mingle in. Grab another towel an my stuff an find a toilet. Stand there in the cubicle an go through all my pockets, trouser, jacket, shirt, one by one, every one a fight to get in. Seekin Arnos papers useless. Cos it aint there. It just fuckin aint.

All the places I been since, things I done, come floodin back. Beckton Alp. Orla. Hikmets pool room. Mortimer Road. H & H Transport. Tilbury. Krypton Metal. Mortimer again. Sunbed in the tile hall. Too many steps to retrace. Other hand how many time I throw my garms off in a rush? Not with Orla. Not round Mortimer. Now, here, is all, is the only time. Which is to say theres every chance its out there by the sunbed. So I dress, still sweatin, everythin clingin. Then with a towel over my head like I was dryin my hair I step back in the busy hall.

Trouble is my beds already been taken. Some geezers sprawl on it face down with *World Trance Millennium* glarin out a green logo on the soles his flip-flops. Ibeefa shorts an tan to match. I go close as I can, proper scannin the floor round him, round his half-unpack bag with Filo, shampoo, comb, shavin kit. Under the see-through plastic of the shavin kit there could be somethin, white, square.

Hes quackin on his mobi. *Yeah baby course it is, it really is, I feel wha youre goin fru, its totally heart-renderin . . .* A builder, obviously. But theres no time to check more closer cos theres Warrens hairdo appearin top the stairs. My instinct tell me to chip, slap my cap back on an just leave. Only I cant, bein as how my insurance policy, my one an only ace, could be down there on the damp floor, about to stick on the sole of a trancedance builders flip-flop. So instead I hunch right down like I was lacin up.

In a almighty hurry, Warren go past me, over to his locker. He get his gear out, an like me he start pullin on his trousers an so forth before hes dry an dusted. I look back across the floor. Trancedance builders slowly sittin up, penny-a-dozen feelins an heart-renderins comin out his mouth. 2 steps, less than 5 an I'm over, liftin his shavin bag an inch, pickin up the paper beneath. He say *baby* as his eye turn toward me, then to his gear like I was a teef.

—— Yeah? he go. *Hold it a sec baby* . . . Want summink?
Whassat?

—— Thought you might like my phone number . . .

I hold the damp paper out to him. He look back at me
like he just hear the most disgustin thing in history.

—— Wha? he go, standin up, glarin. Wha did you say . . . ?
Fuck off. Go on, fuck off out . . .

I shrug. He mutter somethin like *fuckin fag* under his
breath. I think I mutter somethin like *be like that then* under
mine. Then I'm out, walkin fast as I fuckin can, the whole
of me shakin. Cos its like the pretence of wha I just done
is more scarier to me, more scarier to the average Zing
Geezer than anythin, than even listenin to that bastard in
the steam room.

Still, my luck must be turnin cos I beat a traffic warden
to my car. Hes checkin the meter I never fed an course next
thing his brains workin overtime tryin to punch the plate
number in his gismo. When he see I beat him to it he grin.
First time ever a warden grin at me without backin the
grin up with sadism. I nod in return, turn it over, drive
off, pull in 20 feet away round the block. The papers in
my fist, damp an scrunch up.

Take good few secs to unfold it without rippin it. Inks
wet, the letters an numbers is well fuzzy. But my good
luck drain out no sooner than comin through. Cos theres

no mistakin wha is writ on it. Cos wha is writ on it is already familiar to me. An for all the fuzz an damp an dodgy asthmatic handwritin the letters an numbers couldnt be more clearer if they had mega green logo round them. Wha Arno give me is Monicas address. J & Ks address. The BT cunts address. Which is to say 32 Village Road.

Dont need me say the heart-renderins I'm goin through. Not just the dizzy steam. Not just the migraine. Its the picture of me phonin Monica, thats wha flood back. *Baby I understand* an all that bollocks. An now, now wha? Hows this time gonna be any different? Could just be a waste of time, a risk too far an all that. One way its the muffs watchin me to watch Uncle an then certain other muffs bein more equal than the first muffs watchin the muffs watchin me. Make no fuckin sense none at all.

Other way make more. Which is to say how this address arrive in my hand? Maybe Arnos workin me so as he really can be free, so as he can die holdin his own dick. It occur to me before. But compare to other possibility it dont come close to reality. Its more like Uncle puttin the wind up me. Monicas address: his insurance. It guarantee I carry it all out, lick his arse an then thank him as well for the opportunity. *Please sir may I have some more?* An if I dont do as I'm told, he turn enforcer, course he do, he has to, *for my rep J*, he just has to, hes 20 year old an he can carry the fuck out wha the fuck he like. An wha he carry out is mostly his word. Which is one thing more than me.

Meantime maybe Uncles standin in for the BT man, while Mr Answerphones takin a break an suckin on a menthol Locket. Uncles in there now, puttin on a class voice while hes home with Monica all this time an me, me never sussin, an them, them havin a royal laugh, a laugh a day, a minute, whenever they feel like it, him with himself all over her, her with herself all over him, laughin an shaggin an laughin their crooked way round her house. Wha should be my house.

End the day angry patterns an positive thinkin cancel out the one the other. Leave me standin still in a cloud, in a fog. 3 time I'm a digit away from bellin Duane an askin him, beggin him, to tell me wha the fuck to do, to give me an order, any order, cos I aint got a clue no more. Commit, dont commit, go left, go right, I dont know no more. Cos its either that, askin Duane even though I know wha hes gonna say, either that or its writin a letter to *Zing for Geezers*.

Dear Zing, *wha should I do if my wife is slipslidin the gangster wha threaten to put my children in a porn video unless I steal a 40-ton truck?*

The *Zing* expert says: *Do 20 squat thrusts, eat a leafy salad and study the diagram below of the clitoris.*

I swing by Mortimer, see if Sensis still there but course he aint. Vans gone. In a vase on the kitchen table hes left his good-luck bunch. Note under. *Be lucky flowerboy. Bell us ASAP.* Hes probably gone up Frans or the gym or maybe to his crossbow workshop to make new bolts. I have to tell Sensi about Warren course I do. But at the end the day, fool or no or fool committin foolishness or no, theres only one place to go right now. For better or worse, richer or poorer an all that. I take the flowers with me. Not that flowers is gonna make no difference. Its the words wha unlock the doors, same as before, same as always. Before I never had the right ones. Now I got the words. Cos if it aint Arno workin me an it aint Uncle workin a 2-timin bitch then the words is simple, simple an totally unbelievable: *Monica please trust me I cant explain wha it is just stay away from Village Road for a few days until I give you the jolly-hockey-sticks all clear ok?*

Dont need me to say she aint never in a million gonna accept nothin along them lines. She aint never even gonna listen to nothin along them lines. All I'd get is her sassin. Or police arm response. Or her secret BT nose man lover an a fresh batch Uncles goons shootin, stabbin, batterin an generally murderin me before I even get to press her fuckin bell. Which is to say I could do with a personal trainer to train me, kick some ideas about, rehearse my lines, run through it all with me 100 time to get the approach, the timin, the words, the emotion an all that perfect. But.

20 min drive. 30 in the traffic an rain to say fuck about

the flatbed wha shed its scaffold on the Brent Cross flyover or the burst pipe round Kilburn High. An so on an so forth till Monicas neighbourhood. Round there all the churches is convertin. Nobody believe in nothin no more. Geezers swarmin all over them, roofers, lekkies, glaziers knockin out the swankholes for the up an comin. Next itll be the mosque an the synagogue. An after that theyll build phoney churches an mosques an synagogues just so they can convert them, just to keep all the geezers busy.

Anyway. All quiet round Village Road. Her Audis park outside. If last Friday was half-term J & K is gonna be back in school this week. Stand to reason shes either on her own or with Mr Answerphone. Nothins comin out the place. Only noise is from Mrs Nettie Curtain next door, scopin the street, window slightly open while the zom box flash behind her. Cross the green, grass squeakin, avoidin the cack cos it could create the wrong impression. Mrs Curtain watch me go. Dont look at her, I keep tellin myself, dont give her the benefit. Just come back one bitter winter night an stick a brick through her perfect pane. Freeze the bitch rigid in her sleep.

Still, all this dont help me with the right words. Any words is gonna do except *hello*, anythin but that. But wha happen aint wha I hope. Truth be told its the last thing I expect. Cos I'm no more than 20 feet from pressin the bell when wha happen? Godpitikins is wha. Only the door openin is wha. Only her comin out is wha. Not so much comin as dashin. A full-on dash is wha she perform, celeb-style like she was avoidin the media, slammin the door an dashin to her Audi. Instinct kick in. Cant help it. An wha I do, how I react, I know look bad, I know it look bad, very bad even, from her view an to anyone wha care to watch. Cos wha I do is I block her off. Technique I learn off of Sensi. Which is to say I sort of get between her an her car. Which is to say I shock her. I mean, I sort of scare her shitless really. Which is to say I fuck up before I even kick off. After that hell.

Shes screamin, tresses flyin all over, she look so different, screamin at me to get out the way. Me I'm tryin to explain to her hair cos I cant see her eyes. An both us is generally just talkin all over each other as per the good old bad old days. *I told you – I know – I warned you J – It aint about that – Get out of the way* . . . An stuff like that. All that stuff comin out like it was way back when, like nothin move on, like nothin happen between. The net curtains is shiftin next door. Bitch is gonna triple-9 me for def. Can almost hear her describin wha she witness. Neighbourhood like this 2 mins or less is all I got, is all there is. Top that Monica take out her mobi. First I dont know if shes threatenin to call someone or to hit me with it.

—— Are you gonna let me go?

—— I aint holdin you.

—— Well get out the way then.

—— I'm tryin to tell you youre in danger.

—— I can fucking see that.

—— No Monica . . . Fuck . . . Not from me for fucks sake, not from me. Me I've lost. I've lost ok. I'm finish. I'm the loser. I know that. I accept it. Its over an done an I know that I—

—— But?

—— I aint come to stir it.

—— But?

—— Where you goin? I just need a couple mins to tell—

—— I'm in a hurry J . . .

—— I know that. I can see that. You dont have to run—

—— Whos running?

—— Well where—

—— Youre so suspicious. You always were.

—— I just need to talk, to tell you—

The sentence dont get finish cos theres a patrol car turnin in up the top end the street. Like they was waitin. Like it was a sure bet.

—— Monica . . . Monica . . .

She stand there smug as a perfect alarm system, all the angles cover, her blonde-highlight tresses fallin about her face, her sweepin them off, them fallin again, her sweepin them off again like her hair was the only thing goin on in her life. Patrol car creep slowly down like they never receive no triple 9. Or maybe its just them bein cautious apprehendin public enemy number 1.

—— Monica . . .

—— Well talk then . . . Youve got about half a minute till—

—— Dont get me arrested, I'm quackin like I never heard myself quack. Not now . . . I'm the loser like I said. Its done. You win. I just . . . Youre not gonna get me . . . I mean, old days, remember? You hid me. When you hid me that time. Remember? In the bed? When they come lookin, when they come searchin the house an you hid me in the bed, under the covers, under the hand-plucked Siberian goosedown duvet. Remember? *Where is he?* they go. *How should I know?* you go. An there I was, next to you, right next to you, under you more less, all safe, well safe. Hidden. Totally hidden. Remember? You remember that? Help me now. Cos I'm in a bit . . . I mean, I dont— I mean, I cant even treat a boil without you.

—— Is that what it is? she ask, hair fallin over her face.

As she brush her tress off I glimpse an eye, a dark eye, an it throw me cos its a well-sad dark eye wha I see.

—— Yeah, yeah thats wha it is. A boil . . . Wha can I say? I turn ugly innit.

—— An ugly man, she shrug, wouldve tried harder. A lot harder. Ugly men do. Thats what they say.

—— Well I'm ugly now an I'm tryin.

—— Youre not the only one.

—— Wha? Wha you sayin?

—— And your tooth? What have—

—— Dont ask.

—— To be honest I wasnt. Not really . . .

She look up the street. Patrols pullin up outside the neighbours. You can see ones a woman officer. They step out, both them arrangin their hats an genitals.

—— Monica, dont get me done . . . Monica . . .

She start back to the door. First I dont twig. Then I follow. Course I do. Million things about her floodin back at me. New perfume, new garms. Only thing different is her cover-up chest, the way she cover her face too, like she dont show her chest or face no more. Sure sign she got someone, someone else. So she dont need to show nothin except her tresses an her back. An thats wha I'm followin. 2 time I seen her an I seen more her back than her face.

An then shes openin the front door an I cant describe how it feel to go through a front door like this again, with her, sharin a front door again, just with her, if only out her charity for me, if only not to get me bang up all over. Only once we get in she dont close it, the door, she leave it ajar, whether cos she still got the fear or shes waitin for the obvious PC Jobsworth I dont know. I dont know nothin.

Take them a long time comin, a long time investigatin. Durin the long time, now that I got the chance to say wha I come to say, I say nothin. Too busy takin it all in, her an me in her place, wha should be my place, me tryin to smell who else is in here, who else been here. But wha flood back then is Jade & Kylie. I smell their baby smell, their flesh-an-blood smell like they aint grown, aint change, like time is stood still an all that, like its just part of me in here an more parts an nothin else, just my flesh, my blood, no someone else, just me an the smell of wha is still my family. An all them words, baby words, flood back, weird scientific words you learn cos you need to keep up with wha it all mean. Like *vernix*. But wha do I know?

When the knock come, shes there, steppin out to greet them. *Yes . . . ? Oh you got a call . . . problem? No, no problem . . . everythings fine . . . the neighbour mustve misunderstood . . . have a look round if you like . . .* But they dont. *If youre ok we're ok.* They grin I bet. She grin better, better an bigger, grin an bluff them right out. Bluff the muffs. Not like she lose her touch. Then they go. An she step back an still she leave the door open, head down, hair coverin her face, high top coverin her chest, leather jacket over that, everythin a secret.

—— Monica . . . Thanks . . .

I reach out but she pull away.

—— Dont, she go as she take out cigarettes an spark one up.

—— You started again?

No answer. Just stand there waitin, tryin to get another glimpse her eye, wonderin wha I miss, wha signs I miss, who else she got.

—— Look good . . . you do you really do . . . Different but . . .

—— Stop it. I'm going now. I have to.

—— I havent even told you wha I come to tell you. Where you goin?

—— See Tru in hospital.

—— Tru? Why? Wha happen?

—— Her baby. Her baby happen.

—— Course. Shit. Maybe I—

—— No no no, forget it, no way youre coming. No way . . .

An thats the whole past right there. She took my past as

well. It stick in me. Cos they all chose, Duane an Trudy an Monica. Like Sensi warn. An it aint me they chose.

—— You know when I smell Jade & Kylie, you know wha come back? All them words. Remember? *Vernix, laguno an meconium*. Like estate agents innit . . .

Old joke between us, way back when, like an old karaoke number, an icebreaker.

—— Lanugo, she correct, no smile, nothin. Its *lanugo* . . .

—— Meconiums the one you never forget innit. Stink to fuck that first crap . . . You dont ever for—

—— J . . . What did you come here for?

—— Monica, I go, reachin out to her like before. Is there someone else?

Course like before she pull away. But this time as she pull away she turn an my hand brush over her, barely really a touch, just brush over her, the front of her, barely my fingertips but just enough to touch, an just enough to feel, an wha I feel is nothin. Which is to say theres nothin, not like wha I expect. I mean its like wha should be there aint there. Dont understand it. In that split sec both us is actually lookin at each other. First time her hair is out her face an I get 2 sad eyes lookin at me. An in them eyes I see somethin she want to say, to tell me, before she let the tresses an everythin fall back. Again it all stick in me. Cos I dont understand. I dont get it. No idea wha to say. Then she go:

—— Youre not the only one whos turned ugly.

—— Wha? Wha you sayin?

—— My silicone got rejected didnt it.

—— Kiddin . . .

—— No . . .

I look down, cant help it, only now her arms is fold across her.

—— Had to sling all my bras. They were like . . . hammocks . . . Now . . . I dont know . . . Back to size B. Where I was only worse. Cos things are always worse. So . . . there you go . . .

—— When . . . I mean, when this happen?

—— Couple of months. What difference does it make? We both turned ugly and weve both got our problems. Which reminds me: now that you know my address dont go giving it out. Right?

—— Wha? I never give it to no one. Who did I give it to? I nev—

—— NACRO. Ring any bells? I had 2 blokes—

—— NACRO? Rehab? Bollocks. I nev— Wha they look like?

—— Men in black from outer space. What difference does it make?

Could Uncle really have just turn up here? For a recce of his own? At my house. Wha should be mine. Right here. Man in black. Maybe he want to take some more snaps, the fuckin cunt. Thought cut me to the bone. I look at Monica, waitin for me. An again I reach out to her. This time she elbow my hand off.

—— What did you come here for J?

Her voice crack, like she was cryin without tears. Under her tresses she was invisible. The whole time her hairdo cover how she feel. But when her voice crack I cant describe how it make me feel. An wha can I do? Cant even touch her. Even if she feel this way about herself, even if she aint got no one else, even if theres hope or somethin, even then it dont mean shit. Cos I cant touch her. I aint allow no more. So wha can I do? I go:

—— I come here to warn you to stay away. From here I mean. For a few . . . a couple days is all . . . Its . . . complicated . . .

I know straight off it come out all wrong. Especially the

word *complicated* which is a word wha use to fuck her off
bigtime. She half gulp. She stop cryin, then more less groan,
mumble a load *oh for fucks sakes* or somethin, a load things,
laugh, almost, then hang her head, then shake her head,
laugh again, almost, laugh again almost a good few time.
An all this she do cos she dont know how to react to wha
she see is just the same old, the same old J who never had
to stop an think an all that, never had no big Q to answer,
never did get proper focus or his priorities sorted. An all
that. Cant do nothin except put it to her again an hope she
take it serious.

—— Will you stay away? You have to stay away a couple
day is all. Will you?

Dont need me to say how ballistic she go. Which is to
say very fuckin. Like BIM BAM BOOM. Like she throw
the Q back in my face. *Will you stay away from me J?* An
all that. A right earful. A right mullerin. Then her voice
crack again, only now in anger, screamin like before only
worse, cos like she say, things get worse. I try an calm her.
Then I'm standin outside. BAM. Door slam. 6 locks, barrel
an Chubb an the rest. Then she dash. Shout at me a good
few time. All sorts. Stuff like *leave me alone*. Stuff like *stay
away from me*. Stuff like *get a life*. An other stuff. Like I was
one them paparazzi. Like I was zoom-lensin her the whole
time, doorsteppin her at dawn an all that.

But wha she dont say is whether she will stay away or
no. Wha she dont say is whether she got someone else or

no. She drive off is all she do, glarin at me the whole time. An I ask myself, I have to ask myself if it was worth it, the effort, if the effort was really worth it just for this, just to share a front door with her for a few secs, for a *this is your life* moment, for the sake of wha we had, in the name the good old bad old days. An I dont know if it was. How could I know? I dont know. Cos after all is said an done an all that, wha do I know? Wha can I say I know? Wha can I say?

At a bus stop on the North Circ I sit in the car smokin cigarettes, one after the other, water tricklin down the windscreen. All I think about is Monica. How once upon a time when we was less ugly I would wake up with her hair stuck to my nose an mouth on account her hair mousse. She use to like sleepin on her side with me behind. She use to like me to hold her. One her tits was always warm. This was in the days before the silicone. She use to like sleepin on her left side. So it was her left one wha was always warm. An so she use to like me to hold the other one, the right one, the cold one, hold it to keep it warm until she got to sleep, hold it while I was tryin to get to sleep myself. I always did though, always did hold it long as I could just to keep it warm an her happy. An now she tell me its the ugly men wha try more harder.

Eventually I snap out this type negativity. I have to cos I realise its well late, like pushin half 3. Swallow a couple Ibuprofen then get to a phone an leave a message on Duanes mobi just to say *congratulation an jubilation in the nation* an all that. Then course I do wha I been delayin all along: I phone Sensi to tell him about Warren. Only it don't quite come out.

—— You braindead bastard arsehole fuckwit, Sensi snarl under his breath. Where the fuck you been? I told you to chill out not go fuckin AWOL. Where the fuck you been you fuck?

—— I got things to tell—

—— Oh yeah? Well I been busy J, real busy.

—— Where are you?

—— Fuck do you think? I'm up Tilbury in a pub down the road from the Continental doin the fuckin business you should be doin.

—— In a pub?

—— Yeah in a pub.

—— Doin wha business?

—— Well put it this way: I'm splicin the mainbrace with that old Rusky seadog Yurry.

—— Who?

—— Who? Yurry. *Yoori.* Yu-ri. *Yu-ri* Zedski or whatever. You fuckin know who. The international fuckin driver is who.

—— How you recognise the—

—— His Russian-American friendship t-shirt. Like wearin its gonna help him in the afterlife. Sure as shit aint doin him favours in Tilbury.

—— He aint even suppose to be down there this early.

—— Well he fuckin is J, an I've just Rohypnoled the cunt. So get the fuck down here cos hes gonna be blubbered within the hour.

An hour aint wha it take to get down Tilbury. More like 2. By the time I walk in the saloon bar of the Dumb Docker, which is as empty as an open pub can be, Yuris nose is in an ashtray an his breathins swirlin the ash from Sensis cigarette all over the table. His hands still close round his drink. Sensis sittin opposite with 4 pint glasses, 3 them drain down to the suds, an hes well engross in his true-life SAS book.

—— Well about fuckin time, he whisper as he glance about. Lets get him out of here . . .

He down the rest his pint, get up, grab Yuri under his arms, shout *cheers mate* to the absent barman, an we walk Yuri out, short fat Yuri, one either side. We walk him along Dock Road to the Continental. Sensi tell me to wait a minute till he get Yuri back up to Room 11. He open the main door with Yuris keys an leave it on the latch, main door wha lead one way on to a scuzzy wet pavement an other way into a bacon-stinkin corridor. *No Vacancies. No DSS. Breakfast 6 a.m.–8.30 a.m.*

After a min or so I trip the latch back an tread silent up the stairs. The pictures is all wild horses on beaches an cats in baskets. Pass nobody. Only the aftershave an toilet smells tell me theres life about. Room 11 is slightly open. An inside it, inside wha is a shoebox barely big enough for one, is wha you might call a surprisin scene. Sensis got Yuri face up on the bed an hes leanin over him an strippin him stark naked. Bollock naked. I push the door to. Sensi grin as he throw clothes on the only chair.

—— I aint no burglar J but I think I got a definite knack for befriendin lonely Rusky truck drivers. He sinks 2 pints an hes tellin me his mothers middle name, his room number an the address of Svetlana, his favourite whore in Archangel. I gave the cunt 5 Rohyps just in case. By the time he come round hes gonna have a record-breakin beard an Moscows gonna be a Disney theme park . . .

He laugh at his own joke.

—— An now, now for the *pièce de resistance* . . .

He flip Yuri over on his front, face down, pull off his undies an spread his legs.

—— Jesus wept. Wha—

—— Look an learn J, look an learn . . .

From his pocket he take out a tube of Vaseline an start unscrewin it. Then he take a corner the bed-sheet, fold it till he got layers coverin his hand. When hes ready he squeeze the tube on the sheet an give old Yuri a proper smearin between his lifeless cheeks.

—— Tellin you, a little grease on a batty goes a long way . . .

—— Yeah?

—— Yeah cos itll keep him thinkin an his thinkins gonna be the same as 9 out of 10 geezers in his situation. Point bein 9 out of 10 aint gonna say nish if they think they been buttfucked by accident. Hes got his honour. Plus hes a Rusky. So by my reckonin he will most certainly keep *stummski for mumski*. As they say. Not like the mans objectin is it? Anyway he'll come up with a story how he got jumped or dipped or whatever. An lets face it, whos gonna believe a Rusky pisshead with hardly no English . . . There that should do it, go Sensi wincin as he take his hand out Yuris arse. Be useful J an shufty round for the documents . . .

So I do. Wha else? They aint difficult to find cos basically theres nowhere to hide them except under the bed. I pull out a black zip pouch. In it is Yuris passport, licence, driver docs, photo of his woman, kid, currency an use tachos from Smolensk to Rotterdam. Sensi empty Yuris overnight bag an start laughin as he stuff it with Yuris garms, all except the Russian-American friendship t-shirt wha he drop over Yuris arse.

—— J, you are gonna be one authentic trucker: woolly hat, boots, check shirt, chammy gloves, the works, a right job lot innit. Here, grab a hold your new ID . . .

He hand me the bag an slap a Yorkie bar on top.

—— The truckers choice, he laugh. Never know, might come in handy. Right, lets chip . . .

—— Where you wanna go?

—— Hook up with Warren. Hes comin down.

—— Wha for? We dont need him now.

—— Well yeah but hes insistin on *overseeing his investment*. Fairs fair really. Any case we got time cos accordin to wha I could get from Yuri, he can only pick up the truck at 8 from out the depot. So that gives us nearly 2 hours to fix things with Warren an find a place off-road to dump the truck. Which is what you should of done this a.m.

—— Yeah well . . .

—— Yeah well what? I'm windin you up J cos Ive already found one as it goes . . . I even gave them 2 jacks in the box a walkabout an stuck them back in. *Customer aftercare*, its called. What you think of that?

—— Yeah? You took them out an—

—— No J. No I did not. It was a j-o-k-e joke. Yo ho . . .

—— Well thats . . . thats . . .

—— Fuckin hell . . .

Sensi turn round an start washin his hands in tiny basin. If he wasnt so busy cleanin up an makin sure he aint left no clues an makin even more sure I aint brung no fresh ones, he'd see the way I was. Jarred. Cos my mouths movin, about to tell him Warren aint Warren no more but Umar, that Umar been roll over, turned by some iffy muff, that they got him well an truly beggin for biscuits, an that with or without him the chance we got aint just slim, its anorexic. Sensi would see this straight off, my mouth movin like a fish an no words comin out, except maybe words to cover the ones I should be sayin. Which is to say I'm lyin. *All thats ok then*, I'm goin.

Even if I told him, theres a half-chance, more than that, a good chance, that he'd never believe me. Just like Monica. Like weve all gone too far down our own paths to just stop, to just turn round an go back, to just set off again in another direction. Especially Sensi. After all, you dont just grease a sleepin mans arse for nothin. Especially not in a B & B in Tilbury.

We leave Room 11, Sensi lockin the door then slippin

the key back under, an I follow him out into the misty rain, the whole situation attackin me all sides, comin at me from everywhere but nowhere in particular, like the misty rain. An all that. Truth be told I aint goin back inside. I cant. An I aint gonna be responsible for leavin no geezers for dead in no crate. An I cant live with the risk of me doin nothin, takin a risk with Uncle by doin fuck all. I aint livin with no guilt over J & K. I couldnt.

But me doin somethin or me doin nothin, I mean, neither them possibility is even a possibility. Both thems impossibility. An all I'm doin is followin Sensi like a fuckin poodle. Doin wha I cant help doin. Again. Still. Goin for the gear. As per usual. As per necessary. Only this is the way, the sure way wha lead to one thing: sellout. Like someone is gonna get sold out. Betrayed an all that. Way it is. Warren or Sensi. Monica. J & K. Or me. Someone. Cos you cant please all the people. You cant do right by everyone. Someones gonna have to go. Who I dont know an how I cant say.

I aint no shitter. I never took no bog roll on a job. Now my bowels is concernin me more than ever. It aint just sympathy for Yuris arse but its like I want to go back to that once upon a time where it was all simple, when I only felt like a shit once a day an the stool wha form was solid an regular cos the life wha I led was solid an regular.

We drive in convoy part way an I leave the Persona, bonnet up, somewhere useful, where Sensi indicate, like in a layby a couple mile up the 13 toward Canvey Island.

Then I get in the van with Sensi, the van we should of ditch by now, his sport bag in the back with Situsec tools, pick, shovel, sledge, a *men at work* sign, a couple cones an a righteous reek of petrol wha burn my eyes.

—— Fuck're the jerry cans for?

—— *Cos I love the smell of petrol in the afternoon*, go Sensi with a psycho grin like a Vietnam veteran. *It smells of . . . victory . . .* What the fuck you mean whatre they for? Your man said to torch the truck. No dabs, no forensic. *Burn baby burn . . .*

So here we both is, *hey ho hey ho* an all that. I just want to walk away, get out this now. There isnt time cos Sensi drive barely another 200 feet up the road an turn in the forecourt of a Happy Eater. Forecourts only got 2 cars in it. Most likely ones the managers, the others a dead salesmans. Cos the Happy Eater is the sort of place wha inspire suicide notes. But one the cars, probably the Beemer, is Warrens. Hes already there, sittin in a corner on a red plastic chair stirrin his beverage. He dont look so smooth surround by shiny pics of golden plaice an golden chips, electric green peas an radioactive triple choc dessert.

—— Could murder a burger, Sensi go as he park up.

I grab him, stop him before he get out. He glance down at my hand on his arm.

—— Darling, dont tell me, youre pregnant.

—— Very funny.

—— Well what then? Its like I have to operate 2 brains same time, mine an yours. You should . . .

Before he get too much farther with his latest advice, I let him know:

—— Warrens been turn . . .

But Sensi look at me like he aint heard.

—— You need a pint of black coffee an a hour listenin to Warren rehearsin the Oxford English Dictionary. After that—

—— You hear wha I said? I said—

—— Yeah rubbish.

—— Tellin you—

—— What?

—— I'm sayin hes been roll over.

—— J, you know what? I dont believe you. Ok?

—— No it aint ok. Not by a long way. Warren aint Warren. An he aint got no muff. Its the muff wha got him. I was down Porchester this a.m. I heard him Sensi, I fuckin heard them. Theys a double act, Warren & the Muff. The single come out next week. Called Sellout.

I carry on. Course I do. For a moment the detail about Umar an his runnins, his troubles, his twisty life an his crooked times batter Sensi into silence. For a moment he aint jubilatin no more. Maybe for a moment he even think to do to Warren wha he done to Martin & Geoff, an even wha he done to Yuri, only worse. But wha come out his mouth after all I tell him stun me even more than layin eyes on him with Yuri:

—— J, youre full of it. Youre a farty dreamer is wha. Thats you all over innit . . . Innit . . . Cos youve been lookin for a way out ever since you found a way in. Its like your belief span is the same as your attention span, i.e. 10 seconds. Its like you tell everyone how you lost your heavy goods licence runnin over a suicide when we all know it was cos you fell asleep at the wheel innit.

—— Man was juice to the eyeballs.

—— There was no skid marks J.

—— Walked out like—

—— Police sussed it easy. Hand it to em. They could see there was no skid marks, no brakin. Just one long slow drift across the tarmac . . . Farty dreamer . . . You killed a man. You did. Pissed or no, you did. An just like the muffs sussed you, I'm sussin you too. Face up to what you done an what youre about to do. Nothin else is gonna work. So no more of your shit. Youre in too deep to back out. You an me both . . .

Then he nod slowly to himself a couple time before starin at me, his lower jaw juttin like a shelf, an he go:

—— Any case, you know what? I aint gonna let you. I aint gonna let you back out. Simple as that. Nuff said . . .

Course I'm regrettin openin my mouth. Cos wha slip out his is no less than a twist, a whole new twist from a whole new knife. I suppose I just wanted to be straight with at least one person this lifetime. But whoever I try an level with just turn it back on me. Sensi say *nuff said* but thats just his personal cue for another lecture, a new lecture about focus an respect. An all this is his way of waterin down his threat which now stand between us like a gear-stick. He try an joke about all *the lucre we will harvest*, not to mention *the spondooli, the peas, the shells, the dollari, the sobs an the squids we will rake an the spoil we will pluck*. More he quack, more I cant trust him. New stuff occur, like maybe Sensi know about Warren already, like maybe theres double acts out there wha everyone but mes heard of, people pairin off an makin old-style whoopee, an me with nothin, no double, no &, no other half.

Only thing I got is a connection wha spring in my mind like a 50% solution to the hell if not the high water. Accordin to Arno, accordin to his bit of paper, Uncles gonna be at Village Road. But in his right mind he aint never gonna be nowhere near. Not tonight anyway. Its just to let me know, to keep me on the move, to make me cack my pants for now an most likely for ever. Maybe I sus this from the off.

Other hand I could know exactly where Uncles gonna be. I could know that by arrangin it myself. That would take care one the monkeys on my back. The gear I can walk away from. I know that now. I just want to be able to walk away from the rest the monkeys, my monkeys, the animal shadows, the duckholes, the lockups an anywhere shadows live. The last the Ibuprofens is wearin off. Sensi can see I aint focusin, not on him anyway. Hes sittin there vex as fuck, facin me down, waitin for me to say somethin.

—— Mines a pint black coffee . . .

—— Fuckin last, he mumble, no more crazy ideas J . . . thats it . . . call it a day for the love of money . . .

An as he get out in the rain he start singin *pound signs keep fallin on me head* . . . Me I'm wha you call humiliated in myself. My hands aint tied. There aint no crossbow at my skull. Its just the opposite. Its my free hands wha humiliate me. Cos they aint resistin nothin.

We go join Warren, Sensi orderin a burger an fries an me a coffee an Danish. We have to repeat the order 3, 4 time. Sensi reckon its cos the pasty waitress is inbred, which is somethin Sensi say happen a lot round Essex. Then she has to repeat the order 3, 4 time to the geezer behind the food counter. Warren reckon its cos the geezer is both her dad *and* her boyfriend. Maybe there is a bit of confusion round Essex but do them 2 lie half as much as us 3? Sensis settle in the corner opposite Warren. Me next to Warren.

—— Well old boy, looks like its a goer . . .

—— And why shouldnt it be Sensi? go Warren laughin without laughin, adjustin his specs, brushin fluff off of his lapels, glancin down at me, stirrin his cold coffee, almost like he was nervy. I can arrange distribution within approximately 2 hours of delivery.

—— Add an hour cos deliverys gonna be in Canning Town.

—— Fine. I just need to verify the consignment in situ.

—— Youll be told where an when after—

—— J, he can . . . Warren, you meet us where we ditch the truck an do the verifyin there. Thats why I said to meet here cos exactly one an a half mile up the road toward Canvey theres a left. Its just a service road, dirt track really, but its wide an smooth enough for a 40-tonner. Its lined with trees all the way down. Not perfect cover but good as it gets round here.

—— No witnesses either.

—— Specially none of them Warren, Sensi grin like a proper

double act warmin up. End of the service road theres a buildin like a small outhouse, disuse farm or summin. No roof so bring a brolly for your hairdos girls. Oh, an get gloved up . . .

Warren smile.

—— *Gloved up* . . . I like that . . . Youve done well Sensi. Dont you think so J?

—— Yes. Very well.

—— And you will be equally pleased to know that Ive secured a better price than the 50 per unit I mentioned.

—— Yeah? How much better?

—— £90.

—— *The man wheels, the man deals* . . .

—— Or rather: he who wheels deals.

—— No Warren its: he who *steals* wheels deals. Innit, Sensi laugh.

—— I stand corrected, Warren laugh back, actually laugh for the first time, only its still more like a nervy squeal.

They twinkle at each other like a couple right lovebirds. An me I try an make a grin but my tongue touch my metal tooth. I watch Sensis mouth as he stuff it with burger. I watch Warrens mouth as he pronounciate his every dainty dotted i an his crispy crossy t. An it recall to me that settin up Uncle, arrangin for him to be clocked *in flagrante* with his panties ankled, was not my connection at all.

Truth be, it was all Warrens idea. It come from him, from that same mouth. Hes the one wha brung it up all casual, well casual, too casual. Hes the one wha snuck it in the scheme of things back in the pool hall, a casual idea wha he plant deliberate. Other words Warrens gaggin for this information more than anythin else, gaggin to know where Uncles gonna be so he can get himself off of his personal hook. Back when he first say it it was pie in the sky. Now its more like deli on the plate under a pigs snout. An its the only thing I got.

Cos then all of a sudden the time come. When it do Warren pay up an leave. Sensi stay to finish his third coffee an second dessert. Me I go out to the van an get in the back, the back of a Situsec Transit in the Happy Eater carpark. Here is where I sink again more than ever back in the anon geezerhood. Even when I was inside I still had somethin. I had name, I had form. Now as I take off my garms I am nobody, I become nobody. Then I start pullin on Yuris garms, his thick green check shirt wha mix smells of washin powder, sweat, baccy, his boots wha squeeze an his black woolly hat wha is too big. His short fat jeans I leave.

Then about 8 Sensi drive me to the port. No words is spoke. He stop up round the corner from the main gates. Like an authentic driver I jump out grabbin my overnight bag an givin him a wave.

—— Oi. Aint you forgettin somethin?

As I turn back Sensi dangle a small rubber Mickey Mouse in my face which is the keyring holdin the keys to the truck. Before I can take them he close his hand.

—— Eyes open J. Bit of focus. Then you can go back to bed . . .

Prick. I take the keys an start walkin. Behind I can hear him 3-pointin the van an headin off. Ahead all the lights an floodlights is on cos the night is more less come. An the rain is more less stop. Just like Jade prophesy that time to her dad. I throw the overnight bag over my shoulder an put a chunk of the Yorkie in my mouth for special effect. Night come when the rain stop. An at the end the day it aint such a bad night, as bad nights go, to be stealin a truck.

They waited for me as for the rain

On a less cloudy night you could see west to the Dartford crossing. On a clear day you could probably see all the way back to an industrial depot wedge between Beckton an Creekmouth. If I could I would probably see Uncles eye glue to his long-range telescope lookin straight back at me, Arno opposite playin solitaire on a packin crate, a fresh cuttin pin to the board: *Organised crime is thought to be behind a recent spate of thefts from ports around the south-east.*

Right now the only thing visible is the uniform in the booth by the gate. Gulls circlin the blue-black cloud. Saunterin in aint the problem, even with my too-small boots. Its pullin up at the barrier on the way out. For the final check. For the mug shot. I got a good beard by now. Plus a woolly hat. But still.

273

Barriers, channels, arrows in blue, in red, flat space beyond all the way to a smoky funnel 200 foot off. Uniform in his booth glance at me, nod, ghost white under the strips, I nod back, carry on. I try an look like I know where I'm headin. But course I got no idea where Transcargo International Depot 4 is.

Mark on Yuris papers is a whole load stuff, container numbers, haulier name, reg number, size, weight, seal numbers an all that. Can only hope theys all in order but whether they is or aint make no difference till I find a 40-ton Merc with T-O-R on the plate.

Spillers Milling, Elephant House, Port Health, Customs, Giraffe House, Admiralty Marshal. Speed Limit 5 mph. Names wha mean nothin. Signs everywhere but no direction. Depots, warehouses, loadin bays, containers, dumps, restricted areas.

A forklift whine past the Flying Angel Club an on toward tiers of containers, *Deutsche Afrika Linien*, an then on toward the loadin bay of the massive *Hanjin Korea* wha rise empty out the estuary like it was parkin on the pavement. I walk the other way, past port agent offices, the port mechanic, a steam cleanin bay. CAUTION. HARD HAT AREA. Hardly no sound.

On the Thames side theres another berth. Oily river water slap round the *Connemara*. Crews is loadin it. Dozen geezers in hard hats an earmuffs. Hardly no sound. One them, ratchet in hand, wave me away from a movin crane on rails wha loom along 60 foot above me. BEWARE STRADDLE CARRIER, it say on it. Walk under nothin. Beware everythin.

Another forklift whine past an is swallow in a black hangar. Place like this shit me. It dwarf me. Even more than London a place like this crush me with scale. Saunter on, tryin to find someone alone to give me direction without attractin too much attention, only the spaces between people an buildins is big with plenty unexpected fencin an chicken wire an the whole space watch over by big brother, cameras on posts like eyes on stalks.

Speed Limit 10 mph. Warnin left an right. *Marine pollutant. Flammable liquid. Contaminants. Corrosive materials.* An all that. In shore wind across the open space. Near the rail terminal I single out a docker in overalls whos busy hookin up a water pipe. I give him my best stupid Rusky grin, showin him the Transcargo document. He point in the direction the grain silos, *past the weigh station* he say, indicatin second right. I grin like I understood nothin an move off.

Second right take me between 2 warehouses an out more less under one the towerin silos. Light rebound off of the corrugations. Across a loadin bay padlocks an chains shine like jewels. Top the silo is a whole house, a buildin like a haunted house stuck on top the silo, wha must be the weigh station. Docker was right. In the shadow the silo is the Transcargo depots. 4 in all. Each one fill with slumberin trucks. Inside depot 4 is about 6 all line up, gleamin dark. The one on the left has a Merc badge. My heart shift up a gear when I see the registration letters: T-O-R. 40-tonner for sure. Open top for crane loadin with just a tarp stretch over it.

Years since I driven a 5-axle. An my drivin years is times I dont care to remember. Q now is whether I'm gonna remember wha I have to remember. Which is to say how to drive one. But first hurdles even bigger. How to sus the procedure. How to look like I know it.

Next to depot 4 in the Transcargo office theres a couple admin bods chattin over tea an biccies, one with his feet on his desk holdin the *Mirror*. A security guard with a sniffer on a lead walk right past me. Silent rubber stride. Never even heard them comin. Never even see his face. The dog patter along, smell a puddle, piss on a standpipe, look back at me with his tongue hangin before he get drag on, their shadows, the guards an the dogs, splittin under the banks of lights into dogman an mandog.

Approach the office. Through the window the one with his feet up spot me. I nod, point at the truck. He give me a thumb, swivel round on his chair to open a filin cabinet. Obvious I'm gonna have to sign somethin, have a word an all that, compare dicks. Bold is best so I step in the office with a grin an put my docs on his desk.

They got a tv on top the cabinet. Documentary murmurin about the tadpole shrimp wha is over 140 million year old an more less extinct apart from a couple stagnant ponds off of the A40. While the bod search for his file I grin at the other. Hes dunkin a chocolate digestive in his tea an the only thing wha bother him is achievin the perfect dunk. A 1-sec dunk. 2-sec dunk. 3-sec dunk. He keep dunkin an bitin, testin the texture, never really satisfy with the balance.

Meantime the first ones found the file an hes leafin my papers, selectin one doc after another, tickin each off against his file, checkin all the numbers, the VIN, other vehicle idents, chassis, engine, paintwork number, load refs, haulier refs, all the long numbers digit by digit.

Then he move on to the personal ID, my driver docs, flippin through my Rusky passport, lookin at the stamps, noddin to himself without ever proper lookin at the photo. Tickin, checkin, goin through the motion, sleepwalkin through his modus. Then he get me to sign a paper. Which I do fast an confident. By now I'm sure he aint gonna compare signatures, Yuri before, Yuri after.

—— Fine, he go. No probs . . . On the way out, keep left, follow the signs, and hand this in at the gate . . .

I nod, take the form he hold out, grin again an thats that, I'm out the office walkin to the truck. Nothin but my footsteps across the diesel puddles. Trucks standin cold wet lit by yellow balls of safety lights round the depot. 2 things I didnt count on: cab door bein visible from the office an left-hand drive. Take it slow, dont panic, remember the checks, I'm tellin myself. Switch on first, let the engine idle a couple mins for a smooth off.

Pull out Mickey Mouse. Stick the key in the lock. Gloves I forget. Still jam in my pocket. I put them on, keepin my back to the office, wonderin if I already touch anythin. Like the office doorknob. Like his pen. Too late now. Unlock the cab an climb in. More like squeeze cos the fuckin seats right up to the wheel for a fat shortarse driver with no arms. Feel for the lever under the seat an slide back. Pretend to fiddle with the tacho insertin a fresh one. Then I locate the battery master an flip it on.

Whole new layout, whole new truck. Switches I dont recognise. Parkin brake valve dead centre as per usual. Its on, transmission neutral. Ok. Key in the ignition, turn to drive. 3-sec buzzer like an air-raid siren in the silence. Check the warnin lights. Belt an door warnins wha I ignore. Axle lock off. Ok. Turn the key to start. Engine kick in first time, no bollocks, no accelerator needed, no start pilot, well maintain. Near the wheels the idle control. Give it a few extra revs to make sure it dont stall. Check the oil pressure. Ok. Check the Duplex for the tyre pressure. Ok. Fuel, half tank. Headlights on low beam, rear fogs an sidelights. Ok. Then I climb out the cab an make a show checkin the exterior. Lights workin all round, tail, side, beam an fog. Tyre pressure ok, no foreign bodies, no scrapes, no damage. No trailin bits on the vehicle, no drips under. Tarpaulin proper secure all round, ropes tight all round, tied off an padlocked. Load sealed an also padlocked. Roof nobody check anyway. Adjust side mirrors an wipe, left an right.

2 mins later I'm back in the cab. Door close, belt on. Warnin buzzers off. Return idle control to normal, in gear, check mirrors, parkin brake off, hydraulics hissin, thats when the office bods is gonna look up a sec but I dont look back, just a goodbye hand in the air, an I'm rollin smooth out the depot with full care an consideration to other road users. Which lucky for me there aint.

Keep left, follow the signs to the gate. 10 mph all the way. Couple seagulls watch me from their perch on a gutter. Truck hum past opposite direction. Docker runnin against the wind holdin his hat. 10 mph all the way, all the way to the gate. Gull perch on the booth. Pull up at the barrier, parkin brake on, transmission neutral. Uniform open the slidin glass on his booth an wait. One problem. Left-hand drive mean I have to unbelt, buzzer come on again, shift over to the right, search for the assistant-side window switch wha aint easy in the dark.

He take the form I eventually give him, step out the booth an check the plate, haulier data, weight, the chassis an paintwork numbers. All over again. Even shufty inside the cab but only to check the VIN wha is etch into the boardin plate. Then he nod an I slide back left, belt up, buzzer off, in gear, parkin brake off, barrier up, rollin once more. Fuck me. Almost easier drivin out than walkin in. Piece of piss. Piece of fuckin piss. An the concentration an fear work better than Ibuprofen for my headache.

Then I'm out the port, out Tilbury, headin to the roundabout an pickin up the signs for the 13, grateful for the easin weather, grateful I dont have to drive in the rain, grateful that at least Sensis got fuck all to get a temperature over. Unless I get a pull. So I drive well slow, keepin it in low gears, under 30, givin them no excuse, no chance to fuck up in a speed trap. But the traffics light an theres probably plenty bored muffs out there in the dark eatin sarnies made by their mums waitin for the one sad trucker whos got slack time to make up on the overnight.

Still. With the engine churnin an the road open theres a moment when I'm thinkin ok, I aint king my life no more but high up above the tarmac like this I'm king the road. King of somethin. An I get this urge, like people standin on tall buildins get an urge to jump, I get this urge just to put my foot down an carry on east, well east, east as east get. Or as long as the diesel last. Whichever first.

Mins later I'm passin the Happy Eater. Maybe this pattern, this route, is the same as on the hooky tacho, maybe the exact same, I'll never know. See it through J, I'm tellin myself. Keep calm an see it through. Past the Eater I shift right down, scopin for the turn-off. Cant afford to miss it. No way I wanna try an reverse 40 tons back up an A road, or worse, wheel it round. But Soldier Boy is good when it come to the recce an I spot the line of trees easy.

As I brake light an early a figure leap out on the shoulder the road, head consume by night-vision goggles, evil red eye dots starin back like a killer robot, arms wavin, directin me on to the service road. I slow right down an start turnin. Sensi hop on the assistant-side boardin plate. Glancin at him freak me out. Hes black-boot-polished the rest his face an hes grinnin under the goggles like hes just won Alien of the Year award. I give him a thumb an rumble down the lumps an pits killin the rear fogs. Pass Warrens Beemer then the Situsec van, cargo doors open, engine runnin, facin back up the service road ready for the off.

Sensi hop down when we get near the outhouse an direct me in between the wreck walls, brick piles, glass an crack timbers. Pull up scrapin the side against concrete stumps stickin out the wall. Parkin brake on. Shift neutral. Lights off. Engine off. Pocket the keys.

Its only when I get out the cab I realise I'm shakin, my hands is shakin, legs wobblin, an I'm sweatin, almost like a fever. Warrens comin over, hookin his mobi back on his belt. Who the fuck was he talkin to I wonder. Sensi rip his goggles off, vice my shoulders with a glove hand, still grinnin:

—— *He whos got the truck . . . has got the luck . . .* Innit. Any trouble?

—— Nah . . .

—— Good. Lets get the bitch open . . .

Sensi go for the van. Warren stand there in front of me in his *on safari* outfit wha consist of combat trousers, combat boots, woolly hat an black leather drivin gloves with holes round the knuckles. Ex-Falklands, he claim. Yeah right.

—— Excellent J. Well done. Stage one is complete.

—— That was stage one?

Sensi come back, sport bag in one hand, heavy-duty bolt cutters in the other. We follow him round the back the truck. The cutters pinch straight through the padlock securin the tarp. Then he do the same with the lock securin the cargo units lever. We start to untie the tarp an pull it back over the rim the rear doors. Whole load waters been sittin up there on top an it spray down on us like celebration champagne. We share a laugh, a seconds relief. Then Sensi shift the lever an open the back to wha is really a big box with no lid. Neither Sensi nor Warren is prepare for the interior.

—— Fucks sake J, go Sensi shinin a torch. Its stuffed. Look at all this shit. How the fuck we gonna find anythin?

—— It was always gonna be stuffed cos—

—— Dont start J. Not now. Just tell us how we supposed to know? How we supposed to ident the boxes. Where the fucks the gear?

I shrug.

—— Close to the rear doors is all I know.

—— Yeah?

—— Wha I was told.

—— It could still take an age to locate—

—— Warren, its ok. Calm. Everythins still jubbly. *The gear is near the rear*, the man says. *Near the rear is the gear* . . .

—— I certainly hope the man is right, Warren reply approachin the cargo.

—— Wha I was told.

—— Ok then gentlemen, no time like the present. Lets—

Warrens stops, his nostrils sniffin the air.

—— Whats that smell? Can you smell that?

The smells a slow seeper an it must hit me an Sensi same time as Warren cos both us is crinklin our noses.

—— Rotting fruit, Warren suggest.

—— Piss an shit, I go.

—— Livestock perhaps.

—— Deadstock by now. Whatever it is lets fuckin move.

So Warren give me a leg up to the cargo unit, cleanin scuff off of his gloves after, an we start movin the first crates out to make room for a proper search. Then with Sensis torch I'm scannin the crates. Theys stamp with all sorts. Letters. Numbers. Half-words. Dates. Words in tongues. Warnin stickers.

All I know is I still aint told Sensi about the aeroplane logos wha is suppose to be on the boxes. Why exactly I dont know. Just somethin, a piece of information to hold on to. We all need one, one small piece for ourself. The rest you can pass on, like crates. So I'm passin out crates. Warrens examinin them, tryin to make head or tail. Sensis back down to the van bringin 2 then another 2 petrol cans.

I'm pickin out the more likely crates but nothins really got anythin like a plane on it.

Outside Warrens breakin open a couple with a gorilla bar, metal hookin in wood lids, wood splinterin, crackin, wood bits spreadin in a muddy arc round the cargo doors. I'm humpin more crates an palettes an lookin in dark nooks. Sensi begin dousin the truck end to end then circlin it. Hear the cab door openin so he must be dousin in there too. I find nothin. Maybe cos theres nothin to find. Maybe cos we all been stitch up. We should be out by now. Out an gone. Then a feelin come at me, a strong feelin wha make me stop searchin for the boxes. Wha trigger the feelin I dont know. It aint the smell Warren point out. Cos by now petrol stench up the whole area, specially between the walls the truck. An it aint no special sound. Cos all I hears the splinterin goin on outside an Warrens gruntin an the occasional splash of petrol, half-empty can knockin against metal. Aint nothin in particular wha trigger the feelin. Its just that there come a certain point when I know, I just know, that I aint alone no more.

I mean its like youre in a queue an you think youre the last in the queue but then somethin tell you the back your neck is bein looked at. An you know this cos your neck hairs is standin an your body is tense an all of you is shivery. An all this for no reason.

I turn slow behind me toward where the cab is. Palettes an crates. Still silent stack. But not silent an cold. More like silent an warm. Maybe Warren was right. They got livestock. Very well-behave livestock. I grab the torch.

Shine it round the far end. Hold my breath. Listen. Step up on a crate. Shine round. Shine down. Dark nooks. Shadows. Things I cant see. Angles all over. More shadows. Animal shadows wha my imagination play. Stuff wha my para patterns create, wha my splittin head force me to see. To see right—

—— Fuck you doin J . . . ? J . . .

To see right—

—— Get the fuck on with it. You said it was near the rear . . . J . . .

To see right to the back I have to climb up on 3 crates, lie across 2 an look down between them to the far end the cargo unit. I try an listen but all I hear nows my own breathin.

—— J . . . fucks sake . . . you believe this Warren? Look at him . . .

I shine through the gap. Light the dark nooks. Glints. Black shadows. Rabbits out of hats. Animals.

—— J, you deaf cunt . . .

Wha I see down there in among the crates make me do somethin I never done. I swallow an I fart same time.

Cos the torchlight flash back an eye. A whole eye. An the eye look back. Like it was Uncles eye on the other end his long-range telescope. Just one eye. Then gone back in the dark. Human I dont know. Whatever it is it give me instant fear. Like my fear was freeze dry waitin for somethin sudden like boilin water to activate it.

I edge back on the crate, shift angle an shine torchlight between palettes. The light flash back again. This time 2 eyes. Then after a mouth. Human. For def human. No way not. Then 3 eyes. Then 2 faces. Then 3 mouths. Then 5 eyes an 3 faces. 4 mouths or 5. 6 eyes. 3 faces even. 2 for def. 3 ears. Human. 3 faces for def. An 6 eyes or 7. 2 more ears. An so on. Mouths I lose count. 3 faces. 3 for def. Noses. They aint sheep noses. They aint sheep faces. They aint sheep for def. But they aint no different. Sheep or human. Cos whether sheep or human theys just live export all the same. 3 faces, 3 live export. Man. Woman. Boy. An a bundle. Hooky humans. Hooky fuckin humans is wha look back at me, the hookiest gear of all.

I'm almost as scared as them. Cos its like scared animals pass on their fear like a disease. An these scared animals is a family an there aint nothin like the fear a family got, one for the other. I feel my nerve slippin. An it dawn that I been set up, that maybe I was set up the same 9 month ago, that if Uncles bein watch hes just usin me to divert attention from somethin else hes got goin. Maybe the bushes an trees is full of muffs, cammed up with boot polish like Sensi, cammed up an waitin, muffs even Warrens muff dont know about.

By this time Sensis up beside me on the crates, goggles on, killer robot, red dots scopin down into the same nook, seekin the heat, finally seein wha I'm seein.

—— Motherfuckers, the robots mumblin softly. Look at them motherfuckers . . . Now how the fuck they get in there?

I climb down, clear my throat, wipe my face in my shirt.

—— Most likely they just cut through the tarp then sewed it back up from the inside.

—— Youre jokin, go Sensi climbin down after me.

—— My contact will not be pleased about this, go Warren from outside.

—— Dont nobody fuckin check?

—— Dont check every truck. Cant. An they could of got in more less anywhere, some lorry park, depot, who know. Maybe over here, maybe where the ship come from. Maybe even Yuri was never wise to it.

—— Maybe. Or maybe they wedged him up. Maybe theyre loaded.

—— Forget it. Leave them. When wes ready we dump—

—— Dump? Dump who? You think I'm gonna let some

fuckin tarphead tell some fucked-up story to some fucked-up pig in some fucked-up lingo? You think some squeegee refugees gonna mess up my big stroke?

—— Vinegar stroke more like.

I dont get nothin else out cos Sensi knuckle me against the side wall, my head knockin it, settin off the pain again, he blur, close up, his face right in mine, him screamin, at least shoutin, scarin the brickwork, me in a new place, spit flyin in my eyes, a place where things is suddenly clear, my ideas, an all that, suddenly very clear.

—— Funny you callin me a wanker, hes sayin. Funny you . . . funny you . . . funny you . . .

I cant feel my arms. I cant feel my hands. I'm sayin to him, I'm askin him:

—— Wha you gonna do about them?

—— Funny you should ask J, funny you should ask cos I was about to tell you: they aint goin nofuckinwhere J. Nowhere. They piss an shit where they sit. You ever heard of the Wick Effect? With a bit of accelerant workin on what fat they got theyll burn to fuckin dust. No dabs. No witnesses. No bollocks. An one day this nation will personally thank you for gettin rid of a couple of nameless spongin cunts. Now get me them fuckin boxes . . . Warren . . . gis the bar . . .

Warren pass up the gorilla bar. Behind me the humans
is standin up. Their stink rise with them even drownin
out the petrol. I look at them with their sad pleadin
faces. Theyre filthy. Woman with a greasy bundle. Boy
about 6 with dry blood on his nose. Man with hat an
beard. Hes holdin somethin out to me. 2 scraggy notes in
a useless currency wha has been up his arse for hundreds
of miles.

—— Thats more fuckin like it . . .

Sensi push past me, snatchin the notes.

—— Wheres the rest? Then for effect he swing the bar
down crackin one the crates. He order the humans down.
Sit, he say. *Stay*. He hold out his hand. The man give
up his watch which Sensi examine an pocket like it was
a Rolex.

—— I could take a breath an theyd cack themselves, he
tell me.

Then he do, he take a breath, an then he grin when
they cower.

—— Give them a couple of squids theyll do anythin. *Moo*
like a cow, he tell the man, grinnin again before his grin
disappear. Right J, wheres the fuckin petrol tank cos I
dont wanna blow myself up.

I pretend to carry on my search, doin as I'm told, pullin another crate but avoidin lookin at him.

—— The best place to douse, I tell him, aint in or round the cab. Its under. You get a good mixture of combustibles down there, engine fluids, axle grease, tyre rubber, petrol from the secondary tank—

—— They got a secondary tank?

—— Course . . . Best place I'm tellin you.

—— Well at fuckin last, somethin useful that even ring true. Now find the fuckin boxes cos I wanna get the barbie off before it start rainin.

Sensi jump out. No sooner hes gone I pass Warren another crate. He smirk at me, like I'm busted an broken an he got no respect. It wash over me, his look, his words, wha he think, wha anyone think, it wash over me. Because I know wha to do. Warren he take the crate in his arms an lower it to the ground. I wait till hes squattin, head down, tryin to open it. Then I jump on his back, knees first, squash him double, jam him against the crate, fold him like a deckchair, wind him, gasp him, leave him eyes bulgin through his specs, wonderin wha the fuck.

I feel nothin. Take the mobi from his belt an turn back to the humans, put my finger to my lips. Which is to say I give them the international sign wha people trust. I once give the same sign to a man whose gaff I was robbin in the small hours. An he obey. He keep silent like there was a peace between us, a peace both of us should never disturb. Still. Choice is wha they aint got.

I beckon them out. The man help the woman down, me the boy, stale piss follow, an I walk them, man woman boy an stale piss, across the glass, brick an mud to the van. Sensis legs is stickin out from under the cab. Warrens sittin on the ground tryin to call out but he cant even muster a cough. A single match is all. Thats all it would take. Torch them both. Fuck them both. Cos wha is betrayal?

The humans is gettin in the back like I show them. They dont care where theyre goin. Anywhere will do. They only got one bag. An the womans bundle. Which could be a baby, way shes holdin it. But only one bag. Like they just been release. Like they just been strip back down to their pants an wits. To nothin but their heartbeats. To wha they was way back when in their beginnin.

When theyre in I begin to close the cargo door quiet as I can. Glancin back. Silent as I can. But the hinge creak across the dark. Alert Sensi. Hes scramblin out. Gettin up. Takin stock. He stand there confuse a sec, lookin at me then over at Warren pointin at me from the ground. Dont take Sensi long to do his sums. I'm steppin in the van as hes pickin up the gorilla bar again, an comin toward me.

—— *Mother fuckin Teresa*, hes shoutin. What you gonna do? Start a squeegee firm?

—— No a crime wave.

—— You fuckin arsehole, hes goin but hes slowin down, givin up the ghost cos he see he aint gonna make it.

I'm revvin the van, throwin him the keys to the Persona across the dark an puddles an petrol, him still shoutin.

—— *Your shares mine . . . you know that . . . you know that . . .* cunt . . .

—— You can have it. The boxes is mark with aeroplane logos. Near the back like I said. Is all I know.

The gorilla bar wha Sensi fling, his killer mug all bare teeth, bounce off of the side. By then I got the van movin over the ruts an pits toward the road, Sensis crossbow, Situsec tools an hooky humans jumblin in the back. Turn left away from Tilbury. Main junction of the 13 ahead with the one word writ on it wha remind me most of London. Which is to say the word London. Anywhere but there, anywhere.

Other ways Southend, the straight an narrow to the sea. No danger. Holiday instead. Family holiday. Why not? Cos I have a vision, not any vision, more like the head-divin uchi mata of all visions, a holy vision wha personally speak to me. It tell me I aint got no right to spread the fear. Cos who has?

From a distance flashin blue. Coincidence? Or Warrens muff? Fuck know. All there is is the smell of the sea from a long long way off. If Warren made his call he would of said A13 goin west, back to town. Southend will confuse everyone, all them jokers. So I turn away from the blue light. I turn away from London. An I put my foot down.

Does the rain stop when the night come? Like fuck. Children aint prophets. Jade aint. An now I'm travellin hard away, hard an fast away. The rain come down cats an dogs. But mostly dogs. Van steam up an stink. Open window, rain soak shoulder, wipers racin across the screen an back, wall of spray off of a truck in front. Overtake everythin I can, cuttin up the light traffic, comin at them out of nowhere, visibility 20, 30 foot, me pushin it, 60, 65, 70 plus. Cos I dont care an they dont care an my head keep punishin me for all the bad wha has gone through it. In time its a half-hour wha divide us from Southend, a half-hour wha I want to last an last. Cos theres fuck all point drivin like a holy cunt if the place youre drivin to like a holy cunt is the last place.

Course between now an the last place I could get pulled.

An then wha? I cant deny knowledge. I cant say I dont know theres hooky humans in the back, rollin about, humans wha usually wait for a truck to tank up at a service station then cut their way out the tarp an seep off into society. But the muffs ignore us like they was secretly laughin at me, laughin at the dumb pied piper leadin a squeegee refugee crime wave the length the coast, beggin an robbin an stealin. Give them somethin to talk about. But theres no muffs about, no muffs lurkin at the 10, 15 roundabouts wha zig an zag the straight an narrow to the sea, each roundabout planted with earth an bushes an signs to confuse the enemy: *left to the seafront, right to the seafront, ahead to the seafront.*

Then the sea itself crumple an shift out the dark. The dome the Kursaal like a cathedral convert into amusement palace mark the beginnin the front. As I do a right I realise one the humans is leanin across the passenger seat. Its the boy. Hes maybe 6. His smudge face is crease with amazement ripplin the dirt streakin his forehead. He obviously aint never seen no esplanade. He obviously aint never arrive in no neon paradise. He aint never seen Circus Circus. He aint never rid the Barracuda. He aint never experience the American Whip. Or the swings, the roundabouts an the bouncy castles. He aint never seen this many colour lights an flashes an sparkles, doughnuts, choc-ices, rides, games, bandits, galleries an prizes. He aint never even seen fish an chips. Southends the place for all this stuff, a place where the lights an the fish an the chips gather like a community, a place wha is suppose to amaze an bring magic.

My splittin head an the brightness an all that make me feel like the time me & Monica done Es together on our second date. We done an E each, then 2, then split another between us an went up the Gatehouse in Edmonton for a 70s nite. It was a magic time an it seal our deal an we become an item an all that. But wha I remember now is Monicas eyes, cos her eyes had magic in them the whole time, the whole night, like everythin was new an different, everythin seen for the first time with eyes as fresh as the boys, same as the boy, same as him.

I give him Yuris Mickey Mouse key ring. His first bit of prop for his new life. He like it. Its wha they come here for all them hooky humans, cos they think Mickey Mouse is gonna welcome them.

I drive through slow, all the way down the esplanade so as he can see it, all the places an people, take it all in, the good, the bad an the ugly old headscarf havin a smoke in a damp shelter. Or the kids tryin to save their candy floss from the drizzle. Or the 2 bints gigglin their way with their arcade bears, one trailin bog roll from her trotty shoe with stains of lipstick an red wine an chip fat on it like a tacho of her evenin out.

Up the top where the lights is just streetlights but the smells of fish an burnt sugar carry in the van I park up. I turn to the boy an pretend to put food in my mouth. He turn to the others, his mum an his dad. They fear everythin, see danger everywhere, cos they always expect the worst, an experience most likely tell them theyre right. But when the international sign for food come up they dont hesitate.

They frame a grin between them cos neithers got enough teeth for a solo performance. So we get out an I lead these people to the first fish fryer, Enrico of Southend.

Above us theres a million starlings swirlin an divin. Never seen so many. They cut each other up then land in the high dark trees on the slope above the front, before takin off again, circlin an screechin an swirlin. Enricos standin hands on hips, lookin up at them too. He say to us:

—— Ina Italy we call this *lo splendore della natura*, the splendour of the nature. Every night here is the splendour of the nature.

I order up for all of us. Enrico dont mind who he serve. He serve all sorts, the stinkin an the fragrant, all the same, them with boils an headaches an them without. The man try an intro him an his family. Theys call Brim, Stim an Plim or somethin. Plus a baby. Cant even figure out which is which. An their garms is whacked. Man in a fishbone jacket, once upon a time a fishbone suit, once upon a time special an new, worn for big occasions, then smaller occasions, then the trousers wear out an soon hes wearin just the jacket, wearin it for occasions so small they aint occasions no more, just days of his life. An the patchwork colours the womans shawl started fadin once upon a time an never stopped fadin. An the boys shirt is worn until the shirt disappear, until theres more skin than shirt.

When the fish an chips come I put a chip on the table an call it UK an ask them where they come from. The mans brown fingernail point well away from the chip. I try an guess all the countries I know in that direction. But wherever it is its a place well east of Southend, maybe Marbella.

Then we eat. They eat like they never eaten. Their blood flow like it aint flow in a while. Bring life in them dark cheeks. Theys almost embarrass to look at each other. Theys almost embarrass to look at me. To them I most likely look lavish an well healthy. Even the boil is pink an puffy an alive. Its when I start thinkin in this way that I realise the woman aint been feedin the baby in her bundle. First I'm thinkin shes breast-feedin. Cos they do that in public. But she aint. Then I'm thinkin it aint no baby she got but heirlooms. Cos the bundles precious but silent. My hand go to touch it, with a *look at the baby* smile pin to my mug.

The woman look up, stop chewin. For a sec I see Monica, hear Monica, like she was about to tell me not to touch, to leave her alone, to get the fuck out her life. The mans shakin his head, both them lookin at me, only the boy still eatin, an it begin to come to me that it is for def a baby in her bundle, not heirlooms, not a diamond an 2 nuggets in a 18-century cheveret. Only it aint alive no more. An as I'm starin, not chewin no more, just tryin to swallow, it begin to come to me, the when an the where, the time an the place, the how an the why. Which is to say how it happen that a hooky human mother is sittin eatin fish an chips in Southend holdin a bundle with her dead baby in it.

Cos wha else she gonna do? Baby die in a travellin truck, at some place, some point on some international route, an theres nothin to be done, fuck all to be done. You cant bury on the road like you can at sea. I order the boy a banana milk shake an light a cigarette an spark one for the man cos actually I'm tryin to stop the mush comin up. Which is to say I'm fightin the tears in my head. An I hate myself. I drive all the way to fuckin Southend, to the last place, to fuckin hate myself. An its like I seem to carry this feelin, all my crap feelins, round with me like a bag. Like my one bag. *Any luggage sir?* No, just the one bag crap feelins. Wherever I go it come. Maybe back there on the service road Sensi was right. Cremation would of been best an if not best then for the best.

More silent than silent, silent as the baby, we sit a while more. I try an blank it. I try an ignore the bundle. But the silence keep remindin me of it. We wait for the boy to finish. When he look up satisfy, smilin at me, I avoid his eyes, go over to the counter an pay up. We walk out, me with this family by the sea when me I got a family. Only I left them all. Left Monica. Left Jade & Kylie. Left Duane & Trudy an the rest. Left the lot behind for nothin, for wha, for a split-second dream that turn into a long slow drift across the central reservation.

We cross the road. Lights is flickerin, arcades bleepin, puddles like mirrors. I was makin up slack time on the overnight, eyelids flutterin, openin, squintin, then shuttin for a whole split second. It could of been a case of 15 tons blastin through the crash barrier. 360 rotation. Merry-go-round. Flip. Jackknife. Cargo flyin. Palettes snappin. Diesel gushin the tarmac. 60 foot of burnt rubber after a full-lock skid. 20-vehicle pile-up. Fireball.

Only it wasnt like that. It was just a moment shuteye on the overnight is all. Just a long slow drift through the central reservation into a wall. No skid mark. No brakin. Trap 3 hour in the wreckage. Fire crew cut me loose. Ambulance crew take care my busted ribs. Doctor give me dozen stitches. Nothin more. Traffic was light. Never even cause a tailback. Carriageway clear by the a.m. rush hour. Nothin more. Nothin except the dead man they scrape off of the road, off of the wheels, off of the axles, off of the wall.

Man was staggerin, drunk, I told them. No evidence either way. Except the skid marks wha wasnt there. *Did you try to brake?* I try to steer instead, I told them. *In a long gentle curve across 3 lanes?* But they left it at that. More less. Apart from doin me for the paperwork. Or lack of. Lost my licence. Nothin more. Man had no family to take up his cause, no union to fight for justice, no legal team to win compensation. It could of happen the way I said. Only it didnt. Cos I fell asleep at the wheel. Now I'm awake after all this time. An now after all this time only deeds is wanted.

I leave them at a quiet roundabout. I give them the £102.99 I got left. That an a shovel wha the man request. I didnt have the heart to tell him that a grassy roundabout aint no burial mound. With 102 squids an a shovel I pay for my sins. I fuckin pay for them. I scare a family. I help another. An if Monica could see me now. If she could see me. The good I done. The good wha I done. If she could see me.

Anyway. I leave them at the roundabout. Then I'm pickin up the signs for the 13. As I put my foot down I'm wonderin if a bolt from a Panzer crossbow would really split Uncles skull clean in half.

Stuck in traffic round the Hackney Wick interchange is where the last the Ibuprofen wear off. The corners my vision turn white an the pain wha come through let me know I aint got long. Not long enough to sit through a jam. Not long enough to wait for the lights to change. Comin up the 13 I call Uncle from Warrens mobi. Hes well surprise to hear from me. Like he expect Martin & Geoff to call instead, like he expect the muffs to catch me by now. His surprise is wha I got goin for me.

—— Get my flaahs?

—— I got you more than flowers, I tell him.

He hesitate. He aint sure. Hes mullin it, chewin it, schemin his schemes. Then after a sec or 2 hes sure. He go:

—— Meet us . . .

—— Where you wanna meet? An dont send no Arno.

—— Arno? Arnos got a bit of an evil chest infection as it goes. Shouldnt go out on romantic dates in the rain so much should he. Ha fuckin ha. Rain can be fatal for asthmatics . . .

—— Yeah?

—— Yeah. Meet us up Columbia Road. Up top past the Royal Oak theres a block. Guinness Trust estate. Round the back theres lockups. Wheelie bins at the end. Be there in an hour.

I lost track of wha he know or might know, wha he dont know or might not know, whether he was usin me to divert attention from somethin else, whether he really expect some hooky *flaahs*, whether Sensi & Warren got their own schemes or whether Arno play me for a fool or no. Jade & Kylie lost track too. They hardly recognise me.

That night, that summer night way back, Jade was suppose to cut off the villains head in scene 6. Now I will have to do it for her. I aint no killer. I done a triple 9 for Martin & Geoff. But this is different. *Its never too late to do the business on someones head.* Thats wha I told Jade.

Now I must live them words. Which aint the easiest thing. Unless you got the ill-will to see it through.

All I know is that round the Hackney Wick interchange, stuck in traffic, phase fucked on the lights, eyes waterin as my brain scrape skull, I got all the pain I need. Plus the worst ill-will I ever had. Ill-will wha Duane would call plain an simple *murderosity in the city.* Yeah right. No fallin asleep on the job. No accident. This time awake. More wider awake. Enough awake. Kill the cunt so help me.

I leave the van off of Columbia next to S. Jones Dairy. Old dairy wha hark back. Some Sundays me & Monica & the kids come up here for the market, for plants an flowers an soft furnishins. Even on a wet night in the deserted road I see the flowers of Columbia Road. Santolinas, golden plumosas, stargazers, maidenhair ferns, spider blooms an mini gerberas. Names like all the women I never knew. An now I dont want to know them. I had my &. I had Monica. We was expandin all the time. We made the town our own. We shag on Hampstead Heath. We kiss under Nelsons Column. We horse about on Oxford Street. We done some heavy pettin on the District Line.

We always expand our map this city, all the people, all the places, all the friends, all the events, all the school functions. In the few days I been out my map this city become smaller an smaller. I cut people off of it, places off of it, my life mostly taken, the rest left to disappear back to nothin. If I get the chance now, if I get one chance now, I will take my place, I swear I will, I will take my bog-ordinary place an stay there come hell or high. Now all there is is another last place, a new last place, a narrow drive, row of lockups, back of a block, up top Columbia Road. I'm pissin in a corner, pissin up a wall, pissin in a puddle, pissin like no tomorrow. At least me pissin is me pissin no matter where I am.

4 floor up comin through an open window is a documentary about dog-owners dogs wha made friends with cat-owners cats. Water splatter out an overflow. 4, 5 lockups with green doors. Beyond them junk, shoppin trolley, cooker, soakin sofa, the wheelie bins. 25 mins early I find a hide, not the obvious by the bins or behind the sofa or in a corner by the lockups but in a cluster of motorcycles park in a black puddle. Me hidden among them, squattin. Sheet of damp newspaper coverin the crossbow. Crossbow prime an ready. Hand on stock. Finger on trigger. Just a matter of time now. Bide it. Be patient. Drops comin down. Single big slow drops. Bide my time. Focus. Read the newspaper. Check each the items. One by one.

Asthma kill asthmatic gimp.
Two men with cramp found in scrapyard crate.
Boxing instructor caught stealing flowers.
Police informer too winded to speak.
Burglars ex has silicone removed.
Baby buried in roundabout.
Two little girls forget their dad.

Police aint appealin for witnesses cos nobody give a shit. Natural causes the lot. Next of kin on holiday. Everyone else out to lunch. Fuck it. Fuck the lot. Who care? An me? Wha is my cuttin? An Uncles cuttin? Fuck know. None of its gonna flog papers. Be patient. Bide it. Focus. Bim bam boom the rain. Bosch surroundsound. Tepidarium. 3 men in gloves. Warrens drivin gloves. Des an his res. William Morris tiles. Barium enemas. Ibuprofen. Car engine.

A car hummin. A car engine. Merc poke in. Bonnet sleek in the driveway opposite the lockups. Car door open. One then another. Then a third. Martin & Geoff? Or 2 others, 2 new ones? Did I really think he'd come on his tod? I peep through handlebars. I squint through carburettors. I hide my nose behind a tax disc. I bite my tongue.

Theyre movin, lookin about, coverin the angles, murmurin, spreadin out, one left, hands in pockets, one right, gloved, searchin. Uncle half in view. Half blur. White vision pressurin in. His back to me. Footsteps cross grit, puddles. Wha was the range this weapon? Wha did Sensi say? Close up is the only way, the surefire way. Uncles back in full view.

I lean my head, just for a sec, eyes open, not asleep or nothin, eyes open starin at my reflection in the black puddle. Vanity blind me. Pentium processor. 4-piece bath mixer in chrome an gold. Armoire-cupboard. Playstation. DVD. I'm cleanin dog shit off of Jades shoe. I'm carryin family-size Kelloggs cornflakes to the breakfast table. It take a while to realise my life is flashin. One thems sparkin up, havin a smoke while he wait. I lean my head, just for a sec, back against the brick.

It take a while to realise Uncle is out of range, well out,

always was, always will be, his the only name wha liveth for ever more. The rest is just geezers. Stick their names down. Send them up ladders. Order them out in vans. Get them diggin. Keep them fetchin. Time their carryin. Rob them blind. An one them geezers, cackhand by the name Martin, he kill me way back with a single cosh. Bim. He done his chore.

I try an stand. I try an jump a fence. I try an take my place. But I only get as far as 0.99. Even my flashin life dont go all the way. It just stop when it stop. Dawn is when the Onyx bin crew will find me.

Man with headache pulled from puddle

Maybe one the crew will triple-9. Maybe theyll inform Monica, who will inform Duane, who will inform Trudy, who is breast-feedin a healthy 8-pounder. Maybe theyre comin. Maybe Monicas bringin J & K. Maybe the police want to interview me. Maybe they find my lost drivin licence in a stolen Transco van in a breakers yard. *Piping it for you* it says on the side. Maybe. Who know? All I know is theyre comin for me soon.

Man pulled from puddle rushed to hospital

I hope they inform Monica. I hope shes on her way. All I know is theyre comin for me, 3 them, surroundin me, 3 them like surgeons, lookin down at me, starin down. First thing they do theyll get gloved up, cos theyre professional an all that. No dabs. No trace. Clean, simple. No fuss. Next theyll examine the patient, for marks, for damage. Then theyll drain all the ill-will, sluice it all, leave it in a black red puddle. An finally, not before time but before its too late, they will do the business. They will operate on the patient. They will operate to relieve the pressure.